THE PERFECT STRANGER

TARA LYONS

For Nancy
Happy heavenly birthday

'Trust people but remember: Salt also looks like sugar.'

— Paulo Coelho

PROLOGUE

MAY

You. You deserve to die. For the way you've treated people and trampled over their feelings. *My* feelings. You pushed and pushed and pushed until there was no other way out.

No escape route.

The blood glugs along the floorboards, as if it has a mind of its own, spreading dark, thick liquid closer and closer to the tips of my trainers. My own escape flashes before me. I can't stay here much longer, but this isn't finished yet; there were two of you in this dance. Waltzing around like you had no cares in the world, as if your actions weren't painful and hurtful and dangerous.

This was never planned; it's important you know that. It's important the police know that. *I didn't do this.* You did, you attacked me, physically and emotionally. But no, what if there's nothing for the police to find. If I move quickly, there'll be no bodies to find.

I can't bury both of you. A bonfire in the garden could seem a bit out of place, but it could be mistaken for an early evening BBQ. At first, at least. There was a TV programme on a few weeks back, my attention barely on the screen but nobody could

1

ignore the interesting fact about burning human flesh smelling like cooking beef. Add in a touch of pork-like aroma for all that fat inside you both. The presenter explaining this little interesting fact said no one would mistake the smell for a 'back-garden cookout' – so it was an American programme then – but a small window of time is all I need. It won't take long for these god-awful nosey neighbours to notice, but by then I'll be gone and you two... well, you'll both be fried meat.

It's sickening that I want to laugh at my own words, my own plans, I can admit that. This tingling feeling is very new... No, I shouldn't be thinking this way, it's quite awful. But this is *your* fault. Your lies, the manipulation and scheming. I've never been an evil person, a person who would delight in harming others, but a person can change. Grow. Evolve into something new, something stronger.

Your squealing drags my attention back to the here and now. I'm sorry to say it, but you look like a pig, with your mouth gagged and your wrists and ankles tied, crouching in the corner. You look so different to me now, I'm ashamed of myself for how you made me feel at the beginning of all this.

And his bloodied body, helpless next to you. I can't believe you allowed this to happen. Did you know how selfish you were? I certainly didn't. But then, no one ever really knows who they're living next door to. Be careful what you do and say to your neighbours.

I yank the tape from your lips. You suck in fresh air, panting hard like you've just broken the surface of the sea. Greedy as ever.

'Please.' It's barely a whisper, so I move slightly closer to hear you. 'I'm so... so sorry. Please don't do this–'

You're cut short by your own crying as a new wave of weeping begins.

Ah, because you've actually stopped thinking about yourself

for a moment and allowed your eyes to gaze to the floor. Yes, watch the blood leave his lifeless body. Lower your head. Let the tears mix with the pools of snot that have collected around your nostrils. I can't believe how highly I used to think of you. How in awe I was of you. Now look at you... you're useless.

'I'm s...s... sorry,' you stutter.

I grab your face in my hand, grip your cheeks and force your head up. *Look at me.* I'm overcome with how infuriated you've made me. Your face burns white with the pressure of my rigid fingers. Go ahead, whimper and whine. Cry and blubber. Mutter words that make no sense.

Sorry.

Scared.

Selfish.

I see it so clearly now, that's who you are. And you should *feel* ashamed. He's dead because of you. And now, there's no other way that this can end. You have to be next. I don't even need to say those words aloud. Our gaze finally meets for the briefest of moments, but I have to look away, your eyes so wide you look demented. I guess you really are crazy. You must be, to do what you've done to me. I don't even know who you are anymore. But there is something I do know...

He's dead because of you. Now you have to die, too.

Then an ear-piercing wail shatters the silence.

CHAPTER ONE

FOUR MONTHS EARLIER

No one is perfect. No couple has the perfect relationship. If you think they do, it's because that's what they *want* you to see. Be it on social media, celebrating a special anniversary, buying their first home or announcing their miracle pregnancy. Or to your face, telling you about their promotion, the holiday they've just booked, or the weekly date night that is a *must* to keep the fire burning in their relationship. Is any of it really true? Can all your friends, family and colleagues have their shit together?

I'm not so sure. Though I bet most would call me jealous for saying that. Jealous because my family is minimal and my friends can be counted on one hand. I haven't had a holiday – abroad – in at least three years and do not have one booked. I'm self-employed; so unless I hire an intern just to have a 'team', I ain't getting a promotion anytime soon. There's no ring. There's no baby.

But Mike and I are happy. We're content in our little bubble which isn't social media perfect, but is perfect for us. That's not to say it's been easy over the past six years; relationships are messy because people are messy. Would I like a ring on my

TARA LYONS

finger? Yes, of course. However, it's not the be-all and end-all, as I already have Mike's commitment.

Do I want a child? More than anything in the world. I've been ready to start a family with Mike for... well, probably since the day I met him. I've always fancied the pants off that man. The contrast of a permanently clean-shaven face with messy blond hair always gives him that I-just-got-out-of-bed look, but with a flawless edge.

I've always wanted to be a mum. When Mike and I moved here back in March 2020, it was always with the vision of it being our family home.

When Covid took over the world shortly after, it felt like a blessing. At first. The thought of the two of us locked away together day and night... surely I'd fall pregnant. We'd be a family of three by the new year. But, as with so many people that year, and for so many different reasons, our hope was shattered.

While I sat at home drinking in the summer sun and pondering which position Mike and I could adventure into next, my poor mother lay in a pool of her own blood on the cold ground. That image returns to me at some point each and every day, like an unwanted guest who just won't take the hint and stay away. For good. Mum's death has scorched a mark on my heart deeper than any living memory of her.

The rest of that year, and the one after that, is a blur.

Since then I've carried a sadness with me. Even when I'm laughing out loud, there's always a shadow of sorrow tucked away in the nook of my smile. Anger stayed with me for a long time, and I refused to move past what had happened. You see, it's all my fault... Mum's–

'Yes, Carlos, I know we're low on orders at the moment, but customer service is not my remit.'

Mike's booming voice travels around the house and snatches

my thoughts away from Mum. A good thing, really. If I delve into the memory fountain that is her untimely death, I'll be on the floor again – and it's taken me years to drag myself back up from it. I can't go back there. Not again.

Mike's patience, and the fact that he didn't leave my side for one night, was commendable, in all honesty.

It's a real test of a relationship when one of those in it doesn't have the strength to even get out of the bed each morning. But Mike saved me. Even after Covid had long passed, he continued to work from home. When he wasn't busy on an online conference call, he would make me cups of tea or bring me another book.

I didn't have the heart to tell him I wasn't actually reading them. I just stared blankly at the pages, seeing my mum's distorted face jumbled up in all the letters. I didn't have the heart, or the guts, to tell him a lot of truths during those early months...

But, a few years later, I finally felt ready to try for a family again. *Family*. It's the grandest six-letter word in the dictionary, isn't it? Well, it certainly is to me. It's all I want, but each month I'm greeted by another negative pregnancy test. I've changed my diet and introduced more exercise. I use ovulation trackers and I will always initiate sex on my fertile days. I've tried everything I can think of but none of it seems to have worked. Now I can't help but wonder if it's time for Mike and me to see a professional. Get tested.

I feared this was also my fault. Spending so long being down on myself, living in a fog of grief, my body just didn't know what to do anymore.

Matters were made worse when Mike's company started making redundancies and his colleagues began falling away as though a private sniper was stationed nearby. It played on Mike's mind – he's worked there for twenty years – and it showed in his interactions with me. Now it was him who didn't want sex. You can't start a family when you're emotionally drained, and I felt that. So it was my turn to save him. The past six months haven't been perfect, but they've been near-damned close enough.

We've both steamed ahead with work. For me, it's been about starting a new fantasy series. I'm at my best when I'm writing, but I'd let it slip in my lull of grieving. Luckily, being a self-published author, I'm my own boss. I've devised a schedule whereby at least five thousand words must be written before I can plan or factor anything else in. Strictness is the key when you're self-employed, and getting my daily word count comes first. It's been so satisfying to see my hard work pay off with new releases and many book sales.

Mike was one of the lucky ones who was not made redundant – thank fuck for that – and although they've closed down the offices and warehouse in London, he's been part of the next stage. I'd love to share the ins and outs of Mike's job, but I've never been 100 per cent on the finer details. The gist is, he works for a multi-million gambling company that makes and supplies machines to the biggest casinos in the world: Vegas, Dubai, Spain, Australia... Actually, it does sound rather glam, doesn't it? But whenever he's asked, Mike just says he works in the gambling industry and leaves it at that.

'All the cabinets need to be in Barcelona.' Mike continues to project his voice to every corner of the house. 'They should have been freighted from London already, so you give me the update.'

And that next stage of Mike's role has been to assist the company in opening a new warehouse and office in Spain. Apparently it's cheaper than having it in the UK, but they didn't want to lay-off everyone with knowledge. Having worked for the company since he left school at seventeen, Mike knows a lot about each area of the business. He's an asset, and I'm just so thankful they saw that too.

This just feels like our year. We're not very far into it yet, granted, but for the first time in a long time, it's as though everything is aligning. I've dropped the sex schedules and we are just enjoying being together. I know my body is responding to that closeness in the right way. I can feel it.

My books are selling well again. There had been a worrying time when I couldn't shake the darkness to think creatively, to write my books as well as market and promote them so they were found by readers who would love them.

Mike's in a steady position at work and, more importantly, can continue working from home. Though his voice echoes through the walls when he's on a conference call, and other times he plays Capital Radio just a tad too loud, having him close-by feels like a comfort blanket. He protectively wraps himself around me, and the house, and I actually look forward to getting out of bed each morning now. I also look forward to getting back into bed a lot more, too; we have such a connection at the moment.

The thought makes me smile.

While I'm leaving my work desk to go downstairs, Mike begins yet another phone conference. His Adam's apple acts as a personal amplifier and his voice fills the air. This three-bedroom house, and what's happened – or not happened – in the years since, means we're lucky to each have our own room to work from. I wouldn't have chosen the smaller of the two, because there's something about a box room that can squash a person's creativity. But it was the bedroom we'd earmarked for our baby and while we wait for that little bundle of joy to join us, I feel like I'm keeping it warm for them.

Mike's loudness does infiltrate my working day. I can't complain, though, because I leave the door to my office wide open by choice. As much as this room means to me, and as much hope as it should bring to me, it can feel suffocating. Having only the same small four walls to stare at, with no opening, no light other than the small window looking out to the apartments across the field makes it feel as if there's no way out. The door has to remain open, to keep the locked-in feeling away. You have to keep the darkness at bay in any way possible, don't you?

CHAPTER TWO

Lost in a moment at the kitchen sink, my fingers curl around my mug – though the heat has long since seeped away from the colourful ceramic – and I stare out at my postage-stamp garden. My leafy suburb in Hertfordshire is tugging harder on the coattails of winter. We're only a little way north of London, and perhaps we too are affected by the changes to the city's climate, where a milder November and December makes way for a freezing start to the new year. Anyway – the frosty spell of January has clawed its way into February, and I try my best to ignore the neglected ice-scorched plant in the corner of the garden.

I long for warmer days. I've missed the bright mornings, which just get the day started with a buzz. It's easier. And the mild afternoons when I can sit in the garden and type at my laptop with the glistening midday sun and an ice-cold can of Diet Coke. Perfection. If only it could stay that way and not bring with it those claustrophobic weeks of summer, where the heat strangles you day and night. I hate it as much as the dark depths of winter.

I breathe in deeply, attempting to wake my bones from their reverie, when I hear Mike before I see him.

'Ruby, Ruby, Ruby.'

He calls out my name in that sing-song tone; even though he knows I hate it.

Obviously I was born before the Kaiser Chiefs infamously asked if a girl called Ruby knew what she was *doing doing doing*. I'll admit to using the word *infamously* with an eye roll because, personally, it's the most annoying combination of repeated words and whiney tune. But it could also be the fact that everyone I've ever met since 2007 has sung it *at* me as if they've just been welcomed to the karaoke at their local pub.

In recent years, I've noticed people linger over my face, mental cogs turning, trying to decipher how old I am: *could* she have been named after it? No, mate, I was born in 1990 and was worrying about my A-levels. My name actually came from my nan's love of Kenny Rogers and a girl who shouldn't take her love to town. That, and my birth date belonging to the day of love—

'Ruby, Ruby, Ruby,' Mike repeats as he slides into the kitchen.

I pull up a smile and spin around, knowing Mike's playful way of calling me can only mean he's in a great mood. I would hate to burst his bubble before he's even had a chance to tell me why.

'What's got you singing?'

'A promotion.' He opens out his hands and begins gesturing widely. 'This move to Spain, well the guys out there don't know as much as they thought they did. They don't understand the warehouse and how it runs. Not like I did in our London office. It's caused a big delay in the grand opening over there.'

Mike's voice has become as animated as his gestures, but his words are far too rushed. He must misconstrue my frown because he suddenly stops mid-arm-swing and asks why I'm not happy for him.

'I am happy, of course, if you're happy, I'm happy… but what is it we're happy about, exactly?'

'My promotion, Ruby.' His arms fall to his sides.

I've ruined his buzz; I can tell by his tone. His posture. I rush to him, take his hands in mine and smile. 'Slow down, is all I meant, and explain.'

He takes the bait, pulls his hands free and squeezes my shoulders in a bear-grip. 'Ruby, they want me to be involved in the Spanish opening. The warehouse and offices.'

Mike's grin is so wide I'm sure I could count every single pearly white.

'But we live in England.' I sound like a crank.

'Yes, babe, we do.' He laughs. 'But there's these things in the sky, we call them aeroplanes… Well, they can take you to near enough any country you wish to visit.'

'Haha.'

He releases his hold of me and bounces around the kitchen. 'Obviously, I'm still London-based, working from home, helping the team to plan and schedule from here. But they'll also need me in Spain a few times a month to help train and implement and–'

'A few times a month?' I interrupt, aghast at the proposition. 'They're going to pay for you to travel so often. Why can't they just hire someone who lives in Spain?'

Now it's his turn to frown at me. 'Ruby, this is such a great opportunity for me. The company have made people redundant, but they've chosen me – me and my skills – to be a part of this.'

'Of course, it's just so unexpected.' I take a deep breath. 'I'm sorry. Congratulations, babe.'

'You could have started with that,' he grumbles.

He's right, of course, he is. So why can't I cross the kitchen to hug him? I'm stuck to the spot, but Mike's staring at me for a reply. 'Yes, I should have started with that, please forgive me.'

'This is a great opportunity, babe,' he repeats, and guilt washes over me for knocking his spark. 'It will only be a couple of days at a time...'

Mike's words trail off, and it forces me to cover the distance and embrace him. 'I'm so proud of you. And so they should recognise all your knowledge, and dedication to the business.' He looks down at me. 'Congratulations.'

We share a soft kiss before he pulls away and drops another bombshell: 'I head out next week to meet the team and introduce myself in person.'

'*Next week?* What about Valentine's Day?'

Mike laughs and moves away towards the fridge. 'Worried you'll miss all the romance, babe?'

I feign throwing up. Valentine's day itself is made-up. If you only show love and buy overly expensive flowers on one day of the year, it's not real. 'No, I meant—'

'Yes, I know what you meant,' he replies, and peers back at me over his shoulder. He's changed so much over the past six years, but his trademark cleanly-shaven face has never faltered; it keeps him looking young, and very handsome. 'You meant your birthday, and I would never miss that day, Ruby.'

I'm not even sure why that was the first thing that came to mind. It's not as if turning thirty-five is a huge milestone, but I guess the thought of spending it alone... I could call Stef or Nancy, sure, but we all know that friendships in your thirties means more than a week's notice for everyone to be free. And even if they were, I would still be alone come the night and—

'So what do you think?' Mike's voice shakes me from my selfish thoughts.

'About what?'

'I spoke to my boss about dates and flights, and he wants it to work for me as much as the business. So I'll fly back Friday morning and you'll just be finishing your daily word count by the time I'm home. Then I can make us dinner and we can snuggle up and watch a film. You get to pick, of course. Does that sound like a nice birthday?'

'Sounds lovely. As long as we're together how could it not be.' But my stomach clenches. 'When will you fly out?'

'First thing Wednesday morning. It's just a two-night trip this time,' he replies as he closes the fridge door, and then turns to face me with another Cheshire cat grin. 'Now that's settled, do you think we could celebrate my news? We have no bubbly in, though, so I'll quickly nip to the shop.'

'Great. I'll go freshen up.'

Mike only makes it to the kitchen door before he turns back, a playful look dancing across his face. 'Actually... should we pop to the local for a few instead?'

Honestly: no, I don't want to. We never 'pop to the local' and I suddenly feel very nauseous. None of this is voiced aloud. I'm conscious that I've already dampened his spirits enough about his big news. 'Sure, why not? The change of atmosphere will be nice.'

He rubs his hands together in delight. 'But you'll... you'll still freshen up, right? That's where we differ working from home. You look like you've just rolled out of bed.'

Though it's said in jest, I self-consciously run a hand through my unwashed long hair. And when I peer down at my comfy, grey joggers, I notice a small tea stain. Okay, the man has a point. 'Yes, of course,' I say, and hope my can of dry shampoo isn't completely empty. 'Let me go...'

But Mike's attention has been snatched away by his phone. My heart flutters a little faster and my stomach tenses, so I slip out of the room and make my way upstairs. I trudge up them as if it's the hardest thing to do. There's a weight in my thighs, like cement, and it feels as though I spent the entire previous day at the gym working on my legs. Heavy. Non-compliant.

I'm panting by the time I reach the bathroom. Pull the cord to turn the light on, realising that I shouldn't need it as it's only coming up to 1pm, but the room is so dark. Everything *feels* so dark.

Dizzy. Spinning.

I release the cord, but don't trust my legs to keep me upright with no support so I slide down the wall, bringing my knees up to meet me. Adopting the brace position, the tears come without warning. Big, heavy sobs gush from somewhere deep inside me as I attempt to suck mouthfuls of air into my lungs. It's painful.

This has happened before. Just once. I thought I'd buried the feeling. Mike can't see me like this. He can't know... But that extra worry only lights the path for confusion and haziness to enter my mind. It allows the light-headedness to attack further. To take over and control. The room spins. The bath, the sink, the toilet. They're all swirling around me. I can't catch a deep enough breath. My chest is so tight, so constricting, so demanding.

Inhale. Exhale. Quickly. Too quickly, I can't keep up, I can't breathe.

I'm alone.

I'm going to die.

I'm going to die alone just like... just like she did.

CHAPTER THREE

Hump day Wednesdays are for visiting Gran. Well, not every single week, because my little gran can be a cantankerous old fart – which I say with love – who insists I don't smother her. I once went three Wednesdays in a row and as I had no 'new news' for her, Gran had said, 'Ruby, my dear, I'm now living vicariously through you. So please get a life, and come see me when you have some gossip from the outside world.' I can only hope her words were meant with as much love as my own.

Gran lives in a care home in central London. The little apartment block could be located anywhere, in all honesty, as she hasn't left the building since she moved in. Her mind may well be as sharp as a tack, but her mobility is not. The body gave up on her many years ago.

She had lived with Mum, prior to Covid, but it was getting too much for them both. Playing the role of daughter and nurse and caregiver can take its toll, and Gran could see it was wearing Mum down, though neither of them would admit it.

So Gran moved at the beginning of 2020 and I can't help but wonder if we had known what was around the corner, would things be different? Would Mum still be alive?

I wrap my rainbow-coloured scarf snugly around my neck and pull my shoulders back as I inhale deeply. I must stop letting these kinds of thoughts enter my mind whenever they like. They're too dark. Too depressing. One last check over in the mirror by the front door, I look better than I thought I would after last night's bottle of wine in the local. And that's a bottle to myself, because Mike only drinks beer.

Of course, I hadn't intended to drink so much, considering I didn't even want to go. But I got carried away. It made me sluggish in reaching my five thousand words, and it was hard work. I'm sure I'll edit the crap out of them tomorrow, but they are written and that's the main thing. A long, hot shower helped me feel more human; and making the effort with my hair and make-up was a nice change this morning. Heaven forbid I rock up to see Gran looking like an extra from a zombie apocalypse film.

'Mike,' I call out from the front door, and wait for a response with my hand on the doorknob. There's no reply, but he has been quieter than normal this morning. Either the alcohol hit him harder than I thought, or he's busy planning his first trip to Spain. I shudder at the latter, and a heavy rock drops in my stomach. My eyes sting, so suddenly, without any warning. Mike's new promotion has brought with it such fear that the mere thought of it is enough to reduce me to tears.

And these haunting memories... but no, the selfishness has to stop. It isn't about me; it's about Mike, and this is such a great opportunity for him.

I have to stop letting the darkness back in. Shaking it off, I clear my throat and yell louder. 'Mike!'

'What? I'm on a call.'

'I'm leaving to visit Gran, so I'll see you later this evening.'

No reply. I wait a few seconds more, but it's clear he can't talk so I head out the front door. He'll text when he's finished, I'm sure.

Mike knows I'll be gone for a good few hours as it takes flipping ages to get to Victoria. My fault, I guess, using public transport instead of driving when I visit Gran. Parking is always a pain in the arse, for one, but the main reason is because I absolutely hate the roads of London. The too-big roundabout circling Hyde Park Corner, the myriad lanes on Buckingham Palace Road, the double-decker buses and impatient taxi drivers. It's all enough to send a driver insane. Give me an open motorway any day, with each car taking their own pace and space from each other. When it comes to visiting Gran, let the train take the strain – as it's just over an hour's journey – and read a good book I say.

It's bitterly cold and the sharp breeze slaps me in the face when I turn out of the front garden and onto our close. I yank my scarf up further, covering my chin, and stuff my hands in my coat pockets. I've chosen comfort over style, like I do most days of my life, so the big, padded outerwear will protect me well on the ten-minute walk to the train station.

Our house is in the middle of the close, so I could cross over the street and walk up the alleyway – it's a strange little passageway between the two houses opposite us and has no name or signage on Google Maps, but the shortcut is well-known to the locals as a cut-around from this side of the town to the high street. Mike is adamant it's a quicker route to the station, but I hate walking through the hustle and bustle of the high street. I much prefer walking past our neighbours' homes, and then the houses on the surrounding streets before reaching the top of the high street having missed all the shops. Plus my way *is* faster, I just don't like to argue with him about it.

So I turn right and slowly pass by our immediate neighbours' house. On a few occasions I've spoken to the woman – Sharon I think she said her name was – just in polite conversation. But I know nothing about them except the fact they have two very noisy kids who I can hear through the walls. And that they erected a trampoline in their garden last year. Luckily it was right at the end of the summer, so there wasn't much playing time to be had, and I'm praying to God it's blown away in a gust of high wind before the sun makes its annual visit.

Gosh, that makes me sound pretty awful, doesn't it? I do love children, just not the noisy pair next door.

To the left, a little further up, is the dark house. That's what I call it; have done since the day we moved here. I've never been inside, obviously, but it just has this aura about it. Even from the outside, it just feels cold – even during the warmth of summer – and appears *darker* than all the others surrounding it. It's just bricks, like all the other houses on the street, but this one is gloomier. Dimmer. Sadder. Dirty, almost.

Perhaps it's more to do with the man who lives there... The Weird One, I call him. Mike always rolls his eyes at me whenever I do, and says all the true crime documentaries I watch have left my mind scattered in dark places. But it's not. It's the eerie way The Weird One stares deeply whenever we see each other in the cul-de-sac. He stands tall and confident, but in a stiff Michael Myers from *Halloween* type way, his beady eyes unfaltering. You can feel them boring into you long after you've walked on by. Which is the reason why today I quickly avert my own gaze from his shady house, just in case I catch him watching. It would only leave a curdling feeling in my stomach for the entire day.

One house I know I won't be able to pass without seeing its occupant is the last one – or first, depending on which way you're coming from. Picky Patty, as Mike nicknamed her, can always be found at a window, strategically at the front door or even out on the street collaring someone for a chat. I don't think I've ever walked by and not seen her.

The first time I met Patty was because she'd taken in a parcel for us. Now, being a couple who barely leaves their home, this is a rare occurrence for us. I'd seen the delivery card when I returned from visiting Gran, and hoped Mike would pop up to the neighbour at number one to collect it when he was home from seeing his brother. He wasn't in the house five minutes when Patty was knocking the letterbox with a parcel addressed to him. She'd used the visit well, telling us all about the cul-de-sac's WhatsApp group, and the Neighbourhood Watch scheme she manages with some of the locals, and her idea of a local community book club.

Of course, Covid hit a few weeks later and once I had picked myself up off the floor – physically and emotionally – it didn't feel right to introduce myself to everyone as the new neighbour. It probably left a bad impression on Patty, too, so I'm not sure now if it's us who dodges her or if it's the other way round. We like to keep ourselves to ourselves anyway.

And today, as I pass her house with its neatly trimmed and very open front garden, I see the woman standing at the window of her living room – well, I assume it is from the layout of my own house. If I had to take a guess, I'd say she was in her early sixties, but I always think she looks so glam and more fashionable than me. I can just about see a leopard print top with a subtle frill detail on the shoulder today, and her hair is poker-straight to perfection. She lightly brushes her side fringe away from her eyes and just as I think I should look away, Patty gives me a small wave, like the Queen used to from her podium on the balcony. Before I have the chance to wave back, she places a phone to her ear and swings away like a flash of lightning.

That was strange. Patty's never waved at me before.

21

CHAPTER FOUR

It's an awful thing to say, but it was hardly worth visiting Gran this week. She wasn't in the best of spirits, and given the lack of chat from her today, I'm not even sure why. She usually loves a good gossip and catch-up, and I love putting the world to rights with her.

It's hard to admit, but her mood swings have gained momentum over the past few months; they are as unpredictable as the sea waves. At least if she had a mobile, we could chat more often and freely, but Gran despises them, believing they ruin "real" communication. It's a generational thing.

'Plus, you could send me one of those fax messages,' she had said one day – clearly not fully grasping the word text – 'to say you're on the way to see me. When really you're sitting in the local with a G&T and I'd be none the wiser.'

At that point, I gave up with trying.

It's not that I don't want to see Gran, of course I do, but it's not as if it's just a quick bus journey down the road. By the time I finally turn my key in the front door tonight, the sun has long since set and every joint in my body is shattered. I welcome myself home with a huge sigh of relief.

'There you are.' Mike pounces as soon as I'm over the threshold. 'Where have you been for so long?'

'Visiting Gran. I told you that.'

'I called your phone like a billion times,' he continues as he turns to walk off to the kitchen. 'You could have answered, Ruby. I was really starting to worry.'

I take off my coat, pulling my mobile from the pocket as I hang it up. I check the screen: ten missed calls. *Shit...*

'I'm sorry, babe, it was on silent because I hate being on my phone while travelling, I'm always worried I'll miss my stop,' I say in the direction of the kitchen. I'm not sure Mike's listening, until I hear him muttering a remark about my nose being stuck in a book. He's right, to be fair.

My back muscles tense with the cold and I shiver as though I'm still outside. How can he not have the heating on? It's bloody freezing in here. I place my phone on the console table and grab the thermostat. Sure enough, the heating is switched off. I remedy that straight away and whack it up to twenty degrees; bring on the warmth. Now I just need a cuppa.

The kettle is already boiling when I enter the kitchen. I thank Mike and give him a smile, but only receive a curt nod in reply.

'I said I was sorry, Mike, please don't hold a grudge.'

His expression changes, as though I've slapped him across the cheek. 'A grudge? Bloody hell, I was worried.'

'You know I'm gone most of the day,' I reply as I busy myself making the tea. 'Though it wasn't a great visit as Gran didn't seem interested in chatting today, sadly.'

'It's a waste of time,' he mumbles, but continues quickly before I have a chance to argue. 'I just mean, you should call ahead before you head out. It's a long old day for you and if she isn't up to the visit...'

Though I don't totally disagree with what he's saying, it

doesn't feel nice. 'No, I couldn't not see her just because she wasn't feeling chatty. Perhaps those are the days she needs to see me more.'

Mike barks, a horrible sarcastic noise, and continues his dispute. 'So you journey hours around central London and back for what?' He doesn't pause to let me answer. 'I know she's your gran, Ruby, but she's not the same woman she once was. She probably needs more rest, less stimulation. And I'm here, worrying about you when I should be working because I haven't heard from you since you left the house.'

I'm too tired to argue, and I guess there is that sweet nurse who works at Gran's care home. Perhaps I could have a chat with her about calling Gran more often, as a compromise. I bite my lip and nod my head, allowing Mike to think I agree. I wrap my arms around his waist and wait until he hugs me back before apologising.

'You're right, and I'm sorry,' I say into his shoulder, appreciating the warmth radiating from him. 'I should have let you know I was on my way home, at least.'

He kisses my head, letting his lips linger there for a while and my stomach tingles. I caress my hands slowly up and down his back, pull my head up to face him and press my lips against his. That fluttering feeling intensifies and just as it begins to travel downwards, Mike pulls away and winks.

'Let's eat first,' he says. 'I'm famished. Worked up a right appetite waiting for you.'

He chuckles as he moves away from me and then reaches into the kitchen junk drawer. Pulling out the menu of his favourite Chinese restaurant, he beams at me hopefully and waves the paper in the air like a white flag. Except, it's not a peace offering, because I hate the damned place. But then... he has been worried about me, and it was all my fault for getting lost in my paperback and not checking my phone.

'Sure,' I say with a pinched smile. 'Put the usual order in and it'll be ready for me to collect by the time I finish my cuppa.'

Just one of the reasons I hate the local Chinese is that they don't deliver. Who wants to venture out for a takeaway? The whole joy and treat of not cooking is the fact that they're bringing it to your door. But nope, not The White Dragon. And it's right bang smack in the middle of the high street, there's no point in driving because the food would be cold and greasy by the time you found somewhere to park. That's if you find a space at all.

Mike leans down and kisses me hard on the lips. 'You're offering to collect?'

'It's the least I can do,' I say and kiss him back, softer and lighter.

'I think someone's gonna get lucky tonight for that.'

'I think someone should.'

He slaps me on the arse, then turns to leave the kitchen.

The walk back from The White Dragon only takes ten or fifteen minutes, depending on how briskly you want to walk. Tonight, the urge to run is sickeningly intense. But I'm scared I'll spill Mike's sweet and sour sauce from its tiny white container if I start bombing it down the street.

It feels even darker than it did an hour ago on the walk back from the train station. This is unnerving. It's so quiet, and so cold, it's as if I can *hear* the frosty whiteness in the air.

Each time I look over my shoulder, no one is there. No one is following me. But there are footsteps in the shadows. It's not just my breathing in the icy evening. I can hear the steps, and the panting. The brightness of the high street is behind me now, as I walk down the side road leading to the alleyway opposite my house.

The alleyway. *Shit.*

I shouldn't have come this route. The alley only has one streetlamp, in the middle at the bend from one side of the path to the other. In the blind spot where you can't be seen from either this street leading to it or the cul-de-sac I live on.

The footsteps gain speed.

I want to listen, to know where the stranger behind me is coming from, but my breathing is out of control. Like drums banging in my ears, pleading with my body to stop moving, huddle down and pray the person walks on by assuming *I'm* the nutter. But I can't stop, and my own footsteps pick up the pace as though they're the ones in charge. My overactive imagination and penchant of all things true crime has my brain sending signals to my feet before I can even register them.

Fuck the sweet and sour, it's saying now.

I grip the white carrier bags in a fist and jog. Fast.

My footsteps echo as they pound against the ground. Stamp. Second stamp. Is it an echo, or is the stranger moving faster too? I can't bear to turn around. The wind slaps my face and my cold nose starts leaking. My eyes, too. Blurring my vision.

The turning into the alleyway is just up ahead, another fifty feet is all, but that'll be worse. It'll be darker, and secluded. I try to catch a glimpse of the houses as I dash past them. Is there anyone looking out of a window? Could I knock on any of these doors? No one would answer. No one helps strangers anymore.

He's panting behind me. Closer. He's caught up.

I can't stop now. Head down, as though I'll gain more speed, I push myself to run faster. My legs feel as dead as wood, but I thump along the pavement and turn into the alleyway. All I can see are my bright white trainers moving forward as fast as my unfit body will allow. The rustle of the evergreens overhead mingles with my breathing, with the panting in the background.

I hear it right up until I reach the middle of the alleyway, the streetlamp at the bend which leads to my cul-de-sac. The stranger's footsteps stop.

Without thinking I stop. Panting, I swing around and see a shadowy figure a mere ten feet away. His face is dark and obscured by a baseball cap, and he's just standing there. Unmoving. Staring. I mirror his position through pure fear.

The figure jerks forward and I scream. The two bags of food crash to the ground, plastic containers spilling out, and I turn to run. I run the remaining half of the alleyway faster and harder than I've ever run before. The house is in the distance, I can see the light of my bedroom window lighting the way like a beacon. I hear nothing behind me, but dare not stop again. I just need to get home. Just a few more feet.

I crash onto the front door, banging and calling Mike's name.

'Help,' I scream as my fist connects with the glass. Even if the figure has followed me, I'm safe now. He can't attack me on my front doorstep, can he? *Can he?* Oh Christ. 'Mike. Mike, Mike!' I continue to call out and knock simultaneously.

A hand touches my shoulder. I scream and kick, calling Mike's name to save me, while flapping my arms at my attacker. Anything to stop him until someone arrives to help me.

'Ruby.'

Mike's voice drags me from the darkness. I open my eyes and see it's *him* I'm hitting. It's Mike's hands on me.

'What the fuc–'

'Mike, oh my God, what's going on?' I lower my hands and look around him. The front door is still closed. 'How did you get there?'

'I came to find you. You forgot your mobile on the console and you've been gone ages.'

The panting is still coming thick and fast. So is the confusion. 'So it was... it was you, in the alleyway just now?'

'The alleyway?' He frowns. 'No, I drove up to the high street. When you weren't in the Chinese, I knew we must have just missed each other. I just pulled up,' he points to our car parked in the bay to the left of the house, 'and saw you banging on the door like a crazy woman. Why didn't you use your keys? Why are you crying?'

I fling myself into his arms and allow my breathing to return to some semblance of normality before explaining. 'Someone was following me. Then they chased me. I didn't even think about my keys, actually, I just thought you'd open the door.'

'What the hell–' Mike stops, pulls me out in front of him and examines every bit of me. 'Ruby, are you okay?'

I look over his shoulder and see nothing but the bushes of our front garden and houses lit with a warm glow in each room. No stranger. No figure. No one following me.

'Ruby, are you–'

'I'm fine. There's no one there now. But... oh crap, I dropped the food while running back.'

'Are you serious? Let me go and check it out.'

I grab Mike by the arm. 'No. Please don't go.'

'I have to see if they're still there, Rubes.'

'No,' I say, shaking my head, feeling embarrassed and stupid. Surely if someone was following me, they would have continued to come at me in the alleyway. What if it was an innocent person on their way home and I freaked them out. 'Just leave it, please.'

'What about dinner?'

'It's not saveable, I'll sort us something else. Please can we go inside now.'

Mike's sigh is not welcome right now, and only adds to my humiliation. I hope no one saw me crashing through the front garden.

I glance around while Mike rattles his bunch of keys, my leg bouncing on the spot, waiting impatiently. The cul-de-sac is quiet: no cars driving in or out and no footsteps in the distance. I strain my neck, cocking my ear upwards to the black sky, desperate to make out any nearby movement. Nothing.

Mike is all noise. Whining about what to have for dinner now, and lighting up the house like Blackpool Tower. Trainers kicked off. Blowing on his hands like he's just come in from a storm. I glide in quickly behind him, desperate to shut out the world and darkness.

Actually, yes, do turn on another lamp, Mike. Make all the racket you can to shake the grip of the alleyway from me. But as I rush to lock the door, I can't help but peer through the glass panel. For a brief few seconds, a shadowy figure blocks the light from the street.

Then it's gone.

CHAPTER FIVE

The following week, I wake to the muffled hum of Mike's voice bleeding through the walls. His calls have started early, even louder than usual. It's unlike me to sleep in, but sleep itself has been a cruel stranger all weekend. Every time I closed my eyes, I was back in that alleyway – the shadowy figure behind me, the quickening footsteps, the suffocating certainty that someone was following me. It's not that Mike doesn't believe me, but I could hear the annoyance in his voice when he said, 'You've got such an imagination, Ruby. It's a gift. But sometimes you need to rein it in.'

Gift, my arse.

He believes, *if* there was someone behind me, it was probably just an innocent neighbour making their way home. It would have been me scaring the shit out of them: screaming, running and throwing my takeaway in their path. I'm not convinced, but it was enough to shut me up. So much so, I stayed confined to my office for the better part of yesterday, much later than normal for a Monday, and Mike didn't seem to notice. Arsenal were probably playing.

I swing my legs over the side of the bed and rub my face, my palms pressing hard into my eyes. Despite the frostiness of February, the sunlight makes a valiant effort of streaming through the curtains. I need to shake the heaviness from my mind and stop obsessing over the could-be mugger. Mike's laugh booms from his office, snapping me from my thoughts. His voice not only carries through the walls, today, but also through my skull. I need to get out of here. I need air. Space.

After a brief shower, in which the hair did not get washed, I dress quickly in jeans and a comfy jumper. Peeking into Mike's office, I tell him I'm heading to the café to write.

'I thought you were ahead with your writing.' He doesn't even glance up from his screen. 'You were in there almost all day yesterday.'

'I am,' I lie. 'Just need a change of scenery.'

Mike finally breaks from the screen to look at me. 'You going to the usual place, with the little bakery?' I smile and nod. 'Get me one of those old-school slices of cake, will you?'

'Of course,' I reply and slip back out of the room.

I hate lying to Mike, but he doesn't know I'm meeting up with Stef for a coffee and catch-up. We regularly do when she's not on day shifts. It's no secret that Mike and Stef don't get along, but there's no point in making a thing of it. She's my friend and he's my partner; they don't *have* to like each other. But Stef has been my ride-or-die since secondary school, and that's not an easy bond to break.

I grab my bag and car keys, and slip out of the house. The cool air is a welcome relief against my skin.

Stef's already in our usual corner when I arrive at the café twenty minutes later. She looks up and smiles, her face lighting up like it always does. Our drinks are already in place: a green tea for her and a sweet latte for me.

'Hey, stranger,' she says, standing to hug me. The sculpted leggings telling me all I need to know.

'You've already been to the gym.' I roll my eyes and pull my baggy jumper further down my torso.

'We all have our vices.' Stef laughs and retakes her seat. I drop into the chair opposite and let my bag slide to the floor. 'Plus,' she says, 'Once I've dropped Hunter to nursery, I don't like to waste my day off.'

Stef's an inspiration: a paramedic, herbal tea drinker and gym-fanatic. The sigh escapes my mouth before I have a chance to stop it. She notices instantly and asks what's wrong.

'Sorry, it's been a week,' I admit, and take a gulp of the lukewarm coffee.

She nods, as if agreeing, and for a moment I'm tinged with the shame of my first-world problems.

'It's only Tuesday, mate. What's up?'

I hadn't planned on launching straight into it, but Stef has a way of making me open up. Surprisingly, Mike's promotion and upcoming regular travels consumes the one-sided conversation.

'And how do you feel about that?' she asks when I stop for air.

I shrug, forcing myself to sound casual. 'It's fine. I mean, it's not forever.'

She tilts her head, implying that I'm holding something back. 'What's up?'

'It's just... No, you'll think I'm ridiculous.'

'Maybe. But you've started now, so I'll bug you until you 'fess up.'

I roll my eyes at her persistence. 'Well, the thought of being on my own for nights on end... I hate it.'

'Is that it? Jheeze, Rubes, what I wouldn't give to have a few nights a month on my own. I'd have a long bath, paint my nails, watch a film from start to finish without being interrupted.'

I can't help but laugh. 'When you put it like that...'

Stef smiles, but leans back in the chair and encourages me to explain further. But honestly, now, I might sound like even more of a fool to my mate. 'What if something happens when I'm on my own?'

'Like what?'

'There's a fire and I can't get out of my bedroom. Or if I slip in the shower and smash my head and nobody knows because it's late at night. Or a gang of youngsters break in looking for money and jewels but find a woman in bed alone and rip off my nightie–'

'You don't wear nighties.'

I roll my eyes. 'You know what I mean, Stef. When you're alone, you're more vulnerable. One defenceless person in a big old house on their own is just screaming for something bad to happen.'

'Really? Bloody hell, Ruby, what happened in your childhood?'

Stef's quizzical face makes me laugh again, and I wonder if I really do sound crazy. 'Nothing, actually. My upbringing was extremely vanilla.'

'Then where are all these worries coming from?'

I shrug my shoulders, because does there have to be a reason? Doesn't everyone think like this? 'Just thoughts that pop into my mind.'

She puffs loudly. 'Well, that's some overactive imagination. But I guess that's why you're the writer, hey, full-on storyteller.'

That gets me thinking. 'Well, maybe. I guess when everyone was watching *Sweet Valley High*, I loved the Goosebumps books. Then I progressed to Stephen King, *Harry Potter*, *The Twilight Saga*.'

'That's your problem,' Stef says with a click of her fingers. 'All this suspense and fantasy, you don't know what's real or what's fake with all the imaginary worlds you jump in and out of. Then all that true crime shit you watch, it's enough to give anyone nightmares. I see enough horrors at work, so give me Bridget Jones and all of her diaries any day of the week.'

She's got a point, I guess.

'Plus, you've never lived alone.' Stef's on one now. 'You went from living with your mum and your gran, then to halls, then living with me, and then Mike.'

'I hadn't thought of that.'

'Seriously, Rubes, I know you love what you do, but think about switching up your genres. Indulge in a good Julia Roberts film.'

'Sleeping with the–'

'No,' Stef interrupts, knowing exactly where I was going with that one, and we both laugh. 'I mean it, Ruby, enjoy the time alone. Crank the music up and unwind. And if you can't, call me and I'll happily come over. I'm lucky if I get to use the bathroom alone these days.'

Images of Stef's family fill my mind – her beautiful son and wife – and I can't help but smile. 'Yes, enough about me and my *stories*, please. How are Hunter and Kelly? Tell me what's been going on with you.'

'Well...' Stef draws a long pause, her grin widening. 'The IVF worked again. Kelly's pregnant!'

I jump from the table and hug her tightly. She dances in our embrace and her happiness is infectious. For a moment, I let it carry me as I return to my seat.

'That's amazing, Stef, I'm so happy for you both.' I mean it, I really do, but as I speak, a familiar ache knots in my chest. I grip my coffee cup tighter.

Stef keeps talking, her joy spilling over, and I nod along, doing my best to stay in the moment. But the image sneaks in, uninvited: me, telling Mike the same news. His face lighting up. His arms wrapping around me in a tender hug. The vision dissolves just as quickly as it had formed. *How can I be so selfish?*

I raise my cup and say, 'To your beautiful growing family. And to many more sleepless nights.'

Stef laughs, clinking her cup against mine. We continue on about her pregnant wife, their son Hunter becoming a big brother, about her work and the novel I'm writing, when she notices it's past midday and remembers she has errands to run before the nursery pick-up.

Outside, the cold breeze tugs at my coat and whips my cheeks. Stef hands me a pink envelope, saying I can't open it until my birthday.

'Didn't think I forgot, did you?' She winks. 'I'm working Friday, but we could arrange a dinner and drinks for my next night off?'

'Ah, I'm only thirty-five, let's not make a fuss.'

She purses her lips and raises her eyebrows. Full sass. 'Well, you may not want to celebrate *your* birthday, but my son will be partying to his fourth at the end of this month. You're coming, right? I'm sorry it's on a weekday. I know you're busy, but Hunter's told everyone that his "famous Auntie Rubes" will be there.'

I laugh, the nickname warming me more than any cup of coffee ever could. 'Nothing could keep me away.'

'Good. He'd never forgive you. And neither would I,' she teases.

I drive home in silence, the sound of the engine a faint purr beneath my thoughts. The image of Stef's happy, growing family loops in my head, relentless. It all feels like a taunt. Mike and I have been trying for so long. Why can't I get pregnant? When will it be my time?

At a red light, I roll my neck from side to side, and exhale slowly. This despair has to stop. *Do something, Ruby.* Mike leaves for Spain in the morning. Use that as an excuse to take time together. I grip the wheel tighter, determination replacing the ache. We'll have dinner, open a bottle of wine and, for once, I'll push aside the fear, the doubts, the shadows. We'll fall into bed and make our future.

It's a plan I cling to as I turn onto our street, but a removal van is parked across the entrance of the cul-de-sac, completely blocking my way. I hit the brake and horn simultaneously. Nothing. An overweight man sits in the driver's seat, as though oblivious to my presence.

I lean out the window, waving my arm. 'Hey! You're blocking the road.'

He finally looks at me, like I've inconvenienced his entire day. 'Yeah, yeah,' he says, gesturing vaguely. 'Give me a sec.'

I grit my teeth as he takes his sweet time turning the ignition on. My fingers drum impatiently on the steering wheel, surprised the other neighbours haven't already complained and asked him to move. Especially Patty. Crap, I hope he isn't moving into the close. Eventually, the van inches forwards, just enough for me to squeeze past. I don't bother thanking him.

By the time I've parked the car, my earlier resolve has soured into irritation. I take a deep breath and try to push it all aside. The van, the frustration, Stef's announcement. None of it matters. Not tonight. The focus is on me and Mike.

Once inside the house, I'm greeted by a wall of mess and noise. The shoe rack has been given a good rummage, with Mike's variety of trainers sprawled all over the floor. He's even pulled out the tool case which usually lives underneath the racking. Alexa is playing music at full volume, while Mike hums along, moving around the living room and folding clothes into a suitcase laid open on the sofa.

I stare at him from the doorway, my bag slipping off my shoulder. 'Really?'

He looks up, startled but smiling. 'Great, you're back. Where's my blue shirt? You know, my favourite one, with the tiny checks?'

I blink, unmoving, as he returns to his packing. 'In the wardrobe. Where else would it be?'

'Nope, already looked there. Can you find it for me?'

The irritation prickles hot under my skin. 'Seriously, Mike? I just walked in the door. And why aren't you working?'

He doesn't notice my tone, or if he does, he ignores it entirely. He's still half dancing to the radio, his back to me.

'Mike,' I snap.

He finally turns. 'What's your problem?'

'My problem?' I take a step further into the room. 'You're blaring music like you're throwing a party, tossing clothes everywhere like a teenager, and look at the state of the hallway.'

He raises an eyebrow, his easy demeanour evaporating. 'Excuse me for being in a good mood. Damn, Rubes, what's the drama now?'

The heat rises to my face. 'Maybe because I wanted to spend a nice, quiet evening with you, and instead, I walk into this circus. You're packing like you're going on a lad's holiday; you want me to find your clothes; and then I guess I'll have to tidy up all this mess because you're leaving first thing tomorrow?'

His eyes narrow. I've struck a nerve. 'Oh, I'm sorry,' he says, his voice sharp. 'I didn't realise I needed permission to be excited about my promotion. Or to pack a bag in my own house.' He strides past me, sliding the tool case further into the living room with a clatter, and heads for the stairs.

'We're not done talking,' I say, following him.

'Yes, we fucking are.'

'Mike, don't turn your back on me, it's rude.'

At the bottom step, he spins to face me. 'You're being childish.'

'Childish?'

'You can't expect me to cater to your moods, Ruby. Grow up.'

Something inside me snaps. 'I wanted tonight to be special,' I shout, but my voice breaks, betraying me. 'I wanted to spend time with you, Mike. I wanted us to–'

'To what?' he demands.

'To be together,' I say, softer now, the anger draining. 'You're leaving tomorrow, and I wanted to make the most of tonight. But you've ruined it.'

His face grows darker; his shoulders stiffen and his jaw tightens. He steps closer, eyes locked on mine. 'Oh, is that what you wanted?' He grabs the hem of my jumper.

'Mike–'

But he yanks my top off, shutting me up and pulling it over my head in one swift motion. His hands are rough and demanding. He presses me against the staircase. Lips crush against mine. It's not what I imagined: there's no softness, no tenderness. But I don't stop him.

I can't stop him.

Because this is what I wanted, isn't it? This is our chance. This is how we get what we've been trying for. My mind races, the stairs dig into my back, his weight heavy on me. But I let it happen.

Maybe, just maybe, this time will work.

CHAPTER SIX

I wake in the dead of night. The room is suffocatingly dark, the air thick and clammy. My breath is shallow, my limbs heavy, like I'm pinned to the mattress. Something feels... off. I slide my hand across the bed, feeling for Mike, but he's not there. He's gone, and all that remains are cold sheets under my fingers. I go to call his name, but then I see it. The figure in the doorway.

My body stiffens. Someone is standing there, watching me, unmoving. I can't make out who it is, but I know for certain it isn't Mike. A woolly hat, a bulky coat, their hands dangling loosely by their sides. My eyes dart around, my heart pounds inside my chest. I open my mouth but nothing comes out. No sound, as if my throat is locked tight. My fingers twitch under the duvet, I need to grab my phone, turn on the bedside lamp, anything. But I can't move. It's as if, if I don't move, he won't move, and maybe he'll leave.

I'm paralysed with utter fear and all I can do is stare. The figure doesn't shift, but I can hear him breathing now, deeply through his nose. Just staring at me, just waiting.

Sit up, Ruby, shout and scream God damn it, I tell myself.

Call for Mike? Oh God, Mike, what if the intruder has already got to him and he's lying hurt – or worse – downstairs.

Then the figure steps forward.

My breath stutters. I still can't see their face. I don't want to. I squeeze my eyes shut tight, allowing the darkness to press into me, but then something shifts and when I open my eyes, I'm not in my bedroom anymore. I'm in my mum's house.

A stifling heat fills the air, thick with the smell of sickly-sweet incense and burning candles. The walls close in and the silence stretches. I walk, into the living room and turn towards the sofa. She's there. Mum. Curled up under a blanket, her face half-buried in the cushions. The TV is on, but the sound is muted.

I rush closer to her. 'Mum?' I say, but there's no sound coming from me either.

She doesn't move, she doesn't look at me, she just sits there frozen in a strange, twisted angle and stares at nothing. Her eyes glassed over. My pulse slams in my ears and I know this moment, I know what's happening, it's the same as when I found her before. The same feeling – but she wasn't on the sofa. This is wrong, it's distorted, jumbled up.

I shouldn't touch her, I know I shouldn't, but I have to. The longing to feel my mum's warm embrace, to pull her from whatever dream she's in, is too much. I reach out, my fingers so close to her shoulder... but then she disappears into a wisp of smoke, as if I've blown out a candle.

A breathless scream lodges in my throat. I stumble back, but the ground beneath me shifts and I'm gone from her living room. I'm back at home, in the hallway now at the bottom of the stairs, and it's dark and cold and... wrong.

I spring around and find the dark, motionless figure again, standing at the back door. He followed me home, through the alleyway. He's here, but closer now, inches away. He still has no face, no features, no expression. Just a black void. He leans in, and I want to scream, but my mouth is clamped shut with a powerful force. I can feel his breath against my cheek as he comes closer. My feet as fixed in place as the rest of my body. He whispers something, over and over, but the words sound miles away. I can't understand what they mean, what he's saying.

'Shh, shh, shh,' is all I can make out, and the noise slithers through me, twisting in my gut.

A flicker of something behind him catches my eye, a flash of light, and just as the dark figure surges forward, I wake with a gasp.

The room is silent but I'm in my bed. My eyes scan the room, resting on the bedroom door that's fully shut. I reach out and switch on the lamp, welcoming the flood of light. My body is drenched in sweat and my heart beats like a wild drum. I feel Mike's warm body next to me and greedily breathe in big gulps of air.

Just a dream. It was just a dream, Ruby. No one is here but you and Mike.

CHAPTER SEVEN

I find Gran in the common room, parked in her usual spot by the window, watching the world outside with her signature mix of disdain and curiosity. She loves to people watch, but she's never been much of a people's person, and when Mum and I first suggested a care home, Gran was highly offended. If only I'd known then that by leaving Mum on her own, she would–

No. Stop.

I look to Gran again, her hair combed into an immaculate bun of silver. Her slippered foot taps against the side of her wheelchair, waiting, not impatiently I hope. The room is quiet, with the TV a quiet rumble in the background. This room is hardly used. The other residents are confined to their beds, or they prefer the small haven of their rooms. Gran asks to be brought in here most days. I don't think she enjoys that locked-in feeling either.

Gran finally notices me. 'Took you long enough. I was about to call the police and tell them I'd been abandoned.'

I try not to laugh at the dramatics, and wonder if now is a good time to tell Gran of my plan to call in advance. That sweet nurse wasn't around the reception area today when I signed in. I decide against it, for now, and bend down to kiss Gran's cheek.

She lifts her sharp blues eyes to meet mine. 'No make-up today,' she declares, pursing her lips. 'You look very... fresh in the face.'

'Ha. Thanks for the compliment, Gran.'

'It wasn't a compliment, love, you look bloody knackered.'

'I didn't get much sleep last night, that's all.'

'Don't get me started on sleeping in this place. There's always someone up at stupid o'clock being loud. You'd think they'd offer more sedatives in a place like this.' I roll my eyes, but laugh as she picks up her teacup and gestures to the pot on the table. 'Pour yourself one, Ruby, love, if you're planning to stay longer than five minutes. It's like dishwater, but they don't listen to my complaints about it.'

I do as she suggests, attempting to allow the familiarity of our routine settle my nerves. This place always smells faintly of furniture polish and boiled cabbage, but somehow it's comforting. A bit like Gran herself: a tad abrasive, but solid, dependable. Try as I might, I can't shake last night from my mind – the dream and Mike's forcefulness – and not even Mike's early text from the airport could shake the darkness off me.

Make-up sex was amazing. Making me hot just thinking about it.

Am I reading too much into it? Was it just hot make-up passion?

'So, how's your young man?' Gran asks, as if she can read my thoughts. Though the way she says 'young man' makes Mike sound like a door-to-door salesman.

'He's fine. He, uh... got a promotion.'

Gran raises a single eyebrow; a move I've never mastered but always admired. 'Is that so?'

'Yeah,' I say, trying to sound more enthusiastic than I feel. 'It's a big deal for him. He'll be travelling to Spain a few times a month now.'

Her expression doesn't change. 'Spain, eh? How glamorous.' She pauses, her gaze narrowing. 'And what about you?'

'What about me?'

'Well, are they sending you off somewhere nice too, or do you just get to stay behind and mind the fort?'

I feel my cheeks flush. 'It doesn't work like that, Gran. I don't work with Mike. I'm self-employed, I work from home, so...'

'So, you're free to pick up his socks and keep the house ticking over while he's gone? Not the old-fashioned role I would have put you in.'

I can't help but laugh, even though there's an edge to her words and it reminds me of yesterday's shirt incident. 'It's not like that, Gran.'

She leans back in her wheelchair, not looking fully comfortable, her eyes never leaving mine. 'Ruby, love, I'm old, not stupid. I know when a girl's trying to convince herself of something.'

I sip my tea, using the cup as a shield. 'It's fine. We're fine.'

She snorts. 'Fine. The most useless word in the English language. Means absolutely nothing.'

I set the cup down, my hands tremble just slightly. I don't want to argue with her, but her words are pressing against something raw inside me. Something I can't name, but something I can't ignore either.

'Mum would have said something similar,' I say suddenly, and quickly swallow the lump in my throat.

Gran's expression softens, the lines around her mouth ease.

'Well, she learnt from the best. Your mum would be proud of you, Ruby.'

'I hope so.' I pause, swallow hard. 'Do you think she was very unhappy?'

Gran smiles softly at the question I've repeatedly asked her over the years. She never comments on the fact, but is always just patient with me. This time, she doesn't answer straight away. Instead, she reaches out and places her hand over mine. Her skin is paper-thin and warm, and the gesture takes me by surprise.

'We'll never know for sure, Ruby, it's impossible to. Your mum made choices in her life. Some good, some not so good. But she loved you more than anything, and that *did* make her happy.'

'I just... I don't want to...' My throat tightens.

'To what?' she prompts gently, her voice unusually soft.

I shake my head, unable to finish.

I don't want to die alone, I want to say. I don't want to be alone. Mostly, I don't want to wake up one day and realise I've wasted my life. But the words stay lodged in my chest.

Gran watches me for a moment, then gives my hand a squeeze. 'Listen to me, Ruby. Life's too bloody short to spend it waiting for someone else to give you permission to live. Do what makes *you* happy, before it's too late.'

There's an unspoken message in her words, one I'm not sure I'm ready to confront. But as she releases my hand and reaches for her teacup again, I can't shake the feeling that she sees me more clearly than I see myself.

'You're so like her, my darling girl,' Gran says then, but her eyes remain fixed on the window. I don't interrupt her, allowing her thoughts to sit with my mother for a while, but she soon whispers, 'Unruly curls and as pure as the driven snow.'

'It's nice that you think of her in that way.'

45

I regret it as soon as the words are spoken. Gran looks at me, holds my gaze and inhales deeply, but says nothing in response. We move on quickly, not resting there in our emotional mindsets, and ease our way out of the fog by putting the world to rights. As is our routine. I remember to ask about the nurse I haven't seen for a while. Lesley, Gran reminds me of her name, is on holiday with her grown children and young granddaughter.

'I think the crazy woman mentioned Turkey,' Gran adds.

'Why does that make her crazy?'

'Travelling all that way for a bit of sun-worshipping and cheap booze. Crazy.'

I laugh but shake my head. 'Well, I'm going to jot my mobile number down–'

'Don't get me started on those mobiles.'

'I know, Gran. I know.'

I finish writing a little note to Lesley, giving her my number and asking that she contacts me when she's back from her *sun-worshipping*. It wouldn't hurt to have a contact in here who's a direct link to Gran.

As I turn onto the street leading to the cul-de-sac, I glance sideways at the apartments. The moving van is no longer here, but the front door is wedged open with a metal dining room chair, and without the safety of the locks on my car doors this time, I'm desperate not to bump into that portly, rude brute again. The crisp air mingles with my nervousness like a warning not to linger, but as I tear my gaze from the door and walk on, a different man stands in my pathway. Tall, broad shoulders, and a face that makes me freeze mid-step. He's... striking. His dark hair is slightly dishevelled, curling slightly at the top, and his jawline could probably cut through steel. There's an intensity about him that draws my eyes and refuses to let go.

I shouldn't stare. I know I shouldn't. But I can't seem to stop myself.

He notices me a second later. His gaze sweeps over me, not in a leering way but as if he's genuinely curious. Our eyes lock, and for a moment it feels like the world shrinks to just the two of us standing in this ordinary cul-de-sac. I feel a jolt, like the sudden drop on a rollercoaster, and I quickly look away, embarrassed by the heat rising to my cheeks. What the hell is wrong with me? I go to walk by him.

'Hi,' he calls out, his voice deep and warm, with the faintest edge of something – an accent, maybe? He's smiling now, and it's disarming, a mix of polite and... amused, like he knows exactly how flustered I am.

I hesitate, then force myself to respond. 'Hi. Uh, new to the area?'

Brilliant, Ruby. Smooth as ever.

'What gave it away?' he says with a smile, and shifts the box in his arms with an easy confidence. It's then I notice the car, with the boot wide open, packed with things that won't have travelled with the moving van. 'Just moved in to the apartments.' He nods toward the building behind us. 'Henry, by the way. I'd shake your hand but...'

It's my turn to smile at him. 'Ruby,' I manage, my voice quieter than I'd like. I adjust the bag strap on my shoulder, then resist the urge to fidget further. 'Welcome to the neighbourhood, I guess.'

His infectious smile widens. 'Thanks. So far, so good.'

I nod, not trusting myself to say anything more. My pulse is a drumbeat in my ears, and I'm hyper-aware of how long I've been standing here, clutching my keys like a lifeline. I need to go inside. I need to stop staring at the way his T-shirt clings to his chest, the way his forearms flex as he adjusts his grip on the box.

This isn't me. I don't feel things like this for anyone else – haven't, not since Mike. *Mike.* The thought of him jolts me back to life, and guilt twists in my stomach. I don't even know this man.

'Well, I should...' I gesture vaguely down the close. 'Good luck with the unpacking.'

'Thanks.' His gaze lingers on me. 'Hopefully see you around, Ruby.'

I turn, practically bolting towards my house further down the road, fumble with my keys and unlock the door. Once inside, I lean against it, pressing my palms flat against the panel of glass as I take a shaky breath.

See you around, Ruby. His voice echoes in my head, smooth and unhurried. I can still see his smile, that glint in his eye that made me feel like I'd been caught in some invisible web.

I tell myself it was nothing, just a harmless exchange with a new neighbour. But the way my heart is racing says otherwise... and that's what terrifies me.

CHAPTER EIGHT

The house is never loud when Mike's here, but tonight, without him, it's oppressive in its silence. It's a strange, hollow kind of quiet, the kind that seems to amplify every creak and moan of the floorboards. I try not to let it bother me, but it does. I pad around the living room, rolling my eyes at Mike's tool case still underneath the window – I'm not putting it away this time out of principle – and switch on the lamps one by one until the space is bathed in warm, yellow light. It helps, a little, but the emptiness still stretches out around me. I pull a blanket from the back of the sofa, sit down and wrap it around my shoulders, scrolling through the streaming options until I settle on a romantic comedy.

Big mistake.

I try to focus on the film, but my mind wanders. Every cheesy meet-cute or declaration of love by the dreamy male character on the screen makes me think of him. Not Mike. *Him.*

Henry.

I can't believe I'm even thinking about him. He's just a neighbour, who I met for all of five minutes and what we had barely constitutes a conversation. But his lingering eyes, and smile, seem to have lodged themselves in my mind. I push the thought away, ashamed. Mike's only been gone for the day, and here I am, letting my mind wander where it shouldn't. Guilt claws at me. I fire off a text to Mike.

> How was your first day in Spain? Can't believe I haven't heard a word since you landed, hope it's going well. It's crazy quiet here without you! Love you x

The message sends and two ticks appear but then don't turn blue. He doesn't come online. I stare at the screen for a few minutes, willing it to buzz with a reply. Nothing. I tuck the phone in my dressing gown pocket and switch off the TV. The film is no good anyway. It's late. I might as well try to sleep.

Upstairs, the bed feels too big, the sheets too cold. I toss and turn, trying to settle, but every time I close my eyes, the quietness seems to grow louder. It presses against my ears, sharp and suffocating. And then I hear it.

A faint creak, followed by a soft click.

My eyes fly open, my breath hitching in my throat. It's the sound of a door closing. I lie perfectly still, heart pounding. I'm sure I locked the front door when I came in. Positive. But that noise... Did I check the back door was locked? I haven't opened it today, but that doesn't mean that Mike didn't earlier this morning before he left. I should have checked...

I sit up slowly, the duvet pooling around my waist. The sound doesn't come again.

Not wanting to patrol the house unarmed, I slip out of bed and tiptoe to Mike's office. His golf clubs are still propped in the corner, abandoned some months back when he decided the game wasn't for him. I grab one with a thick, heavy head, clutching it in both hands as I creep toward the stairs. The floor creaks softly under the weight of my steps. I pause at the top, straining my ears for the faintest noise.

Nothing.

I wait, holding my breath. Still nothing.

Just as I'm about to let my guard down, I hear something else. From outside my house this time. Perhaps it's a car door slamming shut. My heart lurches as I bolt back to the bedroom, shutting the door behind me. I hurry to the window, but steady myself before slowly moving the curtain just enough to peek out. My room faces *that* alleyway, the one I now hate, running between the two houses across the street. The lampposts cast long, eerie shadows over the cul-de-sac, but there's no sign of movement. No one in the alleyway. No one outside any of the homes that I can see.

I press my head against the cold window and strain to see further down the road. To The Weird One's house. No internal lamps give off any light or warmth. In comparison to the others, it looks like an abandoned house. His car isn't on the driveway either. There's no one there. Just stillness. I stay unmoving for what feels like an eternity, watching, waiting, but the street remains empty.

Finally, I let the curtain fall back into place and retreat to my bed again, the golf club still clutched tightly in my hand. I climb under the duvet, but can't lie down and get comfortable. The stillness of the room is too much, and my heart refuses to calm itself in this darkness, so I reach over to switch on the lamp on the bedside table. The weight of the club is reassuring, though my nerves are far from soothed.

Sleep won't come. I just sit there, wide-eyed in the quietness of my lonely home and listen. For any new noise. For any strange sound.

I contemplate reading a book, allowing the words and characters to carry me from this stifling yet empty room. Whisk me away to somewhere safe, with loads of people and chatter and laughter. To another world, even, where people aren't scared by noises in the night, because there's no need to fear their fellow humans. They wouldn't hurt each other. They wouldn't harm themselves...

Everything feels worse at night, doesn't it? Whether the noises are real or not, you can't ignore them while the world around you sleeps peacefully. You can't be distracted as easily with a TV programme or work project or texting a friend. Because although your body is shattered from the day, your mind comes alive. It can replay your most distressing memory in full HD pinpoint accuracy without any warning. It can force you to believe an intruder is lurking in your kitchen, waiting for you to slip into a slumber before they steal all your treasured possessions. Or worse.

Your mind can make you feel so desperately alone. You hear of parents feeding their babies in the dead of night. Pacing the floor until the carpet is threadbare, feeling as if they are the only person on the planet still awake at 3am, caring for the life they created with a maternal instinct they didn't even know they were capable of possessing. Will I have that, when the time comes? Or will every shadow on the wall and creak of the stairs propel me into a frozen helplessness?

I think of my mum and how, when I was a child, I thought she was so brave and strong. That usually is how you view your parent, until you grow up and enter the adult world yourself. You soon realise everyone is just winging life. But, tonight, I wonder if Mum felt like this, like me, in the days leading up to her death. Was there a warning for her? Were there sounds in her home that sparked alarm and dread? Were they real or just her mind playing tricks? She must have felt so alone... I let her feel alone, so perhaps this is my punishment. My karma.

Perhaps what I just heard wasn't genuine at all, but rather –

as Mike says – my gift of an overreactive imagination. I try to think back to the last time I was alone overnight in this house. That memory is harder to decipher. Sure, Mike has had many nights out with his brother and work colleagues, but he always comes home. Other than that one stag do... yes, that must have been about a year ago, I think. He fell in the door at 6am, still drunk and stinking of cigarettes he doesn't smoke, and headed straight for bed.

I'd watched it all unfold from the kitchen, where I'd spent most of the early hours of the morning waiting, and his self-inflicted pity was quite funny – once he was actually home and I was no longer worried sick about where he had ended up, that is. Prior to him crashing in I had drunk black coffee after black coffee, praying he and his mates hadn't been arrested for being drunken fools and forced to sleep it off in a cell. No, I didn't sleep great that night either, now I remember. Though, I also didn't feel as anxious then as I do now.

The alleyway flashes before me. The faceless figure.

He was real.

And so was the noise downstairs. I'm sure of it.

But just as I begin to believe myself, a sick tiredness hits like a wrecking ball. I stare ahead, focusing on nothing in particular, as the weariness takes control of my mind, my eyes, my body, until exhaustion finally pulls me under.

CHAPTER NINE

The morning light spills through the curtains, harsh and uninvited, and my eyes snap open. I jolt upright in bed and clutch the covers. For a moment, I can't remember where I am, disoriented by the heaviness in the air. My eyes feel raw, as though I've been crying for hours. Maybe I was, in my dreams. Then I see the golf club leaning against the bed. Didn't I fall asleep holding that... Memories from last night flood back – the noises, the terror, standing frozen at the top of the stairs. *Not* a dream.

I listen now, holding my breath for a moment, trying to make out any strange sound. The house is quiet. Too quiet without Mike, and I don't feel I can let my guard down fully. Not yet. Sliding out of bed, I grab the golf club and grip the handle tightly, just as I did last night, but sunrise has brought a glimmer of confidence. The weight of the club is reassuring, even though my heart is racing. I move to the bedroom door, nudge it open and peer down the hallway. Each door is only slightly ajar and means I can't see what's behind them. My breath catches as I push them open with the golf club. First Mike's office, then my own and finally the bathroom. Empty.

Sun bathes the hallway now. When I reach the top of the stairs, still holding the club in front of me like a shield, I pause, staring down into the void below. I strain to hear anything – *anything* – that doesn't belong.

But there's nothing.

I descend the stairs slowly. The living room comes into view first. The couch, the coffee table with Gran's crystal vase, the folded blanket – all exactly as I left them. The kitchen is next. I push the door open, again with the help of the golf club, half-expecting someone to leap out from under the table. My stomach knots as I step inside, my eyes sweeping over every detail. The counters are clear, the back door locked, the windows closed. Nothing. No one is here but me, just like last night. I've worked myself up because it's been so long since I've been alone...

Bloody hell, Ruby, pull yourself together. You're a grown woman.

The house needs some life. I request Capital Radio on the kitchen Alexa, allowing the music to fill the room, and open the window wide to rid it of the stale night air. While the kettle boils, I tuck the golf club beside the fridge and make a mental note to replace it before Mike gets home. I'd never hear the end of his banter if he found out. With the tea and toast made, I turn down the volume of the radio slightly, but not off completely, I don't want to cloak the house in silence yet again.

Picking up my phone and opening Instagram, I take a bite of toast and lose myself in my friends' stories. I don't have many – friends that is – but social media has a way of not caring about personal details like that. You can follow any celebrity, author, blogger, publisher or cleaning account your heart desires. Some of them will even follow you back. And those profiles will all do a fantastic job at keeping you distracted for much longer than you ever intended when you opened the app.

I smile when I glimpse Nancy's face in the small, highlighted circle; I love when she shares a snippet of her life through stories. Nancy's a real friend, from university, not just an account. Though I'm Facebook friends with many people I went to school and university with, Nancy and Stef are the only two I really make time for. Life has a way of scooping you up, moving from day to day, not allowing too many pockets of time for past friends, colleagues or even family. Time is precious, so you have to spend it with the right people.

I come out of Insta, open WhatsApp and scroll to my conversation with Nancy. I'm saddened, and frankly quite shocked, to realise we haven't chatted much at all since the new year. How did that happen? I haven't been *that* busy that I couldn't fire off a message to one of only two close friends. I begin typing:

> Hello stranger... I'm sorry I haven't been in touch for AGES. Please forgive me. How are you?? x

Within seconds, Nancy is online and the three dots tell me she's typing just before the message pings in:

> My beautiful bitch! No, I'm so sorry... it's ME I've been so bloody busy with work. I'll fill you in next time I see you. Actually, why don't we meet for birthday drinks tomorrow?? 😉 xoxo

It's typical Nancy – loud, loving and full of energy. She's always busy, and always up for going *out out*.

> I'm free all day, but Mike's away for work – I'll fill you in too haha – and we've planned something for tomorrow evening xx

> Ah feck I can't do the day. Won't be home until about 5, maybe 6… and my next few weekends are jam-packed xoxo

Nancy is an events co-ordinator, and I couldn't imagine her as anything else. She's gone heavy into weddings these past few years, so naturally it means our schedules are polar opposites. I quickly reply before I lose her attention:

> What about Hunter's party? xx

> That's a Friday afternoon, right? Xoxo

> Yep. And it's a 4th birthday party Nance 😊 xx

> Thanks for reminding me how old he is 😉 it's in my calendar and I promise my best to swing by xoxo

> Okay, well I'll see you there… hopefully… otherwise we MUST get a date in the diary for a catch-up. Coffee. Vodka. Whatever. I miss you xx

Nancy brings out the fun, sociable side of me. Always has. Even if going out for shots of vodka would usually be the last thing on my mind, with her I know it's a good time.

> Deal. Miss you too gorgeous xoxo

And with that message, she appears offline instantly.

I head upstairs, sit at my desk and open my laptop. I'm determined to get some writing done, to focus on something normal. But the words don't come. They don't flow. My fingers hover over the keyboard, useless. Every little creak of the house is still snapping me out of my creative thinking.

How can I create a world of fantasy when I can't escape my own thoughts? I slam the laptop shut, frustrated. I can't do this. I need some fresh air, something to clear my head. After a quick shower and chucking on an outfit, without much fashionable consideration, I grab my coat and head outside. The crisp morning air feels like a slap, but a welcome one. I need it with how I've been acting. I walk quickly, hoping to outrun the tension knotted in my chest.

As I approach Picky Patty's four doors down – we live on the uneven numbered houses of the street – I glance towards her home. The front garden is empty. My steps slow, and I glance toward the windows. Even the downstairs curtains are still closed. It's as if there's no life in the place. And that just feels a little too strange for this house.

I hesitate for a moment, then cross the driveway and step up to her front door. *What are you doing, Ruby?* Patty and I barely exchange pleasantries, let alone hold real conversations. But something pulls me forward, worry for the older woman, perhaps, and before I can second-guess myself, I knock. The sound echoes, loud in the quiet cul-de-sac, and I wait, thinking how ridiculous this is.

When suddenly the door breezes open and a young, beautiful woman I've never seen before is standing before me.

'Is Patty okay?' I ask, instantly hating myself and wishing I'd never knocked.

'Oh great,' she says in an upbeat voice, leaving me confused. 'I'm–'

'Patty, one of your neighbours is here,' the woman calls over her shoulder, then looks back at me. 'Perfect timing, I need to pop up the shops so can you sit with her? Thanks.'

She speaks quickly, grabs her jacket from behind the door and slides past me before I have a chance to reply.

'Well, I don't–'

'I won't be long.' She cuts me off again and walks down the driveway in the direction of the alleyway.

'Who is it?' Patty's voice calls from inside the house. 'Close the door, will you, you're letting all the heat out.'

Standing at the threshold, my nerves still raw, humming inside me like restless bees. I can't decide if I should pull the door shut and run home, or step through it into the unknown neighbour's house.

CHAPTER TEN

I hesitate at Patty's front door, glancing back at the path as if the mysterious woman might return and save me. But she's gone, leaving me to step into uncharted territory. I've never been inside Patty's house before, of course I haven't. Though I've seen her a hundred times at her window, her sharp eyes missing nothing in our cul-de-sac, I've never knocked on her front door. Why? Why did I today? I step inside, and it feels wrong somehow, like stepping into a story that's already mid-chapter.

'Who is it?' Patty asks again, more demanding, realising now that I ignored her the first time.

'It's Ruby.' My voice wavers, and I clear my throat, trying again. 'From number nine, down the road.'

I'm greeted by the warm scent of lavender mingled with the musty aroma of old books. The hallway is wide, lined with shelves crammed full of hardbacks and paperbacks, stacked horizontally and vertically, some leaning precariously as if daring gravity to intervene.

I step cautiously into the living room, where the walls are an eclectic mix of paintings, photographs, and even more shelves. There's more books – on the coffee table, piled near the armchair, on the shelves. It's as if I've walked into a library; even more so because it doesn't look messy. Patty isn't a hoarder: it looks homely. A family has grown here, surrounded by books treasured over the years. My eyes linger and search, spying titles I know and love and others that are brand new to me. Then my gaze finally falls on Patty, lying on the sofa, propped up with cushions and pillows, a blanket covering her legs.

'Ruby?' Her voice is sharp with surprise, but her face softens immediately. 'Oh, for heaven's sake, I wasn't expecting *you*. What are you doing here, dear?'

I falter, aware of how odd this must look. 'I, um...' I hesitate, feeling my cheeks heat. 'I knocked because, well... You weren't at the window, which sounds stupid now I say it aloud, but–'

Patty waves a hand to interrupt, but her face breaks into a wry smile. 'You thought I'd finally keeled over, did you? That I'd died slumped over with my binoculars clutched to my chest before I could make it to my morning lookout post?'

Her laugh is warm, and it washes over me, instantly dissolving my embarrassment.

'I didn't mean it like that,' I say, smiling too.

'Oh, don't be silly. We both know I'm the resident nosey parker around here. It's part of my charm,' she replies, with a cheeky wink.

The tension eases from my shoulders, and I glance around the room again, taking it all in. A framed photograph, of a much younger Patty, tucked away on one of the bookshelves catches my eye. She has to be at least twenty years younger, her arm wrapped round the waist of a handsome man about the same age as her, and sat in front of them is a very proud, and equally handsome, young man in his graduating hat and gown.

'That's a special one.' I turn towards her, to ask more about the snap, but her face is suddenly serious and unsmiling, so I decide against it. Instead I allow my eyes to comb along the books again, their spines a rainbow of colours and titles. 'You've got quite the collection.'

She beams now, a softer reaction, and her pride evident. 'I've been collecting them for decades. Once you let books into your life, they never leave, do they? I'm no book snob, mind you – I'll read anything. Romance, thrillers, history, even a bit of fantasy now and then. Whatever floats my boat, depending on my mood on any given day.'

'Fantasy?' I say, perking up.

She looks at me curiously. 'Why? Is that your thing?'

I nod, feeling a little shy but also eager to share. 'It is. I write fantasy novels. It's what I do, actually, for a living.'

Her eyes widen, and then she claps her hands. 'An author! My goodness, I've been living down the road to a celebrity all this time and didn't even know it. What sort of stories do you write? Dragons? Magic? Hidden worlds?'

'I'm certainly not a celebrity, Patty,' I say with a laugh. 'I self-publish my books. I'm not discovered like, say, Gregory Maguire or Rachel Yoder, and my stories aren't turned into blockbuster films or Netflix series.' I shake my head to dismiss my comment, it's not what Patty asked. 'But anyway, my books, my stories are mostly character-driven stuff, with a pinch of magic. More for the escapism. It's not exactly Tolkien, but I like to think it's still entertaining.'

Patty grins and gestures to the armchair opposite for me to sit down. 'Ruby, dear, I don't care if you write about flying frogs or talking teapots – anyone who can create entire worlds out of thin air is a marvel in my opinion.'

Her words catch me off guard, warming me in a way I hadn't expected. I sink into the chair, the floral fabric beneath me faded but soft. I feel oddly at home in this house, with a woman who seems to understand the weight of imagination.

We talk for a while longer, about books we've loved and

authors we admire. For the first time in what feels like days, I'm not consumed by the noise in my own head, and I relax in Patty's company. Although there's a tinge of guilt for stereotyping her as a nosey neighbour without getting to know her. There's something about Patty – her wit, her unforgiving views on everything – that puts me at ease.

'So,' I say, realising that she's barely moved since I stepped foot in the room, 'what's been keeping you indoors, and not at your window?'

Patty chuckles, the sound rich and warm. 'Oh, so you *have* noticed me being a nosey old bat, then?'

'Well, let's just say I noticed you not being there.'

'Tell you what, why don't you be a dear and make us both a cuppa,' she replies, gesturing through the alcove to the kitchen. 'Strong and no sugar for me. I'm sweet enough.'

'Of course,' I say, standing.

The kitchen is as cluttered as the rest of the house but in a cosy, inviting way. Every surface is dotted with knick-knacks – ceramic cats, potted herbs, a row of mugs hanging from hooks. I find the kettle easily enough and fill it, opening a few cupboards until I find the teabags and sugar, because I am definitely not sweet enough and will always welcome a sugar rush.

Patty's voice drifts in from the living room as I go about making the tea. 'Going back to fantasy, I've just finished a marvellous book – *The Night Circus*. Have you read it? It's like magic come to life. Completely captivating!'

'I have,' I call back, smiling. 'Loved it, too, and the second one is waiting impatiently on my Kindle.'

'Of course,' she replies. 'I could've guessed you'd have good taste in your line of work.'

I return to the living room with two mugs and set one on the coffee table for myself and hand the other to Patty. She takes it gratefully, wrapping her hands around the mug.

'You're a gem. I'd get it myself, but this old back of mine has other ideas.'

'So that's why you're laid-up. Your back. What happened?' I ask, taking a sip of my tea.

'Oh, nothing too dramatic.' She waves a hand again. 'Just an injury from when I was a teenager. Fell off a horse, would you believe? Thought I was indestructible back then. These days, it flares up pretty bad every now and again. I just have to sit still for a while, take some medication, and wait for it to pass. I'll be fighting fit soon enough.'

Her easy tone makes it seem like no big deal, but I can't help but feel a pang of sympathy. Will there come a day when the flare-up doesn't pass, I wonder, though I dare not voice the question.

'The woman who answered the door,' I say instead, 'is she your daughter?'

'No,' Patty says with a heavy sigh. 'Just a family friend.'

There's something in her voice, a soft sadness, that tells me not to pry any further. I mean, of course I want to, but as oddly comfortable as I feel in my neighbour's home, probing further seems a bit too familiar.

Patty's face suddenly lights up and she changes the subject. 'Ruby, you must join the book club.'

I frown. 'Book club?'

'Yes, yes. Everyone from our little close is in it – or at least the best of us are,' she says with a mischievous smile. 'We usually meet once a month, and it's my turn to host the next one. Once I'm up and running again, I'll send a date out, but... it might be too late for you to catch up.'

'What are you reading?' I ask, now remembering Patty mentioning a possible book club that first time we spoke. I'd been interested then, but Mike said I'd be a saddo to join.

'Well, it was a curve-ball suggestion from yours truly, but I wanted to read something a bit different. You know, something a bit controversial, that we could really sink our teeth into when we meet up. *In Cold Blood* by Truman Capote. Have you read it?'

'I have,' I admit, feeling a small swell of pride. 'I actually used it in my uni dissertation.'

'Oh, fancy that. Brilliant, though, because now you're already ahead of the game. Oh, you'll love it – we've got some real characters in the group, let me tell you. It's the best way to stay connected around here.'

I smile, a little taken aback by her enthusiasm.

'And while we're at it,' Patty continues, 'we should get you and your fellow added to the cul-de-sac's WhatsApp group. I never did hear back from you before Covid hit.'

I flush slightly, embarrassed. 'We've never really...'

'Interacted with the neighbours?' she finishes for me, laughing. 'I know, dear. I'm only teasing. But there's no time like the present, is there? Give me your number, and I'll add you later this evening.'

Her warmth and humour are infectious, and before I know it, I'm rattling off my mobile number. Patty jots it down in a little notepad I hadn't even noticed wedged between her thigh and the sofa. And as we settle back into our conversation, I feel excited at the possibility of a new connection. A new friend.

CHAPTER ELEVEN

I wake after a more peaceful sleep than I had expected, the quiet not nearly as oppressive as the night before. Perhaps it was the exhaustion of the first evening alone, or maybe it's the golf club resting in the bed next to me like a silent partner. I've never even slapped a person across the face before, so I can't help but wonder if I'd have the strength or gall to whack someone over the head with a 9 Iron. Still, it's a strange comfort to have it within reaching distance. I stretch and blink into the dim morning light, my phone screen lights up with a notification. There's multiple unread messages, which is very strange for my phone.

The first I open is from Mike:

> Sorry I haven't been in touch as much as I would've liked. I'll catch you up on everything tonight. Happy birthday, beautiful. Can't wait to see you. X

I exhale a quiet sigh. I hate that I'm alone and that he isn't here with me this morning, but his short message still manages to warm me.

The next is Stef's:

> Happy birthday, my dearest friend! Sorry I
> won't see you today, but I hope you're doing
> something special. Look forward to seeing you
> in two weeks! Don't forget your card. Love
> ya xx

I laugh out loud. Stef knows me so well: I'd completely forgot about the card she gave me earlier in the week, and make a mental note to rescue it from my handbag when I go downstairs. Then, there's Nancy's message:

> HAPPY BIRTHDAY, you beautiful creature! I
> hope you're treating yourself. With lots of fun
> and bubbles... not the bath sort, either ⩗ You
> deserve it! Xoxo

My heart pines for time with my friend. Her vibrant nature is infectious, and I need more of that in my life. The final notification is to tell me I've been added to a new WhatsApp group. A group called The Blackwood Close Community. Ah, the one Patty said she'd invite me to.

> Patty: Morning neighbours. I'd like to welcome
> Ruby from No 9 to the group. She's actually
> lived here quite a while, but she's kept herself
> to herself – we won't hold it against you ☺
> Nice to finally have you join us.

Her introduction is then followed by a flurry of welcome and hello messages from neighbours I don't know. Well, at least not by their names, and the ones who have cats or children as their profile pictures I've got no hope of figuring out.

> Patty: Excitingly, Ruby is an author! Yes, a real published author – I've already checked her out on Amazon, 😊 so I've said she must join our next book club meeting. I know you're all still waiting on a date for me. Don't worry, I haven't forgotten.

Messages continue to ping in from these neighbouring strangers, but there's now a fizz of excitement at the prospect of them thinking they live next door to Agatha Christie. They'll be sorely disappointed, but I know I have to send some kind of reply or else be shunned for being a shut-away.

> Ruby: Thanks for the warm welcome, everyone. Look forward to chatting and meeting properly at the next book club 😊

As I press send, I can't help rolling my eyes and wondering what I've gotten myself into here, agreeing to be added to this tight-knit neighbourhood chat is completely out of my comfort zone.

I scroll through the previous three messages again, the weight of the day settling on me. My birthday. A day that should feel special, but the quiet lingers, a reminder of the emptiness in the house. Maybe I'll do something nice for myself today, because each birthday is a privilege. It's denied to so many. My thoughts turn to Mum. This is her special day, too, the day she gave birth to her only child, and I swallow the sadness that's threatening to overspill.

But, hey, it's my birthday and I'll cry if I want to. I just wish she was here to celebrate with me, and then perhaps I wouldn't feel so lonely... I draw in a deep breath, widening my nostrils and lifting my chest, so I can really feel that air. Then I wipe the small droplet of tears from the corners of my eyes. I'll never be sure of Mum's mental health when she felt she couldn't go any further in this world, but I know with all the certainty in my heart that she would not want me crying today.

I glance at my phone one more time before setting it aside. It's still early, and my mind drifts to work. I haven't been sticking to my daily writing target, and it's so unlike me. But this week has been strange. There's been a lot of change, and too much on my mind. Overcrowded with new people and new sounds – both real and in my head. I'll have to treat this week as if I had a little holiday, and catch up next week. I can put in double the time once Mike is home and things settle back to normal. For now, I'm going to leave work behind me and embrace the day.

The only way to break out of this funk is to start with some lightness. I yank open the curtains, and the cold sunshine floods the room, the sharp light hitting my face and shocking my system so the room seems brighter, more alive. I tell Alexa to play my favourite songs and she delivers with Florence and the Machine. The rhythm fills the space and it's enough to make my feet tap as I shuffle into the bathroom. I take a long, hot shower, letting the water soak into my skin.

When I'm finished, I take my time drying off, carefully doing my hair and applying a touch of make-up, things I haven't really thought about for days. Weeks, even. I give myself a quick look in the mirror, satisfied I've done the best with my unruly hair and plain features, then head to the wardrobe and select an outfit that's just a little nicer than the norm.

I feel fresh, and head downstairs to treat myself to a proper breakfast. I usually like to keep things simple, but today I make an exception. I pull out the eggs, bagels, avocado – nothing too fancy, but more so than the usual tea and toast. Despite the grey clouds bubbling past the kitchen window, my mojo is back and I'm excited to see Mike later, and to celebrate being another year older. I grab my phone and make a shopping list. I'll pick up something nice for dinner and have a bottle of bubbly on ice for when Mike gets home from Spain. He'll love it. I run through the list in my head, feeling a little giddy as I check off each item. It's silly, I know, but we all deserve this feeling from time to time.

A few hours later, after being sidetracked by all the clothes and homeware in the supermarket, I'm back home, my mind already on the delicious dinner I'm about to prepare. The ingredients for my signature spaghetti Bolognese are all laid out on the counter when a wad of envelopes are pushed through the letterbox.

I head to the front door and, lifting the post from the mat, smile when I spy Gran's handwriting. She didn't mention my birthday when I visited this week, and I didn't want to highlight the fact she'd forgotten, fearing it would upset her. Looks like she hadn't forgotten after all. Even through her spidery handwriting, I can hear her demanding voice:

> *To our shining gem,*
> *Wishing you the happiest of birthdays, and hoping it's as special as you – but don't wait around for something to happen. Go make the day what you want it to be. We're so proud of you.*
> *Love you so very much,*
> *Gran (and kisses from heaven too) xx*

The *our* and *we* reference is her and Mum. I slide down the wall and sit cross-legged on the floor like a child. She probably sent it before my visit on Wednesday, or asked one of the carer's to, just to make sure it arrived today on time. And so, she just knew *that* question would be – always is – swirling around my mind. I re-read Gran's message over and over. *We're so proud of you.* How she knew it's just what I would want to hear. But my attention is stolen away when a notification pings into my phone, a message from Mike:

> Flight's been delayed. Only about an hour, at the moment, but I'll keep you updated. I will not miss your birthday! X

A disappointed sigh slips out before I can stop it. I'd been looking forward to seeing him tonight. An hour might not seem like much, but it's enough to disrupt the rhythm I had imagined. Still, I won't let it ruin my plans. I'm not going to let this, or Gran's touching card, get to me. I shake off the little twinge of frustration – it's only an hour, after all – and send him a quick message back:

> No worries! Just looking forward to seeing you later. Let me know when you can x

I pull myself up from the floor, return to the kitchen and select my usual radio station via Alexa, letting the upbeat song fill the space, just as it did this morning. I'm determined to make this evening count, even if Mike's a little later than planned. With everything laid out, I get to work with the ingredients. I'm soon swinging around the kitchen, the music filling the spaces in my head. I drop everything into the slow cooker. The food will simmer on low for hours, melding together perfectly, ready for whenever Mike gets in.

The clock's ticking slowly, but I feel calm now. A strange, relaxed energy settles over me, and I decide to keep the momentum going. With all this time ahead of me, why not turn my focus to work? Why wait until next week? My feet race upstairs, and the manuscript is soon open on my laptop; urgency pulling me forward to make headway with my words. I dive in, pushing aside the thoughts of Mike's delay, and feel a shift in my mood. I bury myself in the world of my characters and get lost in their narrative.

After a solid writing stretch, one of those rare, rewarding sessions where the words flow effortlessly, I finally push myself away from my desk. My fingers are stiff from typing, but my mind is alive with the new character arcs I've woven into my story. The sense of accomplishment feels satisfying, but it's also a reminder of how easy it is to lose track of time when I'm really in the zone. I glance at the clock. It's already well past the time I had expected Mike to be home. My stomach twists at the thought of him still being delayed. I check my phone and notice another text from him.

> The airline's been cancelling flights because of the weather. We're all waiting to hear about the next flight options. I'll let you know as soon as I know more x

Shit! It's an hour since he sent that. Concern nudges at me, though I'm not entirely sure why, it's not as if he's been stranded in some remote country for God knows how long – it's just the weather. But surely he must know more by now... I quickly fire off a reply, hoping to catch him before he's in the air, while also hoping he's already flying home. Almost immediately, the little bubbles show that Mike's replying. He must be keeping his phone close.

> I've got a flight, but it's the later evening one. They're rebooking a bunch of people. I'm not sure I'll make it home before 10... maybe even later, but I'll keep you posted. Don't wait up, okay? I'm really sorry I missed your birthday. I'll make it up to you tomorrow. I promise. X

The words slap me twice: a disappointment that he won't be home sooner, and a small tug of guilt that he's apologising for something that isn't his fault. I don't want to sound upset, his situation is frustrating enough as it is, so I reply with a light-hearted message.

> It's fine, don't worry. I'm sure you'll make it up to me. Safe travels, babe. X

I place my phone down on the desk and swallow back the tears. It's an unavoidable delay, and I'm sure Mike's feeling pretty shitty about it, but the emptiness of the house quickly has me in a chokehold again.

CHAPTER TWELVE

You. You are my shiny new gem. A real ruby in the rough, aren't you?

Yes, I can tell that about you already. I am completely and utterly shocked at the way things have changed. The way my head has been turned, and the way you've played on my mind. *Too much,* probably, because I'll let you in on a little secret, Ruby, this shouldn't be happening. Watching you, studying you, wanting you. It could get me into a lot of trouble. And I've been trying really hard to not get into trouble.

It wasn't meant to be *you,* that's another little truth you need to know. Don't take it personally, Ruby, but you were just another face, another movement in the background of this street, this place, this life. I had no reason to notice you. But then you stepped into my view, and suddenly, there was no one else. So, that makes this your fault, not mine, doesn't it? This *need* to know more about you. How can I be blamed for wanting to know more about you when you've eased yourself into my life? So unexpectedly and uninvited.

My interest was piqued, as they say in the books. It started small, at first. Just a passing glance, a passing interest, a small impulse. Yet, I followed. And you never noticed; you never saw me. You walked ahead, oblivious, carrying yourself like someone who belonged here, someone who had been in this place for years. You probably thought you knew it well. Knew its rhythms, its people, its safety. But you don't – and I think you know that *now*.

I kept my distance, testing the space between us. Close enough to watch, far enough to be nothing: a ghost, a shadow. And I told myself this was nothing, that this wouldn't last because you're the total opposite to the one before... But then you did something that changed everything. You smiled. What a stunning smile you have, Ruby. It wasn't at me, sadly, it actually wasn't at anyone in particular – just a small, fleeting smile to yourself as you walked by. A private moment that shouldn't have been mine to see, and yet it was. That's when I understood that I needed to know more about you, Ruby.

I started paying more attention. Watching the way you walked, the way you tilted your head when something caught your attention, the way you fiddle with your bag strap or charm bracelet, anything to keep your fingers busy when you're nervous. It's the small, quiet things I notice. The things you don't realise you're giving away. Not many people do realise how much of themselves are on show.

Let me tell you, there's been a change since then. Why don't you carry yourself with confidence anymore? Perhaps you don't actually feel like you belong... Could it be that you *feel* me? That you're yearning for me as much as I hunger for you. Could it be, Ruby?

I think we may be one of the same. We don't want to make a fuss, and that's why I need to watch you for just a little while longer. I need to know if this really is you, or if you're like so many other people in this world who lie and cheat and show a fake persona. I don't think you're like that, Ruby. I fucking hope you're not like that... but time will tell. For now, I must be patient, and learn what I can about you from the safety of the shadows. The shadows that allow me to see so much. So much of what people think is private. But nothing is ever truly private, Ruby, and I am watching you.

CHAPTER THIRTEEN

Mike is downstairs. Moving around the kitchen, the clink of mugs, the hum of the coffee machine, his footsteps across the tiled floor. For a moment, it's just noise, ordinary sounds that have been part of our routine for years. But today, it all feels... different. Like there's too much space between us, too much distance that hasn't been there before.

I lie in bed for a moment longer, the covers pulled up around me. I heard him last night, finally coming home – his suitcase, the click of the door – but I stayed still, eyes closed, pretending to be asleep. I'm not sure why. It wasn't his fault, but I didn't want to face him then, in the cold shadow of the night. Now it feels weird.

I push the covers off, forcing myself to get up. The house feels alien, it's changed again. I make my way downstairs and as I enter the kitchen, Mike's face lights up with that familiar smile. His eyes immediately soften as he sees me, but I don't feel the rush of comfort I usually do. There's a fog between us. A crack.

'Morning,' he says, his voice warm, but there's something in it – something I can't place. It almost feels like he's trying too hard to be... normal. He probably feels guilty.

'Morning,' I reply, with a stiff smile.

He hands me a mug of coffee while apologising about yesterday, about last night, about missing my birthday, but I cut him off.

'I wanted tea this morning.'

'Oh, right, sorry. I shouldn't have assumed. I'll chuck it and make you a cuppa.'

'No, you've made it now. I'll just have it.' My stomach clenches.

A slight smile appears on Mike's face. Not a sarcastic or happy one, but a sad one. A knowing one. I can't argue with him over flights out of his control, so I'll pick a stupid fight about tea and coffee. I hate to even admit it, but it's exactly what I'm about to start here and Mike has seen straight through it. Even quicker than I did. He reaches out, pulling me into a hug, and I let him, even though it feels... Off. Unwanted. A hesitation that's never been there before. Maybe it's just the distance, the days apart, making it seem this way.

'I missed you,' he murmurs into my hair.

'I've missed you too.'

And I have. The comfort of our routine. The ease of being together. The way he holds me. When he pulls back, he gives me another soft smile, but his eyes are searching mine, like he's waiting for something. Waiting for me to say more, but I don't know what it is I'm supposed to say. Maybe my reply didn't sound convincing, though it was genuine.

'I thought we could spend the day together,' Mike suggests, finally breaking the silence. 'Catch up. Just the two of us.'

What else would we do? That *is* our routine. So why is there a niggling sensation radiating all over my body? It's as though we're covered by a cloud, the weight of things unsaid. Mike has apologised for missing my birthday, and I have accepted it, but there's a weirdness between us that I don't know how to shake.

'I'd like that,' I say, though the words feel like they were dragged through dirty gravel and spat out. 'It's just... it's been a weird week, hasn't it?'

He nods, but there's something behind his smile that doesn't quite reach his eyes. 'Yeah. We'll figure it out. One step at a time.'

And for a moment, I wonder if *he* feels it too – the change between us. He turns away, switching the kettle on and humming a tune. No, he doesn't notice anything different. I'm overthinking everything. It's probably just an adjustment period, this travelling back and forth, it's new for both of us. We're still figuring it out, like he says. Then throw a lonely birthday into the mix... This is all just in my head. I glance at him as he absent-mindedly scrolls through his phone, his expression blank. There's a silence hanging in the air, but rather than feed into it, I cast it away. This is us. Ruby and Mike, who know how to enjoy quiet moments without all this... heaviness.

'Hey,' I say, my voice a little lighter than before. 'Why don't we *do* something together? Make up for the past few days.'

Mike looks up from his phone, a slight frown creasing his brow. I'm not sure if it's from hearing me or because he's still lost in his own thoughts.

'Ruby, I just said that. What do you mean?'

'I know you did, I just meant... Let's... *do* something. We could go out. Jump on the tube and see where we end up in London, for a laugh. Go out to eat some place new, a meal date. Just... different.'

For a moment, he doesn't respond. His eyes flicker between

me and the phone resting in his hand, but then he seems to focus on me, as if realising I'm genuinely asking for his time. A soft smile tugs at the corners of his mouth, but there's still something absent in his gaze, a distance I can't quite place.

'I'm shattered, you know, from all the travelling,' he says, 'but how about we close the curtains, yank the heating up, and get all snuggly together with a film?'

I don't hesitate. 'Yeah. That sounds perfect.'

His grin widens a little more now. I didn't really want to go gallivanting all over town; the idea always seems grander than the action. This is our chilled, quiet normal. That's what we need to feel right now. I leave the kitchen and start pulling the curtains shut in the living room, ignoring the overspilling tool case, and watch as the room dims, the outside world disappearing even though it's late morning now.

Mike follows me to the sofa and starts fiddling with the remote. 'I'll put something on for us. How about that one we watched last time?'

'Sure,' I reply, nipping into the hallway to turn up the thermostat.

The radiators hum to life as I sit down next to Mike. He's still on the edge of the chair, clearly not selecting what we watched last time and now clicking through action movies. Not what I would have chosen, but I settle back, soaking up the cosy atmosphere and allowing the warmth of the room to wrap itself around me. But just as we're getting comfortable, my phone buzzes on the armrest. I glance at it. It's a message from the Blackwood Close WhatsApp group. I'm inclined to ignore it, another stupid request for food or beverages, no doubt, but I noticed it's Patty's name and my interest is caught.

Patty: Hi everyone, just wanted to introduce and welcome our new neighbour, Henry, to the close – and to the group! He's just moved into the apartments on the green behind my house and he's delightful. I hope you'll all make him feel welcome.

I stare at the screen, a warm, slightly nervous feeling blossoms in my chest. *Henry.* The flutter of excitement comes unannounced – and unwanted – and I barely notice when Mike catches the expression on my face.

'What are you smiling at?' he asks, peering slightly closer to my phone.

I quickly look away, taking a moment to place my phone on the coffee table and switching it to silent. To give myself a minute. 'Oh, nothing. Just... Picky Patty finally cornered me again, and now I'm part of the cul-de-sac's WhatsApp group. Someone asked to *borrow* milk. They're always asking for something or other.'

The words are casual, with a slight laugh, but I feel guilty referring to Patty as picky. Now I know her, have connected with her and actually enjoyed her company... I'm also not completely lying to Mike about the milk message. As I glance over at him, I catch the small flash of something in his eyes – amusement, maybe, or even a hint of unease. He laughs, but the sound is low and slightly teasing.

'Be careful, Ruby,' he says, half joking. 'Don't go adding me to that group. I'm not the type who enjoys knowing everyone's business. Or dairy needs.'

'I promise I won't,' I reply, a little too quickly, too eager. But the thought of Mike and Henry in the same group, interacting with each other, makes my stomach somersault.

I move closer to Mike, waiting for him to drape his arm

around my shoulders, so we can get comfortable. Now this feels familiar, nice, as we sit in unison, despite the lingering undercurrent of guilt.

CHAPTER FOURTEEN

I turn onto the street which opens up into my cul-de-sac, passing the apartments to my left. Just before Patty's house on the corner, I spot him. Henry. He's crouched over, tying his shoelace and dressed in what might be the tightest white sports T-shirt I've ever seen. The sight of him catches me off guard and the annoying flutter from yesterday returns. My footsteps slow. I can't get to Patty's house without passing him, and she'll be waiting for the bits of shopping I collected for her. I can't actually get anywhere without walking past, but it's not as though he'll even recall who I am: we spoke briefly for a few seconds–

'Ruby,' he says, looking up at me.

Wow. He remembers my name.

'Hi... Henry, right?' My voice betrays me.

He stands, then bridges the gap between us in just a few strides. I hadn't noticed how tall he was before and the balance is tipped now as I look up at him.

'Fancy seeing you here.' He smiles at his own joke. It's warm and captivating. His brown eyes never leave mine, inviting and mischievous.

'Heading out for a run?' I break away from our stare, pointing at his trainers. Take a quiet deep breath.

'That's the plan,' he says with a chuckle. 'But I can't seem to get my laces to cooperate. I'm all fingers and thumbs, and they have a mind of their own.'

I laugh at his turn of phrase. It's something my gran would say. 'A rebellious pair of Nikes – who would've thought?'

Henry shakes his head. 'Exactly. The struggle is real. You'd think I'd have mastered this by now.'

'Practice makes perfect.'

'Perhaps I could do with some extra help.'

Heat creeps up my cheeks. 'How are you settling in?' I offer, ignoring his flirtatious comment... in case it wasn't flirtatious at all, and I'm allowing myself to be utterly mislead.

'I'm getting there,' he replies, brushing a hand through his hair. 'My apartment still looks like a storage unit. Boxes everywhere. I told myself I'd unpack last weekend, but... well, let's just say I haven't made much progress.'

'It's just you moving in, then?' The question escapes my lips before the thought matures in my mind.

He smiles. It's perfect. 'Yep, just little old me.'

Stupid. Why would I ask him that? It's none of my business. A silence passes over us, but it doesn't feel awkward. Henry's gaze never leaves me, it just lingers between my eyes and lips. I see the subtle movements and mirror them until I feel a snake-like grip of guilt coil around me once again. I have to break the tension.

'When Mike and I moved into the house, I swore I'd have it all done in a week. Three months later, we still had boxes in the hallway.'

Mike. I fidget with the shopping bags, moving them from one hand to the other.

'Can I help you with those?' Henry offers.

'No, it's fine,' I shake my head while lowering them to the ground. Why have I done that? Talk about an invitation for more chatting.

'So Mike...' Henry pauses. 'Is that your dog, your cat, your–'

'Partner.'

'Of course.' The glint in his eyes is back. 'I'm kidding. How long have you and Mike lived here?'

There's a tone to Mike's name that I know I shouldn't ignore, but the butterflies in my stomach carry me along in this dance of meeting someone new.

'Coming up to five years now. But it was just before the pandemic so we never really did a meet the neighbours thing.'

'How did Patty let you get away with that?' Henry's laugh is infectious, and I join him. 'I mean, don't get me wrong, she's lovely, but I'm already in some street WhatsApp group.'

'You're lucky she's been on bedrest lately or she would have caught you on your first day.' We laugh again. 'I've actually only started talking to her recently. Some of that shopping there is for her as she's still recovering a bit.'

'Well, aren't you the perfect neighbour.'

His wink catches me off guard and I fumble over my words. 'No, not really... I mean... it's been five years.'

I clear my throat, but Henry's smile widens, his eyes crinkling at the corners as he does. There's something about the way he looks at me – as though he's fully listening to every single word I say. Does he know the effect he's having on me?

'Well...' he starts, 'I guess I better let you get on with your good neighbourly deed.'

'And I should let you get back to your rebellious trainers,' I say, and sweep the shopping bags back up into my hands.

Henry barks a genuine laugh. 'Maybe we'll bump into each other again soon.'

'Yeah, maybe,' I reply, trying to sound casual. 'Good luck with the unpacking, Henry.'

'Thanks, Ruby.'

He doesn't take off, to continue his run, so it's clear I'm the one who must walk away. I feel his gaze follow me as I do, and I don't dare look back. I also don't trust myself to knock at Patty's house right now, so I walk straight past hers to my own home. The warmth spreads from my face, into my heavy chest and further down my body. By the time I step through the front door, there's a tingling sensation taking over.

I lower the shopping bags and my attention drifts to where Mike's voice carries down from his office. Before I can second guess myself, I'm climbing the stairs, my heart racing for reasons I don't want to examine too closely. Mike's office door is ajar, and I can see him inside, leaning back in his chair, headset on, laptop glowing in front of him. His voice is calm, measured, mid-conversation. My body doesn't hesitate and pushes me further into the room.

Mike turns, frowns and holds up a finger to his lips, silencing me. Fine by me, I didn't come here to talk. I pull off my coat, throw it onto the floor and do the same with my jumper. Mike's scowl soon softens and he attempts to wrap-up the call. Tension falls away the second I unhook my bra and step closer to Mike, our eyes never leaving one another. Just as he ends the conversation and pulls off the headset, I slip onto his lap. My hands rest on his chest and I feel his heart beating fast beneath my palms.

'This is a surprise,' he whispers, an eager huskiness to his voice, and I'm turned on even more by the instant attention he gives me.

'You work too hard.'

'Spain. Threw everything off. Trying... to catch up.' His

words are broken with my light kisses on his lips. His cheek. His neck. He promptly caresses my breasts.

'Well,' I say, leaning into his touch, 'maybe you should take a break.'

'What's come over you?'

'Maybe I missed you.'

It's not entirely a lie.

His hands move down and settle on my waist. Everything feels... easy. Natural. His touch is familiar and grounding. But as his lips hurriedly move against mine and I close my eyes, I see him. *Henry*. It's Henry's face that fills my thoughts while Mike's hands glide further down my body. Henry's dark eyes, that half-smile, the way his lips said my name.

What is happening?

This isn't right. I'm seeing another man's face while with I'm Mike. This has never happened before, but I have to admit it was my conversation with Henry that pulled my body here, to Mike, craving to be satisfied.

No, Ruby, stop. Stop this.

I push those thoughts away, focusing on Mike – on us – on the life we're building. The life I've wanted for so long. This is all that matters. He continues to kiss me deeply, his hands moving fast and impatiently around my body, and I let myself surrender to it, hoping it's enough to drown out this cocktail of emotion. Enough to drown out Henry.

CHAPTER FIFTEEN

The night air is sharper, biting against my face as I step outside to finally deliver Patty's shopping to her. She didn't sound mad, when I'd texted her after leaving Mike's office and having a shower, but maybe a bit distracted. Her messages were short and to the point, with no emojis, which is very unlike Patty. She probably wanted this sourdough bread for her tea, and is waiting until we're face to face before unleashing her disappointment with me. Strange how I care what this woman thinks, when two weeks ago I would have waited until she was out of sight before leaving my house.

The street is cast in heavy shadows, with only a few faint orange glows emitting from the lampposts and houses flanking either side. I don't want to feel afraid. This is my neighbourhood, and while it is a very quiet cul-de-sac, I've lived here long enough to know it's safe. Other than the takeaway incident the other week, nothing has ever happened to me here... but then I haven't been one to walk down to my neighbour's house before. The dread sits heavy in my chest as every noise feels amplified – the rustle of leaves in the breeze, the distant hum of a car engine, the faint clink of something metallic.

It's so dark that I long for the brighter summer nights... but I'm being ridiculous. Patty's door is just four houses away: it's a minute's walk. Even so, the irrational knot in my stomach tightens. I peer back over my shoulder at the alleyway, the black hole in the cul-de-sac, and listen carefully for any footsteps in the distance.

Get a grip, Ruby. I curse under my breath. Pulling my coat tighter, I divert my eyes from the void and quicken my stride.

As I reach Patty's house, the faint prickle at the back of my neck returns. The kind of sensation you can't shake, the one that makes you feel like you're on display. Turning around, I glance up and down the street again, trying to find the source of the feeling. Then I catch it – a movement. A curtain shifts in the upstairs window of the house across from Patty's. The Weird One's house. I squint, sticking my neck out to get a better look. There's someone there. I'm sure of it. A dark silhouette, standing perfectly still behind the curtain. My pulse races. I want to look away, but my eyes are frozen on the dark house.

Then the curtains snap shut and there's nothing to see.

I take a shaky breath and knock on Patty's door. The sound is loud and jarring in the stillness. I glance back across the street, but the window remains lifeless, the curtains a barrier to what's beyond the glass, as if no one had been there at all. My fingers fiddle with the shopping bags while I internally scream Patty's name over and over again. *Hurry up. Please.* The wind whistles past, grabbing my hair out of place as it goes, and the front door finally opens. My stomach tightens all over again. It's *him*. The Weird One.

For a moment, I just stare at him, my words having slipped away. He looks as he always does – too pale, with wiry hair sprouting in uneven tufts, and a grey bushy beard speckled with the last remnants of black. His clothes slightly hang on him today, like he's borrowed them from someone twice his size. They're not tattered or ripped, but it's as if they're from an old black and white film. He has no joy, no colour, and his face carries that same unnerving blankness, like he's not quite real. But his eyes – those sharp, beady eyes – lock onto me with a precision that makes my skin crawl.

'Evening,' he says, his voice thin and raspy, like he smokes twenty cigarettes a day.

'Hi,' I whisper and quickly clear my throat. 'I was just bringing these for Patty. Is she there?'

He doesn't answer right away. Nor does he call back to the homeowner. Instead, he leans against the doorframe, his gaze lingering up and down. 'Patty's not taking guests at the moment,' he finally replies, his lips curling into something that could be a smile on a normal person but looks more like a grimace coming from him.

'Oh.' I glance down at the bags in my hand. 'I said I'd drop these off earlier for her–'

'She won't be needing them now,' he cuts in, too quickly. 'She's... resting.'

I frown, trying to peek past him into the house, but he shifts slightly, blocking my view. I want to call out, shout Patty's name, but who do I think I am? She could be quite friendly with this weird little man. How could I possibly know when I've only just built a friendship with her?

I meet his ugly scrutiny. 'Resting? Is she all right?'

His grin widens, showing his coffee-stained teeth, and it's even more unsettling up close. 'Oh, she's fine. She just needs her peace. You understand, don't you?'

'Of course. But she was expecting this food. She asked me to get it all for her and I texted to say I'd bring it over.'

He leans forward slightly, and I instinctively step back. 'But that was earlier, wasn't it? And then you were busy. With Henry.'

'Henry?' I flinch, caught off guard. 'What do you mean?'

He waves a hand, dismissing me. 'Never mind. You young ones are always flitting about. Anyway, I must get back now.' He steps out onto the doorstep, forcing me further back down the pathway. 'Just remember – don't disturb Patty while she's resting.'

I bristle at his tone. 'I wasn't going to, I just–'

'Because I'll know,' he interrupts me again, his eyes glinting now. 'I see everything. From my house. You know that, don't you?'

He doesn't wait for my response. He pulls Patty's door firmly behind him and steps past me, whistling softly to himself while walking away. I turn slightly, and then just stand there, staring at him retreat as if my feet are stuck in giant ice cubes. I glance back at Patty's house, scan the windows, but there's no sign of life behind any of them. I consider banging on the front door, despite what The Weird One said, but his final words linger, heavy and oppressive and as I watch him again, his figure seems to shrink into the shadows.

What a creep.

But as he opens his front door, I inhale sharply. If that weird little man was in Patty's house... who was watching me from his upstairs window?

CHAPTER SIXTEEN

Mike and I glide around the kitchen, around each other, with ease. Like a winning couple from *Strictly Come Dancing*.

I decided it was time to try something new together, and declared a Friday-Night Fajita-Night, where we can share the prep and cooking tasks. I cut the chicken and veg while Mike gets busy with the guacamole and salad. We've got our favourite songs shuffling on Alexa, which is always a laugh with our differing tastes in music. He's waiting for Eminem while I'd rather hear a bit of Lana Del Rey. Opposites attract.

The rhythmic clink of plates and cutlery on the dining table alerts me that Mike's ready for Ruby's sizzling chicken and stir-fry. I transfer it from the pan to a serving dish and place it in the middle of all our culinary delights. Mike cracks open bottles of Budweiser for us both and we toast to our greatness. It's been a good week. Normal. Not perfect, but does anyone ever have a perfect week? My writing has poured from me effortlessly and even when I'm not at the laptop, my characters have been running through my mind.

Mike and I have spent most evenings on the sofa bingeing the latest true crime Netflix series. We haven't had sex, not since that afternoon in his office, and I can't help but wonder if I came on too strong. Doubtful, I know, Mike clearly enjoyed it, but he hasn't instigated anything since. I'm hoping tonight will remedy that.

The meal starts well, with Mike taking an interest in my latest book. But while explaining the next plot twist, his eyes glaze over. I've gone too far. Only deliver an elevator pitch when Mike starts asking. He isn't a bookworm like me, or Patty, I have to remember. But there's something else, a shift in his mood as he fidgets in his seat.

'Everything okay?' I ask, worried when he lowers his fajita wrap to the plate – Mike usually wolfs it down.

'The boss has requested I head back to Barcelona.'

'Right.' My voice is too quiet. 'When?' I try again, then continue eating. It's no big deal.

Mike grimaces. 'Next week.'

Don't huff. Don't sigh. 'That's soon... after the last trip, I mean.' I put my own food down.

He guzzles a mouthful of beer before replying. 'I know, Rubes, and it's not ideal. But it's this early period, while we're setting up the office and warehouse, this is when the team needs me the most.'

His voice carries a little excitement with it. Whether that's for the job or the trip itself, I can't be sure... but I know I can't linger in those thoughts. He should feel excited, and I should feel proud of him. I do. He's worked hard for this. For us.

'Yes, of course, this is important. I really do understand,' I say, hoping my tiny smile doesn't betray me.

Mike's hand reaches across the table and softly holds mine. 'I know it's not easy with me being away. You don't like being alone... but it's only a few nights here and there.'

'Exactly, it's just a few nights.' I don't trust myself to say anymore, because I haven't fully told Mike about how I felt, or what I heard, while I was alone. I don't want him to think of me as childish, or holding him back.

He nods, withdraws his hand and returns to munching his way through the meal. I don't pick my wrap back up, because as content as Mike is that he has settled things, the memory of his last trip creeps back. Uninvited and unwanted. That first night... the suffocating feeling, the creaks of the house, the noise downstairs.

'I'll be fine.'

'Yeah I know, Ruby. Why wouldn't you be?'

My eyes meet Mike's confused gaze. *Shit, I said that out loud...* Perhaps I should just be honest, and explain what it's like in this big house when he isn't here. But what if he laughs at me? Tells me that I'm a grown-arse woman and shouldn't be afraid of shadows in my own home. Gran definitely would if I confided such immature thoughts to her, so I can only imagine Mike would be the same. But, if he did understand... that would make him feel guilty for leaving me, especially after what happened to my mum. Here he is, trying to build a good career, not just for himself but for us, for the family we want, and I could ruin it all by clinging to him. By turning his opportunities into my fears. *No, Ruby!*

I shrug. 'I was just reassuring you, babe. I don't want you worrying about me... so I was just saying, I'll be fine, you know.'

'Yeah, you'll be so consumed with your new world and new characters, and this new main man... what was his name?' Mike pauses to cram more fajita wrap into his mouth. 'You won't even realise I'm gone.'

New man? Could he mean... Henry. No. How could he—

My book! *Frank*, the new character I'm introducing. Of course, that's what Mike's talking about. What's wrong with me? He *was* listening earlier.

'Oh, I notice when you're not here, Mr Sheridan,' I reply

with a cheeky wink, hoping it will mask the flush of guilt. 'And you're right, about me using the time to focus on my books and the marketing side of things. It's easier when the house is quiet.'

Mike chuckles, but barely looks up from his plate. 'See, that's the Ruby I know – always making the best of things.'

His words are warming, but when he continues with more talk of his trip I can't help but feel that I – and my anxieties – have been dismissed.

'So, it'll be three nights this time,' he says. 'Fly out Tuesday morning and back Friday late afternoon. It's good to get into a routine with these trips, and this will be the norm now. Mind you, I chose the earlier return flight this time, because I'm not getting stuck in any late evening delays again.'

'Makes sense.'

Three nights. I know it's not long, but the thought of being alone again, I can't help it... It strangles me with such dread, it's difficult to ignore.

Oh, get a grip, Ruby.

I change the subject. 'Do you think you'll be back in time for Hunter's birthday party?'

'Probably not, babe.'

'I haven't told you what time it is yet.' I'm teasing, but Mike sighs and looks me dead in the eyes. 'Just kidding with you. It's 4pm at Stef's and Kelly's house.'

'Well, I will have landed then... but I'll be tired from travelling, Rubes. A kid's party is the last thing I'll need.'

'Fingers crossed our friends don't feel that way when it's our child's birthday, someday,' I say with a hopeful smile.

'Ruby, I can promise you, I'm not the type of guy who would pressure my non-parent friends to attend a party full of hyperactive, sugar-high kids.'

His tone stings, and it feels like a losing battle, so I say nothing in return. He rises from the table, having finished his meal while I'm still only half a fajita in. I've lost my appetite anyway, so I stand with him and start clearing the plates away.

'The football's on soon.'

It's a statement, rather than a question, but I can sense Mike's unspoken meaning. I push aside the kid comment and offer to do the washing-up while he relaxes with another beer. Though, if truth be told, does any supporter *relax* while watching their team play? He'll be yelling at the TV within minutes of being in the living room.

'Actually, Mike, before you go... have you seen my phone? I was sure I left it here...'

He laughs out loud from where he's standing at the fridge. 'What the hell–' His own chuckling cuts the sentence dead as he reaches inside the fridge and brings out my phone. 'Seriously, Ruby.' Mike laughs again as he hands my cold mobile over and then grabs himself another beer.

'I didn't put that there.' I frown at his ongoing sniggering. 'I left it over there, by the kettle.'

'Well, I'm sure you didn't put it in there on purpose... and look, the milk is still sat on the counter; you probably just took the wrong thing.'

'Sounds like something my gran would do.'

'You're no spring chicken anymore, sweetheart,' he says with yet another chuckle, and walks out of the kitchen.

'Still younger than you,' I banter, but his attention isn't with me anymore.

Later, after the football, Mike heads upstairs for a shower and I linger in the kitchen, absently tidying up even though everything's already clean. I catch my reflection in the back door window. The glass is dark, turning the garden and the outside world into an abyss. For a split second, I swear I see something move in the reflection – just a flicker. My stomach tightens, but when I look behind me, the kitchen is empty.

'Mike,' I call out.

He can't hear me from down here. I turn back to the door. My eyes dart around my silhouette in the glass panel, trying to make out any kind of movement... perhaps it hadn't been a reflection, but something, *someone* in the garden.

It's too dark, and I'm not brave enough to step any further, to squish my face up against the window and glare wide-eyed outside. I don't want to be that person who dreads being alone, but that familiar, uneasy fear continues to worm its way to the surface. It makes me wonder if I'm strong enough to cope.

CHAPTER SEVENTEEN

I've been dreading this week. Knowing I'd wake up lonely once again, having missed Mike quietly leave, and just an empty space next to me. His side of the bed is already cold, the duvet flung back, allowing a chill to seep into the sheets. I feel a pang of disappointment, until my eyes settle on a folded piece of paper resting on his pillow. I sit up with a huge smile. How romantic and personal.

> *Ruby, Ruby Ruby!*
> *I didn't want to wake you. I know how much you love your sleep. I'll text when I land, but remember, it's only a few nights. Keep busy with your writing and I'll be home soon.*
> *The OG main man*

It's sweet. I can't remember ever getting a note from Mike... even when we first started dating, he would slip out of my apartment early to go home and get changed before work without so much as a goodbye. He lived with his mum until we moved into this house – yes, he was still living with mummy at thirty-two, but I think it's just more socially acceptable now, isn't it? Also, Mike isn't frivolous, so it meant he'd set up some decent savings – better than I ever did. I could have scraped together my half of a deposit for a mortgage, but Mike thought it best we rent first and not jump into buying the first house we saw. He doesn't like pressure. But this house has grown on us, and the landlords have been clear they want a long-term rent, so it works for us.

I snap a quick picture of Mike's note and send it to him with a short message:

> Well, that was very cute and it made my morning! Travel safe and call if you get a chance. Love you xx

Sliding my phone onto the bedside table, I stretch out in bed, and listen to the hum of the house. It's never *completely* empty, is it? The vibration of the fridge making itself heard from downstairs, the patter of next door's feet on their stairs, the flicking red standby light of the TV... with the sunshine breaking through the curtains, all those things are explainable. Normal house noises. But at night, when they're shrouded in darkness, it's easy to believe you're not alone. It's just so easy to overthink things when you don't have the stability of another person to hold on to. But I've made the decision to not let my mind wander there this time. To not be sucked into a downward spiral. I force the unease away, determined not to feel so untethered while Mike's gone.

Swinging my legs out of bed, I pull open the curtains and let the daylight fill the room. As I make the bed, my mind drifts to Patty. The weekend flew-by in a quiet normalcy, and even though I wanted to check in on her – I still have her groceries and the bread will be as hard as a rock by now – I held back. When I briefly mentioned it to Mike, he said not to bother, that she was probably unwell, if that's what the *other* neighbour said, and she'd knock for them herself when she could.

I hadn't explained that I'd been in her house, that I happily offered to go shopping for her and that I actually really get along with her. Now time has passed, it feels strange telling him... like I've held something back from him and made it weird. So even when he popped out to see his mum on Sunday afternoon, I'd done as he suggested and left Patty in peace. Though my restraint snapped yesterday, and I sent her a text when I still hadn't heard a thing from her. But she'd said it wasn't a great time to visit because she had a family friend over... I wonder if it's that same blonde from before.

I grab my notebook and pen from their place on my bedside table. They're both special to me, and I'll hate when the pages of this book are full of my scribbles and thoughts and I'm forced to buy the next one. The notebook was a Christmas gift from Gran, a beautiful black hardback with gold foiled butterfly detailing, and though the silver sleek pen could pass as any other pen, Mum had it engraved for me with the words, *write your own story*.

I need to plan out the next few days. I don't want to continually overthink everything, and writing things down has always anchored me – fiction or reality, there's a sense of purpose and achievement in writing things down and giving yourself a little tick. Perhaps that was my downfall during Mike's last trip: I hadn't been mentally prepared.

1. Hit the halfway mark on book one in this new series.
2. Get round to Patty's and ask her about the weird one.
3. Visit Gran... bring her something nice.

4. Buy Hunter's birthday present before Friday's
   party.

I tap the pen against my lips, staring at the list. It's not bad for a start, but it's the evenings I worry about the most. It's in those long, quiet hours, when the house feels too big and every creak makes my stomach twist, that I could be dragged away with a tidal wave of loneliness. I've always found it strange that Mike can fall asleep in seconds, even with the glow of the TV as it hums in the background, or the lamp bright beside him. I like to quietly read a book and let myself shut down before drifting off. But I'm used to having the security of Mike's warm body snoring next to me. Before that, I had the safety of living with Stef, or an entire floor of fellow students in halls of residence, or Mum in our family home. It never used to be the darkness I feared, because I was never alone. But now, it's that darkness mixed with a silence that makes my pulse race a little faster. Even just anticipating it increases my heart rate. Because the silence lets thoughts creep in... thoughts I'd rather keep out.

5. Think of something to help in the evenings...
   Wine?!

That'll do for now. Time to move on with the day, but I take the notebook and pen with me next door to my office and place it next to my laptop. Just in case – and eternally hopeful – that a better idea than wine comes to me during the day.

I clutch the shopping bags as I step outside the front door, the cold air brushing against my cheeks, while the bright sun does little to bring any warmth. The bags feel weightier than they should, like there's a heaviness in my arms, telling me not to deliver them to Patty's house. The awkwardness of arriving days later than promised, the probability that the woman's already stocked up on everything now, and the worry that she'll be annoyed with me. But she seemed normal in her text messages, so it's just my imagination playing with me again.

I walk down my pathway, wanting to avert my eyes from what's ahead but find myself looking anyway. I can't help it. Even in the brightest daylight, the alleyway looks barren. The weak fences line the thin pathway, while the bushes and trees do everything in their power to keep it secluded and dim. Leaving my front garden, I briskly turn in the opposite direction, shaking off how much I hate it being the view from my window, wishing it hadn't become such a beacon of unwanted attention since the incident earlier in the month.

Patty's standing at the gate of her next-door neighbour's house, and it's a welcome sight to see. And not just because she's back on her feet. Patty's clearly in her element: chatting animatedly, with her hands moving widely in front of her, as she holds court with a tiny elderly woman. I wonder if I should join them, embarrassed that I don't know the woman who lives at number three, but Patty notices me approach and stops the conversation to welcome me with a genuine smile.

'There she is,' she calls out, her voice bright. 'Ruby, come meet Mrs Shah.'

Mrs Shah does her best to look up, though her stooped body doesn't offer much movement. Her face is kind, but worn with deep lines and she grips the handles of her walking frame as though she's been leaning on them for decades.

Patty gestures between us. 'Mrs Shah, this is Ruby. She lives just a few doors down at number nine.'

Mrs Shah smiles, her dark eyes twinkling. 'So nice to meet

you, dear. Patty's just been telling me what a lovely young lady you are. And an author too.'

I smile back, but heat crawls up my neck and cheeks as I realise I don't know this woman at all. Can you really live a few doors down from a person for five years and never see them? I can only hope that I'm right in thinking she doesn't venture far from her front garden – she is, after all, wearing what looks like a nightdress.

'It's nice to meet you, too,' I say.

Patty, the queen of smooth transitions, links her arm with mine. 'Well, we're off for a cuppa now, aren't we, Ruby? I'll see you later, Mrs Shah, and I'll confirm the next book club date soon. Promise.'

Mrs Shah nods, lifting one hand in farewell. 'You girls enjoy yourselves.'

As Patty leads me up her driveway, I can't help but marvel at how easy she makes this all seem – the introductions, conversations and connections. It's so different from how things felt last month, last year, the year before that, when the cul-de-sac might as well have been a ghost town as far as I was concerned. Patty unlocks her front door and pushes it open, but stops when she catches me gazing across the road.

The Weird One's house looks like any of the others. Black painted front door and clean windows. The front garden is neat enough, though there's probably fewer flowers and more shrubbery – no one can compete with Patty's green fingers on this cul-de-sac. But there's still something about it that sets me on edge. I can't fully explain why, but the house makes me shiver, the way some people do when they hear nails on a chalkboard–

'You okay, Ruby?' Patty pulls my attention.

'Yes. Sorry. I was just thinking... wondering about the man

who lives over there,' I say, nodding my head, but not turning back to the house.

Patty peers over my shoulder. 'Oh. That's Norman, dear, why would you be wondering about him?'

'I saw him, last week, when I had your shopping.' I lift up the bags, as if she needs a visual. 'But he told me not to bother you.'

She laughs and lightly slaps my shoulder. 'He never did.'

'Yes,' I reply slowly, emphasising the word. 'He came out of your house and said you were resting–'

'Ruby, love, Norman wasn't in my house last week.'

'When I went shopping for you–'

'I went upstairs and took a nap. Your text later that evening woke me up.'

I look back across at the dark house and notice the curtains in the top window. They're drawn, but there's a sliver of space where one doesn't quite meet the other, like a mouth left slightly ajar, a gap that seems deliberate rather than careless.

'Does he live alone? The weir– I mean Norman?'

Patty hums for a few seconds, as if she needs to think of the answer. 'Well, he did for a long time. As long as we've been neighbours, but then recently his nephew moved in with him and he's a bit...' I turn to face her again, and she shrugs with a smile. 'Let's just say he's even less sociable than you were.'

A nervous chuckle follows, and I'm unsure if it's for my benefit or not, but I ignore it and probe further. 'So you've never met this nephew?'

'Well, yes, but he's not very chatty. Norman said he wouldn't be one for joining us out on the grass for a summer cul-de-sac soiree. But it makes sense, really, as he's in his early twenties, so I'm sure none of us would be cool enough to *hang* with. And I have wondered if he's non-verbal. Billy, that is, not Norman, obviously.'

No, I know Norman isn't. I heard him loud and clear last week. But perhaps it was this Billy who was watching me from the window. My fingers pick at the bags in my hand, poking and pushing at the thick plastic, until a subtle cough from Patty interrupts my thoughts. There's a crease to her brow, questioning me.

'When was Norman last here, Patty?'

She turns down her mouth. 'Last time I hosted the book club, I guess. It definitely wasn't last week, dear. Norman can be a bit quiet, maybe even a bit *queer*, some might say, but he really is a sweet man.'

Sweet... really?

'Maybe your friend, that blonde lady, let him in like she let me in,' I argue.

'Well, even if she did, I still would have known he was there, wouldn't I? And he wasn't. Sorry, Ruby, love, you're mistaken.'

There's a tight, pinched smile on her face. She looks as unconvinced about this exchange as I am. Why can't I find the words to explain *she's* mistaken. She's got it wrong. Not me. She's been resting for days and days now, I'm sure they've all just merged into one. She's probably on strong painkillers for her old injury, so wouldn't those only add to her confusion. How can I make her believe me? Book club can't be the last time he was in Patty's house, because I know what I saw, I spoke to him. I know Weird Norman was here.

CHAPTER EIGHTEEN

The common room in Gran's building is alive with quiet activity today – muted chatter, the soft clink of teacups and the slow shuffle of fellow residents in their slippers. It always feels warmer in here when it's not just Gran, alone, staring out at the world. Although, that's exactly where I find her – in the usual spot – wheelchair pulled up close to the window, but there's a glow to her cheeks. As I approach, she's even lightly humming a tune I know well. The paper opened at the crossword sits on her lap. I love to see her with a newspaper, something which feels so alien to me because I read all the news through an app on my phone. The paper sets the mood for the visit, because I know she'll be as sharp as a knife.

I feel guilty now for saying one of my recent visits was a waste of my time. How could I even begin to think that? Perhaps I need to check my own moods before I judge Gran.

Once I'm standing right next to Gran, I softly sing the lyrics to the song she's humming. A personal serenade, quiet enough for just her to hear and none of the other residents. Knowing them, they'd all join in and karaoke Wednesdays would be a new event on the schedule.

Gran lifts her hand to mine and smiles. 'Who sings that song, dear?'

'Kenny Rogers, of course.'

'Let's leave it to him shall we then, Ruby, love,' she replies, and chuckles hard at her own joke.

I feign shock, but can't keep it up for long. 'That's mean, Gran. Here I am, travelling all this way and giving you a private rendition of one of your favourite songs, and you basically tell me my singing is rubbish.' I bend to kiss her cheek, inhaling a smell of the coconut lotion that she's used for as long as I can remember. Then I get a chair from one of the tables and pull it up closer to her and the window, exhaling hard as I do.

'Tough day, love?'

'Mike's gone to Spain again,' I say, glancing out at the swaying trees beyond the glass.

Gran makes a noise, one of those sarcastic, all-knowing sounds that seem to be expelled from the nose. 'Didn't he just go?'

'Earlier this month, yes,' I reply, fiddling with the edge of my sleeve. 'It's fine. I just... I didn't think he'd be off again so soon. The house feels different when he's not there.'

She studies me, her finger rolling the pen back and forth. 'Different how?'

'Too quiet,' I admit. 'But it's not just that.' I hesitate, unsure if I should say more.

Gran's sharp eyes narrow slightly. 'Out with it, love. You've started, so you have to finish. You know that's the rule.'

I sigh, leaning back in my chair, a heaviness in my chest. 'It's one of my neighbours. I've always found him a bit... odd. I don't know why, and I can't explain it, so I know I shouldn't judge someone so quickly without knowing them but–'

'You don't have to explain any of that to me,' Gran interrupts. 'Tell me how you feel.'

'Well, I've made friends with one of my neighbours, which isn't like me. Patty, her name is. Anyway, I bump into this weird neighbour guy leaving her house and well... he said I shouldn't knock for her and that she was resting. He shut the door on me and walked away.'

Gran's lips tighten for a moment, in that way she does when she's trying to make sense of something unpleasant. 'And you didn't think to press him further on it?'

'Well, I probably didn't push hard enough, but that wasn't the strangest thing he said.' My voice hitches up a notch. 'He said he sees everything that happens on the street. You know, like he's watching me, and it made my skin crawl.'

She leans forward, lowers the pen to her lap and rests her hand on mine. Her grip is strong, despite her frail body. 'Have you told Mike about this?'

I shake my head. 'What's the point? I think he'd say I was imagining it. And actually, with what Patty said yesterday...'

Gran listens intently as I delve into my very strange chat with my newest – only – friend on the street. And that, although Patty is mistaken, it would only add fuel to the fire if I mentioned it to Mike. Gran's eyes narrow further, and for a moment, she looks just like she did when I was a child, ready to march down the road and give someone a piece of her mind.

'You listen to me, Ruby,' she begins, her voice low and demanding. 'I couldn't give a rat's arse what Mike says, or what this Patty believes. If that weird neighbour makes you feel uncomfortable, you trust your gut. Your instinct has never let you down before. Even that night with your mum, you knew something wasn't right... that was your instinct. Don't ignore it, and don't let anyone make you feel like you're overreacting.'

Her words hit me harder than I expect, and I find myself blinking back tears. I wish she hadn't put Mum in the mix, because my instinct *was* off. Completely. I missed all the signs that something was wrong there. So then, maybe, I shouldn't ignore the warnings I'm feeling now.

Gran sits back, her face softening. 'You've always been sensitive to these things, love. You have such an imagination, but that doesn't mean you make things up. It means you see things differently; you analyse things in a way people don't. I'm sure if you weren't a writer you'd be a copper.'

We both allow a short laugh to break the moment.

'Listen,' she says. 'I'm sure every neighbourhood has a strange one; it was different in my day because everyone knew everyone. Knew their husband's name, kid's shoe size and what they were having for dinner. That's just how things were back then. But now... you youngsters don't have a clue who you're living next door to. So, maybe it is nothing... But maybe it's not. Either way, love, keep your eyes open. Okay?'

I nod, not trusting myself to speak right in that second. Gran doesn't press me further, but picks up her pen, as if to say we can move on. And just like that, saying how I feel out loud and not being dismissed or told I'm imagining things, the heaviness in my chest slightly lifts.

'Thanks, Gran.'

'For what?'

'For always knowing what to say. For always making me feel better about things. For not making me feel like a right crank.'

She throws her head back and laughs before giving me a slight wink. 'That's what grans are for, my love.'

I lift the newspaper and take the pen from her, to give her fingers a break, and start reeling off the clues to the crosswords. She's quick at answering most of them, as always, her mind never faltering.

When I leave the care home an hour later, Gran's words echo in my mind. *Trust your gut... Don't ignore it... Keep your eyes open.* It's all good advice, I know, but will I be able to follow it with such conviction once she's not here, once I'm alone?

———

The living room feels colder as soon as I flick the light off. The darkness surges forward, eager, and for a moment, I freeze. My hand hovers over the switch as if I might turn it back on. Instead, I breathe out slowly, step into the hallway, and turn the light on there. The warm glow settles around me like a shield, but the silence of the house hums, too loud and too quiet all at once.

I make my way to the kitchen, my footsteps quick and hurried, desperate to complete the downstairs lock-up routine. I did it all earlier, of course, before the sun setting welcomed the night, but you have to check these things again, before you can actually go to bed, right?

The kitchen light floods the space and chases away the shadows haunting every corner. My eyes dart to the back door, its glass a dark rectangle at the edge of the room. It feels miles away from me, but I walk towards it and check the lock with trembling fingers. I test it twice, pulling hard on the handle, to be sure, then step back.

Don't look outside. Don't look at the glass.

I shudder and turn away, switching off the light and stepping quickly back into the hallway's glow. I swap the downstairs light for the upstairs one simultaneously, so there's never a shroud of darkness, but my pulse still quickens as I climb the stairs. I run up them swiftly, but then hesitate at the top, glancing towards my bedroom door. It's half open, from when I changed into my nightclothes earlier, but walking straight in feels impossible.

I move away from it and open my office door at the back of

the house. My hand reaches into the room before me, flicking the light on. I step in and scan every corner. The spare wardrobe is ajar and I curse under my breath, willing myself to stop being so ridiculous. But I can't help it. I yank it open, fully expecting something to leap out. It's empty, of course, nothing but the faint scent of wood and the jangling of a few unused hangers. I turn to leave, but something stops me. The window. I step closer, pulling the curtain aside and staring out into the darkness. It's the same as in the kitchen – just my reflection, faintly distorted, looking back at me. The garden is a black void, the apartment building beyond it even darker. There's nothing. I swallow hard and let the curtain fall back into place.

Out in the hallway, I move to the next room, again flicking the light on first. The bathroom is empty, the shower curtain pulled back, no hiding places here. Mike's office last, going through the same ritual – though I didn't dare look out of that window towards the alleyway, comforted by the fact Mike never opens it anyway.

By the time I finish, my heart is racing and my hands are clammy. There's nothing up here. There was never going to be anyone up here but me. Finally, I step into my bedroom, closing the door behind me and releasing the tight grip on my mobile. I jump into bed, under the cool sheets, and check my phone to see Mike has finally replied to my earlier message:

> It's too late to call now, and I'm shattered from work, so I'll speak to you before I board Friday, babes. Hope you haven't missed me too much! x

His message does nothing to calm me, and I don't turn off the light. I just can't. Its brightness keeps the shadows banished from my walls. The golf club is tucked up next to me. I'd never admit my new bed companion to Mike, and it's returned to his office when he's home. I reach out towards the white noise machine I bought through Amazon Prime. It was advertised for a baby's nursery, which made me feel like a total idiot buying it... but maybe it will be used in that room one day... when I grow up. Just as I'm about to switch it on, the faint sound of the front door clicking shut catches my attention.

My stomach clenches so hard I have to hold my breath. I listen. The creak of the floorboard, the kitchen door handle squeaking, footsteps on the laminate flooring... Nothing. None of those sounds follow. I turn on the white noise machine and let the static fill the air. *It's just my imagination. It's just my imagination.* There's no way I can go check, go investigate. No, I'll just have to lie here, my hand now gripping the golf club, my body frozen in place, and hope the sun comes up before any intruder does.

CHAPTER NINETEEN

I knew deep down Mike wouldn't make it back in time to join me at Hunter's party. The plane has landed – I checked online – but I'm still waiting for a text from him to say he's in a taxi on his way home. He's dilly-dallying no doubt. But I guess, so am I. Ever hopeful, peeping out of the window each time I've heard a car pulling in or out of the cul-de-sac in the past hour. Stef's house is only a twenty-minute drive away, but if I hold on much longer I'll miss the start, and I'm sure she'll need an extra pair of adult hands. The ping of a message on my phone is my cue to stop dithering.

Prosecco on ice, Ruby. We're waiting!

I reply with a smile:

Is that even allowed at a kid's party, and when your wife is pregnant?

It's because the house will be full of kids and pregnant hormonal ladies... so don't make me have to drink the whole thing myself.

Looks like I won't be driving then, so I quickly reply:

> That means public transport... I'll be there within the hour.

> Don't be a cheapskate, call an Uber. Hurry!

I laugh as I slip my phone into the back pocket of my jeans, and then push my feet in my trusty Dr Martens, grab my favourite rainbow-coloured scarf, black duffle coat and handbag. If Mike can't make it, that's on him, but I'm not about to sit in the house alone, stewing over it. I'm going to have me a few glasses of bubbles with my friend... albeit at a kid's party, but beggars can't be choosers.

I lock the front door behind me, ready to speed walk to the train station. Stef knows me too well. Not that I'm a cheapskate, but I refuse to pay for taxis both ways. So, if I'm having a drink, then I'll definitely want to get an Uber home, but travelling there, that extra cost is not needed. It's a lovely crisp day, but there's a slight bite to the breeze. I keep my head down, not wanting to even look at any of the neighbours' houses today; I'm fed up with them. But just as I turn the corner out of the street, I'm jolted out of my thoughts, quite literally, when I bump into someone.

'Ruby!'

I step back, startled, and look up to see Henry in front of me, a bunch of keys swinging in his hand. He's wearing a black hoodie under his jacket, so casual-looking yet so... stylish.

'I'm so sorry, Henry, I didn't see–'

'Clearly,' he teases, though his tone is warm. 'You in a rush?'

'No. Well, yes.' I backtrack. 'A party.'

'A party,' Henry repeats and raises his eyebrows. 'Starting a bit early, aren't you? One of those bottomless brunches.'

I adjust the strap of my bag. 'Erm, it's actually a kid's

party...' I laugh. 'My best friend, Stef, is about to have her house filled with four-year-olds, so I'm going for moral support.'

'So you're a perfect neighbour *and* a perfect friend.'

His smile is beautiful and I'm lost in it for a second, without replying to his comment. Remembering our last conversation when he called me perfect. I'm far from it... Patty didn't get her shopping then, and while I may be supporting Stef today, I haven't seen Nancy for ages. Hardly perfect when I can't keep up with the two friends I have.

'Sounds... chaotic,' Henry continues, breaking through my thoughts. 'And brave of you to volunteer for that.'

I shake my concentration from his lips to answer this time. 'Ah, I love little Hunter... that's Stef's son. Plus, there's Prosecco waiting, so that will help.'

'Prosecco at a kid's party. Now that's smart.'

'It's for the parents, obviously.' Although I'm not a parent.

'Obviously,' he echoes. 'I didn't imagine bubbles being poured into the sippy cups... but it could have its benefits.'

We laugh lightly in unison, then Henry shifts his weight and begins fidgeting with his keys. He actually looks nervous. It's endearing.

'Where does your friend live?'

'Not far, St Albans, only two stops on the train.'

'I'm heading out anyway. St Albans wouldn't put me out of my way...' He smiles again. 'I'd love to drop you.'

I hesitate, caught off guard by the offer. 'Oh, I couldn't ask you to do that.'

'You're not asking; I offered.' He shrugs casually. 'You'd be doing me a favour. Better company than the radio, and I'd love to get to know you more.'

That was very upfront. Honest.

I glance towards the station, then back at Henry. This man is a stranger. But then, so is any Uber driver I'd voluntarily get in the car with. At least I know where Henry lives. His easy grin is disarming, and there's something about him – a combination of charm and sincerity that I'd like to get to know more, too. It's enough to make me nod and thank him; and within seconds we're both climbing into his car.

'Where am I heading?' he asks, buckling his seatbelt.

I give him Stef's address, and he nods, entering it into Google Maps before smoothly pulling away from the kerb. We're both quiet at first, and I peer out of the window as though I've never seen these houses and trees and streets before. As if this is all new to me. I guess, in a way, it is. My right leg dances on the spot, bouncing up and down, and I can't deny the surge of heat in my stomach. I'm nervous.

'So, this friend of yours – Stef, was it? – she's got a house full of teeny-tiny kids and you're willing to jump in and help out. You don't have kids, do you?'

I don't turn to look at him, just shake my head and murmur no.

'Sorry, I didn't mean to pry about your personal life. I just... I just wanted to get to know you, like I said...'

'It's fine.' I inhale a smile and angle my body and eyes to him. 'Stef's one of my closest friends. I'd do anything for her. And, like *I* said, there's Prosecco on ice. That's the real reason I'm going.'

'Ah, now the truth comes out,' he says, chuckling. 'I knew there had to be a catch.'

I laugh, brushing over the question of children, and fall into the rhythm of banter with him. 'Are you saying you could handle it without the need for alcohol?'

'I've got a high tolerance for chaos,' he admits, glancing at me briefly before turning back to the road. 'I'd be able to survive. Just ask my sister, who regularly makes me dress up for my niece's and nephew's parties.'

'You're lying.'

His mouth drops wide open, make-believe shock at my comment, and from my side view of him, I can't help but study his defined jawline. The few days' old dark stubble forming a perfect shade over his tanned skin.

'I'll have you know I've been Spiderman, the Hulk, a red Power Ranger and a dinosaur. That one was the worst, I could hardly breathe in the suit and needed a chaperone to lead me so I didn't fall over.'

'Bet you made a good Spiderman.' I cringe inside.

'Oh yeah, sure. In that tight spandex, all restricting and sweaty.'

'Was it now?' I tease, but then scold myself and push the images from my mind. Henry gazes at me again briefly, and I hope he didn't catch the simmering undertone.

The conversation continues to flow naturally, the pauses comfortable rather than awkward. For a moment, I forget about the nagging loneliness I've felt these past few days. About Mike not joining me today... That's awful, but yes, even Mike... Sitting in this car that smells of a woody aftershave, everything feels... lighter. As the car hums along the road, Henry steals a quick glance in my direction. It's subtle, but I notice it, and my breathing hitches.

'So, Ruby,' he says, his tone softer now, almost intimate. 'What do you do for fun when you're not rescuing friends from their kids' birthday parties or helping old neighbours with their shopping?'

'For fun?' I repeat, seriously considering my answer because when do I have fun? 'Not much, really. I write. I read. I go for walks... when it's not freezing outside.'

'Sounds peaceful.'

'Sounds lonely,' I admit, glancing at him.

He doesn't meet my gaze, but gives me a small smile.

Knowing, maybe. The silence that follows isn't heavy, but something simmers beneath it. A charge I can't explain, but can feel in the air. The way my skin prickles. My fingers fidget with the charms on my bracelet.

'Do you always do that?' he asks suddenly, his tone laced with curiosity.

'Do what?'

'Play with your bracelet when you're nervous.'

I freeze mid-fidget, caught off guard, and drop my hand into my lap. 'I'm not nervous.'

'Good.' His voice a note lower again. 'I don't want you to feel nervous around me. Unless...'

'Unless what?' I match his decibel.

'Unless you enjoy having that feeling with me.'

And there it is. A low, unmistakable charge that's cloaked with a sexy and hungry tension. I don't respond, but my lips let loose a small giggle. It doesn't sound like me. I don't giggle, and this isn't funny. But my heart races a little faster, and I glance out the window again, trying to distract myself. The streets blur past, but all I'm really aware of is the way Henry's presence now seems to fill the car: his confidence, his warmth, his way of looking at me.

The car slows as Henry pulls up outside Stef's house. She's hung blue balloons on the front door, and they're billowing off each other in the breeze. Not a dissimilar action to the butterflies swarming inside me now. Henry parks and turns off the engine, and the quiet brings me back to life. To reality. But when I glance at him, I'm suddenly unsure of the right way to end this. He's just my neighbour, doing a neighbourly favour that anyone would. But this has felt like something more than that. More than friendly banter.

'Thanks for the lift.' I finally decide on, my hand hovering near the door handle but not quite making the move to open it.

'It was my pleasure,' he replies, his voice still low and smooth, the hint of a grin tugging at his lips. He leans back slightly in his seat, one hand resting casually on the steering wheel as he studies me.

I feel pinned under his gaze, but know I have to make the first move because I'm the one who has to leave. 'Well, I should–'

'You owe me now, Ruby,' Henry interrupts, his tone playful but laced with something else... something that sends a pleasant shiver down my spine.

'Owe you?' I repeat, clearing my throat.

Henry tilts his head, squinting his eyes like a smouldering literary character. 'That's right. I don't just give out free rides, you know.'

His words hang in the air between us, the double meaning impossible to ignore. The heat spreads up through my body from the pit of my stomach. I force out a laugh, hoping it doesn't sound as breathless as I feel, and although I try to match his tone, I'm unable to look him directly in the eyes.

'I'll be sure to repay the favour, Henry.'

Before he can respond, I pull the handle and push open the car door. The cool air hits my face like a welcome splash of water, and I'm drowned with the weight of mixed emotions. I step out quickly, clutching my bag as if it'll steady me. I don't turn to wave, to say thanks again, or even goodbye. I don't trust that I won't jump back in the car and tell Henry to drive away, take me anywhere his heart desires. Anything that allows me to be swallowed by the bubble he's created. Carefree, exciting, thrilling. As I hurry up the path to Stef's door, and press the doorbell, I hear Henry behind me.

'Enjoy the party,' he calls, his voice following me like a shadow.

CHAPTER TWENTY

Stef opens the door and the sound of laughter and music filters through, grounding me slightly. My friend's smiling face, so pleased to see me, is a warm greeting tugging me further back to reality. As soon as Stef hugs me and ushers me inside, I plan to leave Henry, and all thoughts of him, on the other side of that door. I manage a smile, and take a moment to slip off my boots and hang my coat and bag up. But the thud of something heavy hitting the floor, followed by a loud child's cries and parents' concerns, pulls my feet in the direction of the kitchen rather than into the centre of the party.

I make a beeline for the counter where the Prosecco bottle sits, half-empty and gleaming like a beacon. Grabbing a glass from the side, I pour generously, not caring about the bubbles spilling over the edge.

'Ruby!'

Stef's voice comes from somewhere to the side of me, but I ignore her, bringing the glass to my lips and taking a long, desperate gulp. The fizz hits my throat with a shocking tingle, making me cough slightly, but I don't care. Another gulp, and the glass is nearly drained.

'Bloody hell. Steady on, girl,' Stef says, her eyes wide with amusement and suspicion when I finally look at her. She snatches the glass from my hand before I can go for round two. 'How bad was the journey? Why are you necking Prosecco like it's water?'

I laugh it off, waving away her questions, but she's not having any of it. With a firm grip on my wrist, she pulls me towards the other side of the kitchen, away from the door and the chaos spilling out of the living room.

When we're tucked further away, she releases her hold of me and folds her arms. 'You've got a funny look about you, Ruby. And I haven't seen you down a glass in years. Don't make me drag it out of you.'

'There's nothing to tell,' I say, a little too quickly.

She raises an eyebrow, waiting.

'Really, Stef, it's nothing.' I pause, looking past her to the Prosecco bottle across the room, wishing I hadn't given her the glass. 'I just... I got a lift here from a neighbour. That's all.'

'A neighbour,' she repeats, her eyebrows arching even higher. 'And this neighbour of yours, do they usually make you guzzle alcohol like a woman possessed?'

'It's not like that,' I protest, but my voice wavers, betraying me.

'Uh-huh... So, tell me, what's this neighbour's name?'

'Henry.'

'Henry,' she repeats, again. 'And what's this Henry like? Old? Married? Hot?'

I let out a nervous laugh, but stop myself and frown. I haven't asked his age. Or his relationship status. Or even what he does for a living... what his hobbies are. He knows a lot about me and all I can tell my friend is his name. And that he's incredibly hot.

'He's... He's just a neighbour, Stef. He gave me a lift and that's it. Let's forget about it now.'

She narrows her eyes, studying my face like she's looking for cracks. 'But you do think he's attractive, don't you?'

'No,' I say, too forcefully. 'I mean... I haven't thought about it.'

She bursts out laughing, swatting my arm. 'You are a terrible liar, Ruby. You always have been. Come on, admit it. You've got a thing for the new guy on the block.'

'I do not,' I insist, but the memory of Henry's lingering gaze and that playful smirk flashes through my mind. Without thinking, I nibble my fingernail.

Stef's laughter softens into something gentler. 'Look, I get it. Mike's away, the house feels empty, and then this Henry guy shows up. But just be careful, yeah? I don't want to see you get hurt.'

Her words land heavy. It should have been me who mentioned Mike, not my friend. But I nod quickly, brushing it off and repeating myself.

'It's not like that, Stef. Really.'

'All right, all right,' she says, holding up her hands in mock surrender. 'But I'll be watching you, Miss Ruby.' She winks, turns back for the Prosecco bottle and tops up my glass. 'Here, drink up, loosen up, and come help me wrestle these kids.'

I smile, but as I sip the Prosecco slower this time, her words echo in my head. *Just be careful.*

The party is in full swing, a chaotic masterpiece of shouting children, rustling gift bags, and the occasional crash and bang. In the corner of the room, a group of women – all mums, no doubt – sit together chatting and laughing. Kelly sits with them, and I hope there will be a chance for me to congratulate her and ask about the pregnancy later.

A dad stands nearby, holding a paper cup awkwardly, his attention flickering between his drink and the child shrieking with glee as they bounce out of a ball pit onto a soft mat. It's incredible what parents can create in their living rooms for the ideal birthday party. I linger at the edge of the doorway, watching it all. It's pure mayhem, but there's a warmth to it, an energy that feels alive in a way my house never does. I take another sip of Prosecco, hoping it will push down the ache creeping up my chest.

Stef appears beside me again, balancing a tray of fairy cakes she's rescued from a little boy with icing smeared across his cheeks. 'You all right?' she asks, nudging me gently with her elbow.

'Yeah,' I say, forcing a smile. 'Just... taking it all in.'

Her eyes follow mine around the room, to the mothers' meeting, the children running amok and the smashed crisps on the floor. 'It's a lot, isn't it? Hunter wanted a soft play party, but also a party at home. So, here you have it... I've been questioning my life choices since I agreed to it.'

I laugh, but it's short-lived. Stef doesn't notice, already moving to rescue another snack from the growing chaos. I sip my drink again, letting the noise wash over me. I glance at my friend, now pulling Hunter off the dining table as he tries to launch himself into the ball pit from a new height. I envy her, I realise. Not in a bitter way – but in a longing, wistful way. It's strange how much I crave this. The noise and mess, the laughter, the family. Even the exhaustion Stef complains about is something I'd welcome. Mine and Mike's house is so quiet, so still. Even when he's home. Some nights I lie in bed and try to imagine the cry of a baby needing comfort or the sound of little feet running down the hall to get into bed with us.

Instead, I have an empty house and a... a Mike — not even a husband — who's too busy with work to share this with me. I shake the thought away, forcing my mind back to the present.

Stef catches my eye and smiles, her cheeks flushed, her hair coming loose from its braid. 'Ruby,' she bellows, beckoning me over with a finger. 'You're not getting away with just watching. Come help me with these little monsters.'

I set my glass down, plastering on another smile as I join her in the fray. But even as I laugh and chase after one of the kids trying to climb the back of the sofa, that creeping ache refuses to be pushed down. Refuses to go away.

***

The party winds down in a blur of sticky fingers, torn wrapping paper, and sugar-fuelled exhaustion. Parents round up their children like they are herding wild animals, gathering coats and shoes as the kids whine for 'just five more minutes' in the ball pit. Stef sighs, slumping against the kitchen counter as the last guest finally leaves, and Kelly takes Hunter upstairs for a much-needed bath.

'God, I don't think I've stopped moving since 8am,' Stef says, pushing strands of hair back from her flushed face. 'This is more hectic than being out on the ambulance.'

'I very much doubt that.' I offer a faint smile and swipe empty paper cups into a black bin bag. 'You did good, though. Everyone seemed to have a great time.'

'Yeah, great for them,' she mutters, tossing a handful of leftover party hats into another bag. 'Next year, I'm outsourcing the whole thing. No soft play at home. I'm booking a place that takes care of everything — entertainment, food, the lot. I'll just sit in a corner with a coffee and let them get on with it.'

I laugh, collecting a tray of cake crumbs and half-eaten sausage rolls. 'Not a bad plan.'

We work in a comfortable silence for a while, the chaos gradually giving way to some kind of normal order. By the time the counters are wiped clean and the leftover snacks are packed into Tupperware, Stef collapses onto one of the kitchen chairs, gesturing for me to sit across from her.

'Thanks for coming, Ruby, it does mean a lot to me,' she says tiredly, but pours us both another glass of Prosecco. 'It's a shame Nancy couldn't be here. You two mean the world to me, and to Hunter.'

I pause, setting the glass down on the table. 'I haven't seen Nancy since the three of us went out for Christmas,' I admit, guilt flickering in my chest. 'We've texted, but it feels impossible these days to find a date that works for everyone.'

'Tell me about it.' Stef rolls her eyes, then straightens and points at me. 'But that's more Nancy's fault than yours, or mine, what with all the travelling for work.'

I flinch, caught off guard. 'Travelling?'

'Yeah, her events company have expanded to weddings abroad now. She's already been to Cyprus and Amsterdam, and I think she's in Spain at the moment. She didn't mention it?'

Stef's words slap me around the face. *Spain.* My thoughts stumble, trying to piece them together. Nancy's in Spain? Since when? For how long? Why didn't she tell me?

'Spain,' I murmur. 'That's where Mike's been going for work, too.'

'Oh yeah, bloody hell,' she says with a laugh, oblivious to the shift in my tone. 'Everyone's travelling these days except you and me, Ruby. I'm saving lives while you're inventing them, but we could do that anywhere in the world, you know, not just rainy old England.'

I force a chuckle, but my mind races on. Questions swarm in

my head like an angry nest of wasps, each one more unsettling than the last.

Nancy's in Spain. Did she see Mike?

That's daft, Ruby, for crying out loud. It's a massive country. They might not even be in the same city. *Are* they in the same city? Did she know Mike was there? Why didn't she tell me she was travelling at all? We spoke a few weeks ago.

I try to shake it off, focusing on Stef as she rambles on about the nightmare she'll have later getting Hunter to bed. But I can't ignore the images that are trying to hook on to the edge of my mind.

By the time I leave Stef's house, the sky is a dusky grey, moody and heavy. Much like the weight of my thoughts. I pull out my phone and order an Uber. The lampposts flicker to life, their orange glow casting eerie shadows on the ground. But for once, I don't care, because right now nothing can steal my attention from the shadows of my own mind. The tightness in my chest is forcing me to frown and huff and grit my teeth. Can this be true, or is it really my imagination?

Spain. Mike. Spain. Nancy.

I can't seem to make sense of it, but one thing is clear: this feels like too much of a flipping coincidence.

CHAPTER TWENTY-ONE

The Uber pulls up, and I slide into the back seat, muttering a quick 'hi' to the driver. I stare out of the window as we pull away, but I'm not really seeing anything out there in the darkening streets. My mind is somewhere else entirely.

Mike in Spain. Nancy in Spain.

The two facts keep colliding in my head like magnets, impossible to ignore. Why am I even thinking this? It's ridiculous. Mike wouldn't... Nancy wouldn't. But something has sparked the thought, and now I can't put out the fire burning its way through my brain.

Nancy. Gorgeous, confident Nancy, with her big laugh and sparkling eyes. Long, model-length legs and slim physique. The kind of woman who lights up a room without even trying. The total opposite of me. She's been one of my closest friends for years. Way before I was even with Mike. We've barely socialised with my friends since moving into this house. She knows him, of course, from our earlier days of dating, but there's never been anything between them. Never even a hint. So why am I questioning it? I press my fingers against my temples, trying to block out these intrusive thoughts. I'm being stupid.

I'm tired, and my imagination is running wild with the effects of being lonely this week. And the Prosecco. That's all it is.

But Stef's words echo in my mind, and they won't let me go. They're forcing me to make connections: *Nancy's in Spain right now. Mike just flew back from Spain today.* I pull out my phone, my fingers hovering over the screen. There's still no communication from Mike.

I don't want to do this. I don't want to be the paranoid woman who can't trust her best friend or her partner. But the niggles won't leave, and I know it's going to eat me alive if I don't do something. So I type out a quick text message. Keep it light. Keep it casual.

> Hey, Nance. How's things? Missed you at Hunter's party today. x

I hit send and immediately regret it. What am I even expecting? Nancy doesn't owe me an explanation. She's allowed to have her own life, her own work trips. But when the typing bubbles pops up instantly, my breath catches. The Uber driver glances at me in the rear-view mirror, but I ignore him and focus on the screen. Nancy is always quick to reply, always online, but the speed feels different this evening. Like she's been waiting for something.

> Hey! Sorry, couldn't make it. Work's been hectic. Hope Hunter had a great time. Xoxo

I read it over and over, searching for something, anything, in the words. It's fine. It's normal. But it feels... flat. Why hasn't she mentioned Spain? Surely she'd tell me she's not in the country. She told Stef, so why not me? My discomfort grows, the fire now radiating all over my body, the heat spreading and leaving a lump of dread wedged inside my chest. I force myself to reply, keeping the same breezy tone.

> He did. Stef pulled out all the stops, as always.
> How are you? We still haven't arranged a date
> to meet up! X

Nancy's reply is slower this time, as though she's thinking carefully about what to say.

> I'm fine, just really busy with work. Hope you're
> good too xoxo

It's short. Too short. Nancy is never short with me. Even if she's busy, she'll usually send a voice note or a string of emojis. But this message feels like a door shutting in my face. She didn't even acknowledge us not meeting up. I bite my lip, my teeth picking at the skin, and stare at the screen. I could let it go. I *should* let it go. She clearly doesn't want to chat right now... but this is precisely why my unease won't let me end the conversation.

> We missed you today. It's not the same without
> you. When are you free next to catch-up? X

I send it before I can second-guess myself, before I can stop myself, my heart thumping in my chest. What if she says she doesn't want to meet up? The Uber driver slows to a stop and I glance up, realising we're in Blackwood Close. Home.

I say thank you and slide out of the car, my phone clutched in my hand. At the front door, I linger, watching the typing bubbles dance on the screen, before they disappear completely. The agitation curls around me like thick, black smoke. Nancy didn't send a reply. She's gone offline.

The sound of the TV greets me the second I step inside the house. Not just the murmur of a show, but the unmistakable roar of a football crowd. The absolute irony of life. Of course, I'm happy Mike's home and the house is filled with noise, but for once – right now – I could really do with being lost in my own quiet thoughts. I close the door behind me, letting the latch click softly into place, and drop my bag on the console table.

When I step into the front room, I see him, Mike, sprawled on the sofa with a beer in one hand and his feet propped on the coffee table like he's been there for hours. He probably has. He's shifted Gran's beautiful crystal vase from the middle of the table, as he often does because apparently the flowers block his view of the TV. I rarely bother mentioning it to him, or make an obvious fuss, but this evening it adds to my irritation. I bulldoze into the room, lift the weighty vase from the edge of the coffee table and place it on the side table with a thud of annoyance.

'Hey, you're back,' he says with a grin, his eyes flicking to me before returning to the screen, not even noticing that one more jerky movement could have shattered one of Gran's most special possessions. 'Didn't hear you come in.'

I force myself to steady my breathing, to push away the ugly thoughts eating at me. 'When did you get back?'

'A few hours ago.' He lifts the can to take a gulp. 'Must have just missed you. How was the party?'

'Hectic but... interesting.' I stare at him, wondering if he'll catch my tone there at the end, ask me what was interesting.

'Come on, sit down,' is all he replies, patting the cushion beside him without looking away from the match. 'Arsenal's just scored. It's been a cracker of a game.' He pauses, glances at his drink, and then at me. 'Actually, grab us another beer before you join me, will you? You're a star.'

I freeze for a split second, but he doesn't notice. My mind screaming a million different thoughts and ideas and questions.

Confront him.

Don't confront him. It's just a bloody coincidence.

Ask him and see how he reacts.

You can't ask him. He'll be furious and feel betrayed.

I can't focus on one path to choose. I'm giving myself a migraine, and head to the kitchen on autopilot. The fridge light feels unnaturally bright as I open it and grab a beer. My hand lingers on the cold can for a moment, my thoughts churning.

No, I can't bring this up with him. It's ridiculous. What would he think if I said, *Hey, Mike, so... I was just wondering, were you in Spain with Nancy?* The very idea makes my skin prickle with embarrassment. But the uncertainty of it all digs deeper.

I take the can to him, setting it on the coffee table, and take a seat beside him. He mutters a thanks as he switches it out with the empty one, yanks the ring-pull and slurps another gulp of beer. His focus is entirely on the screen, his face alight with the kind of excitement I never understand with this sport. He's shouting encouragement at the players as if they can hear him, completely oblivious to me. I sit there, staring at the side of his face and something sharp flares in my chest. I should be happy he's home. I should feel relieved, comforted. But instead, I feel... annoyed.

After days away, where all I've felt is loneliness and the fear of every creak and shadow, this is the reception I get? A grin, a beer order and a seat next to him while he cheers Arsenal on? I cross my arms and sink back into the sofa, my eyes fixed on the TV but not really watching. His hand rubs my thigh, a casual, absent-minded gesture, but it doesn't soothe me. I can't shake this. The unease, the doubt, the irritation. It's all swirling together, making it impossible to relax.

'You know,' I finally say, desperate to keep my voice calm

and level, and not sound like a moody teenager. 'I don't think you've even given me a hug or a kiss.'

'Well, you haven't given me one,' he says with a loud laugh, but still doesn't look at me. 'We're sitting together now. This is nice.'

'That's not the same thing, Mike,' I snap before I can stop myself. 'You've been gone for days, and you didn't even–'

'God, Ruby, not with the moods again,' he cuts me off, his voice sharper but his eyes still on the TV. 'What is your problem?'

'My problem? You've set up camp with beers and football, your suitcase is still there in the corner, you haven't asked anything about my week or how I am. You barely check in while you're away, so the least you could do is have a conversation when you get home.'

He finally looks at me, a heavy sigh, his brows knitting together. 'It's been a hectic week, Ruby. I'm tired. The case can wait until tomorrow. I asked how the party went. Can I not just chill with a bit of footie without you starting something?'

His hostile tone tightens my chest further. 'I'm not starting anything, Mike. I'm just saying it'd be nice if you acted like you were happy to see me.'

'I am happy to see you,' he says with a frosty bite. 'But you're being childish about this.'

That word. *Childish*. It slaps me again, just the same way it did weeks ago when he first said it. My eyes sting, but I force myself to hold his gaze. 'Don't call me that,' I say, my voice low, trembling with a mix of anger and hurt.

'Then stop acting like it,' he fires back, sitting up straighter. 'You think I don't want to relax after the week I've had? Do you even know how exhausting it is, travelling back and forth, helping to set up a warehouse when I don't speak the lingo? But no, God forbid I have a quiet Friday evening without you jumping down my throat!'

I stare at him for a moment, my face heating with frustration. 'This isn't about the football, Mike. This is about you not caring how I feel. Do *you know* how lonely it's been here while you've been off in Spain?'

He scoffs, running a hand through his hair. 'Bloody hell, Rubes, I'm not on holiday. I'm working. They could make me redundant at the drop of a hat, and then who would pay the bills? It's not as if writing is a steady and reliable income. I'm working my arse off. The least you could do is not ruin my evening when I don't have to get up early in the morning.'

'Ruin *your* evening?' I snap back, my voice rising. 'You've been gone most of the week. But sure, I'm the selfish one.'

His jaw tightens and he reaches for the remote. 'Fine,' he says, switching off the TV and tossing the remote onto the coffee table, the noise making me recoil. 'You've ruined the game anyway, I'm going out.'

'What? Where?'

He stands up. 'I don't know. Maybe I'll meet my brother for a drink, or maybe I won't, but I want to salvage what's left of my Friday night.'

My mood drops as he grabs his jacket from the back of the chair, the anger quickly turning sour on my tongue. 'Mike–'

'No, Ruby. I don't have the energy for this. For you.'

I follow him to the door, my stomach knotting tighter with every step. He's shoving his feet into his trainers, his jaw set, his shoulders tense. I hate this. Hate the way I started it, knowing I was picking at something, anything, purely because I was confused about what Stef said and Nancy's messages. But what I hate even more is where this is leading now.

'Mike.' My voice is barely above a whisper. 'I'm sorry. I didn't mean to ruin your night.'

He doesn't even look at me as he straightens up, grabbing his keys from the little dish on the side table. 'Sure,' he says, flatly.

'Please,' I try again, swallowing the lump in my throat. 'I was just... I don't know. I've been feeling a bit... off. I shouldn't have taken it out on you.'

He pauses for a moment, fingers on the door handle, and for the briefest second, I think he might turn around, tell me he overreacted and that he won't leave. But then he shakes his head and pulls the door open.

'I'll see you later, Ruby. Don't wait up.'

I step closer as he strides out, leaving the door wide open behind him. 'Mike, wait–'

But he's already heading down the path, his back to me, his steps brisk and deliberate. My voice falters, and I don't follow him out. Instead, I stand there, watching helplessly as he walks away.

Then I see it. The hooded figure walking up the alleyway.

Mike is in such a furious, oblivious rush that he storms on by. The dark figure moves easily, like something from *The Matrix*, bending around so the two of them don't collide. And then, at the mouth of the alleyway, the figure slows to a stroll and looks up at me. I can't see their face, but it's as if their eyes are boring into me. I quickly skim over their silhouette and am just able to make out a phone in their hand. Then they peer down, busy looking at the screen, and the hairs on the back of my neck stand to attention. Why would they need to slow to a stop and stare at me first? Am I being paranoid?

Mike disappears completely into the shadows and out of sight, and the figure slips the phone into their pocket and looks up, directly at me again. They *are* watching me, but as I squint to try and make out the face underneath the peak of the hood, they move forward. My pulse quickens as I grip the door and slam it shut with such force, the echo is deafening.

Were they marching over to me, or just crossing the street to walk out and through the cul-de-sac?

I curse that there's no flipping chain on this stupid door, but I press my forehead against the cold glass panel anyway to look out, to search, to see if the figure is now coming up my path. I can see a dark figure so clearly... but is that image now imprinted on my mind, or is someone really there? The tears that had been threatening before now overflow with ease and everything before me is blurry.

Tall, slim-ish build, dark clothes, face obscured. It could have been *anyone*. Just as much as it could have been no one of any significance, just a person using our street to walk through. They weren't really watching me, they were just using the alleyway on their way home, heard me calling out to Mike, stopped to be nosey... just another coincidence.

Then, Gran's voice echoes in my head: *Trust your gut.*

Could it... Could it have been Norman? No, I shake my head, confused and doubting myself once again. But even still, I grab my mobile from my bag and leave all the lights on downstairs as I rush up to the safety of my bedroom.

CHAPTER TWENTY-TWO

I check out of the bedroom window like a demented woman for the next five minutes, but there's no one there. Not anymore, anyway.

When I finally give up, telling myself it was just a fluke and might not have been Norman, I grab my phone to text Mike. The whirling sensation in my stomach makes me feel sick. There was truth in what I said to him, but I picked that fight and it was wrong of me to do that. Yes, the idea of regular round trips to Spain do sound appealing, but when you think of the hanging about in airports, security and passport control and then taxis to and from... not so glamorous. I'd have been pissed off if he complained about hugs and kisses.

There's a WhatsApp message already waiting on my screen, but it's not from Mike. It's a number, so no one I have stored in my phone, either. While reading the text, I impulsively nibble on my thumbnail. At the end, I dither, only briefly, over WhatsApp's options to ignore this unknown number, mark it as spam and delete, or save the number. I type in Henry's name as the new contact and quickly re-read his message:

> Hi Ruby. A bit forward of me, so I hope you
> don't mind, but I nicked your number from the
> Blackwood Close group 😊 Hope you're not
> too shattered from the party – how much
> Prosecco did you have to knock back... haha.
> I'll have a chilled bottle in my fridge waiting for
> whenever you want to return the favour. Henry
> (your new neighbour).

Yes, it is very forward of you. And cheeky and... I can't decide if it's naughty or plain rude when he does know I have a partner. Though, why should he care? I know I have a partner, so I shouldn't have saved Henry's number and even be entertaining the idea of replying.

Then I do think of Mike and how he's made me feel tonight: first, unloved, then hurt and then guilty. Surely he has a responsibility in some of this, too. It's not all just me. And with that U-turn in emotions, Nancy flashes in my mind once more. Her short replies, and then her ignoring me. I'm the one sat here alone, again, left feeling confused and downright annoyed, not knowing where Mike is or who he's with.

Without another thought, I reply to Henry:

> Well, hello new neighbour! Yes, very forward...
> but I'll forgive you, considering you gave me a
> lift today (party wasn't too bad and I probably
> had a few too many glasses). I think that
> makes us even though, no more debt to repay
> 😅

A frisson of excitement – and fear – runs through my body when Henry instantly shows as being online. I re-read my message, as though I'm reading along with him and wonder how long it will take him to answer. The bubbles appear, and he starts replying straight away. I inhale deeply, waiting.

> Haha, nice try but no cigar. A debt is a debt 😅

I may be a wordsmith, but I'm thankful for the introduction of emojis. The tone of a person's message can swing either way – especially in contexts like this, when you're unsure if the person is flirting or not, and when you don't know that person very well.

> I'm sure something can be arranged, but I'm not agreeing on anything right now…

Oh yeah, and why's that?

> Because I don't know enough about you.

Fire away!

What does he mean? For once I have no words, but reply quickly:

> ???

You question, I answer. Whatever you want to know. Go!

I wasn't expecting that, and let my thumbs rest from replying for a few seconds, contemplating what is it, exactly, that I want to know.

> What do you do for work?

Firstly, you assume I work…

> Well, you've just moved into a new apartment. So, if you don't work, does that mean you're wealthy?

Are you after me for my money, Ruby?

> Ha! You said to ask questions!

Fair enough. I'm a software engineer. I'm not well-off, but I'm comfortable enough.

So you've moved in alone, but are you involved or married?

Single. Are you married?

I didn't say I'd answer any questions.

Oooh, touché!

Our messages ping back and forth like a tennis ball on Wimbledon's centre court. I ask about his family and hobbies and background, and he replies effortlessly, answering as promised. Just as I'm running out of steam with what to ask next, and not wanting him to feel like he's being interrogated, he serves a curve ball.

So you're an author... I'd love to read something of yours. Or maybe even have a private reading, followed by a signing 😉

I don't remember telling you that?

No, Patty did...

Of course!

I smile, not really surprised that it's my newest friend – can I call her that yet when I still know so little about her? – who has spread this news about me. I just hope it wasn't in true gossip-girl fashion, but rather it was more like I've been embraced into the community of the cul-de-sac and therefore an introduction to our newest neighbour. I'm not really sure why it matters so much to me now, when a few months ago I'd be none the wiser if someone had moved into the apartments, let alone that they knew anything about me. My phone pings another message from Henry:

> I hope you don't mind me mentioning it. I was only kidding about the private reading...

> > You gave up easily 😌

> Haha! I feel like you keep catching me out... so clearly you have a way with words more superior than I ever could.

> > Flattery will get you everywhere.

> Thanks for the tip 😌

The slam of a car door yanks my attention from Henry and I jump from the bed to the window in seconds. Pulling the curtain back, I peer down at the darkened street and watch a car drive out of our road. Most of the townhouses opposite are in complete blackness, including Weird Norman's house, on the far end.

I quickly look down to my front garden, wondering if I'll see Mike walking up the path, a stab of guilt twisting deep. Nothing. No one. I return to bed, drawing the duvet over my legs and realise, without Henry's distracting texting conversation, how quiet the house has become once again. Without Mike. Alone. I reach for my phone and shoot off a message:

> > It's been great chatting to you, Henry, but it's time to say goodnight!

> This feels like an unsuccessful end of date goodbye... but I get it, I've taken a lot of your time. Sorry!

> > No, don't be sorry. I've enjoyed it...

You don't have to explain, Ruby. I really hope it
was okay that I text you though??

It was!

Then maybe it wasn't so unsuccessful 😉
Goodnight Ruby!

Goodnight, Henry!

Just as I'm about to put my phone down on the bedside
table, it beeps again. I roll my eyes at the thought of Henry
needing to get the final word – though, I'm not entirely sure if
he's that type of guy – but to my shock, it's Nancy's name that
appears on the screen.

My breathing quickens, and I just stare at her name for a
few minutes. I'll open it, of course I will, but there's something
that holds me back, something that makes me drum my finger on
the screen, waiting. Wondering. What can she say after ignoring
me for hours? I work my thumbs across the screen, slowly,
tapping in my passcode and opening WhatsApp again...

Sorry about earlier... I'll explain everything.
Can we meet for a coffee, tomorrow, let's say
noon? Xoxo

Explain everything? I haven't even had the chance, or
courage, to ask her anything yet, so what could she possibly
need to explain? Before I allow myself to question further, I
send a simple reply:

See you at the usual café x

The calendar has stared at me all morning. Not just because I'm meeting Nancy for a coffee later, but because we're in a new month. That means new opportunities and new beginnings and new chances. Spring is finally on the horizon, and for that I'm pleased, but every new month is also a reminder that my cycle has started again, and that another period is due. And they come like clockwork and without fail. I have a routine and today is no different.

Mike is still in bed, where I left him hours ago, stinking of booze and fully-clothed, so I slip into the bathroom and lock the door. My toiletry drawer has a supply of pregnancy tests, and I select one from the box, pushing the heady mixture of nervousness and excitement away. Ignoring them both equally, pleading my body not to overreact, because if it doesn't, if it doesn't get too hopeful, then perhaps there'll be two blue lines. For once.

I'm quite the pro at angling the stick so my stream of urine hits it perfectly. I'm not the first woman to have pissed on her own hand while taking this type of test. But I remember seeing a meme on Instagram that said if the idea of pee – or any other bodily fluid – touching your skin gives you the ick, you're probably not cut out to be a parent. I set the stick down and busy myself for the longest two minutes of each month. I don't peek early, not once, because if I play by the rules then surely this one will be positive. This test is just for me; I quit doing them with Mike.

He said it was torture, taking the test before I'd even missed a period. As if I'm going against the natural order of things, even though these tests are designed to do that exact thing. Tell you early.

He just doesn't get it, so I don't involve him at this stage. I'm not sure what I'll do, the day it's positive, if I'll run out and barge into his office squealing with excitement, or if I'll wait on tenterhooks another week, tell him I've missed my period and allow him to be part of this with another test. As if it's the first time. Share the moment. Fathers miss out of so much in the beginning, when the pregnancy is just a word, just a scan, until the moment the baby draws their first crying breath in the delivery room. Mothers feel it from the second they find out. Or perhaps I've watched too many episodes of *Call the Midwife*. But that's how I expect it to feel.

I inhale deeply and peer at the stick. One blue line. Negative. Again. I chuck it in the bin and slowly lower myself to the floor. I don't cry. I gave up crying a long time ago. Though my heart is crushed, my brain tells my body not to react with tears. Instead, it creates this numbness. I have too many feelings and thoughts and doubts and sadness rushing around me, that I become numb to them all for a while.

Grieving something you've never had is a strange notion to explain to someone else, let alone yourself. How can you miss something you've never had? Oh... but how I do. With every negative pregnancy test I see, another piece of my hope dies and splits me in two. One part wants to get back into bed, curl up and cry forever, but that would be wallowing. The other part wants to brush myself off and continue with the day as normal, but that would be aloof and uncaring. The pressure to think of others, and how they perceive you when you're grieving, is exhausting. So no one knows what I do in here every month. No one needs to. I do the British thing of keeping calm and carrying on, with a small chink added to my armour each time.

I take a deep breath and pull myself from the floor. I don't focus on my sad eyes for too long in the mirror, it won't help to dwell, instead I splash my face with cold water and then plaster it with primer and foundation and bronzer. A woman's war paint. I'll need it more than ever today, as I decide to channel all my pain, all my hurt, all my anger – and all my strength – into getting answers from Nancy.

CHAPTER TWENTY-THREE

The café door swings shut behind me, and the scent of fresh pastries and cakes is warm and inviting. The low murmur of different conversations blend with the hiss of the coffee machine and the clatter of cutlery. I take off my coat, feeling the faintest promise of spring in the air – not quite warm enough yet, but at least the bite of winter is finally fading. I glance around – no sign of Nancy – and pick a table near the window to watch out for her. It's bang on noon – the time she asked me to meet her.

When the waitress comes over to greet me, I order a coffee with no cake. Don't get me wrong, I love cake – all kinds and flavours – but it doesn't feel right. I don't want the sweet enjoyment to turn sour with Nancy's confession.

When the lady returns with my drink, I curl my fingers around the mug and zone out, watching perfect strangers pass me by as they go on with their lives. Mothers and pushchairs, men in jogging attire and teenagers laughing with their mates. It's quite incredible how many people we see, walk past or sit next to on a daily basis and never interact with. How we all share this tiny space of the world and know nothing about each other, our own stresses and worries, dreams and achievements keeping us in our own little bubbles.

Ten minutes pass. Still no sign of Nancy.

I check my phone, but there's nothing. No message to say she's running late, no last-minute cancellation. I leave my phone on the table, just in case, but it's no surprise really. It's Nancy. She's always late. I take another sip of coffee, leaning back in my chair as memories of our university days drift in. Waiting outside the lecture hall, waiting at bars, waiting in taxi queues while Nancy promised she was 'literally five minutes' away. She never was. How ironic now that she's top of her game in the events industry. A role where everything must run to strict timings. Nancy can get a whole wedding party down the aisle on time, but she can't make it to her own meet-up.

Twenty minutes. My cup is empty, the faint taste of coffee lingering, and my stomach rumbles at the glorious smells. I glance at my phone again, thumb hovering over her name. Maybe I should call her quickly. Maybe something's come up. Or maybe she's just running late as usual, and I need to bide my time.

But it was Nancy who suggested we meet today. It was Nancy who wanted to 'explain everything' even though I hadn't questioned her on anything yet. If she's so desperate to explain, there can only be one reason. Guilt. The longer I sit here, the worse it feels. My fingers tap restlessly against the table. I stare at the door, willing it to open, for Nancy to rush in, flushed and breathless with some perfectly reasonable excuse. But she doesn't. The café door swings open a couple of times – an elderly man, a mum with a toddler – but not my friend.

Thirty minutes late now. She's taking the piss. I exhale sharply, my mind turning over every possibility again, each one worse than the last. Mike and Nancy. Have they arranged this together, to get me out of the house? Has Nancy joined Mike in bed, *my* bed, because they couldn't get enough of each other in Spain? Maybe he didn't meet his brother at all last night, but instead met Nancy and they planned all this together. I mean, she did text me after my fight with Mike. He could have been sat right next to her while she messaged me asking to meet today.

And perhaps Nancy *was* the reason Mike was so eager to take that promotion, so they would be flying back and forth together all the time.

Maybe while I was sitting at home, trying to shake the loneliness, hearing every creak and groan in the house, Mike wasn't lonely at all. Maybe he was with her. My partner and my best friend… they both know how much I struggled after Mum died. In their own ways, they had both worried about my mental health and helped pulled me from the abyss of grief. Could that have been the catalyst that brought them together. Poor old Ruby, worrying everyone again, wallowing in her depression and giving no one a second thought. Is that how it was?

I shift in my seat, run my fingers across my forehead and temples, trying to massage these unforgiving thoughts from my mind. I don't *want* to believe any of it, but why else would she be late? Why else would she want to meet up only to keep me waiting? I close my eyes for a second, willing myself to stop this way of thinking. But as the minutes tick by, the images flash in front of me: Mike with a drink in his hand, leaning in close to Nancy, whispering, *She's already suspicious.* Nancy nodding, biting her lip, *I'll handle it, let me talk to her.*

Except she isn't handling it, she isn't talking to me, and I feel as if I'm about to be stood up. I grab the phone, my pulse hammering now, the café suddenly too warm, too loud. I scroll to Nancy's name and hit the call button. It rings. And rings. And rings. Then her voicemail kicks in.

'Hey, it's Nancy. Leave a message or, better yet, text me.'

I hang up without speaking. Fine. A text it is.

> Hey, you okay? Where are you??

I hit send and wait, my eyes fixed on the screen, expecting the usual response – the double ticks turning blue within seconds, the telltale typing bubbles popping up right away. But nothing happens. She doesn't come online. Nancy is *always* online. It's not a habit for her, it's a reflex, she lives on her phone. So why now, of all times, is she suddenly unreachable? I check my message again. Two grey ticks. Delivered, but not read. Minutes pass and the screen stays the same. I know she isn't going to come online while I stare at the phone, but this isn't Nancy being her usual late self, this isn't her getting caught up with work. This is something else. It feels deliberate and planned, as though I'm being played. As much as I don't want to be this person – the paranoid girlfriend, the suspicious best friend – this *stinks* of guilt.

I open Mike's chat:

> Hey, how you feeling? How's the head?

Almost instantly, the double ticks go blue. At least he's online.

> Rotten. Still in bed.

That's it. No *Where are you? Are you okay?* I didn't say goodbye before I left the house, so if I'm texting him, why wouldn't he wonder where I am? Unless he already knows... I grip the phone tighter. Maybe he's still holding a grudge from last night, or maybe he's just too hungover to care. Nancy. Mike. One unreachable and the other one unbothered, but both making me feel like a fool. My friend may well have welcomed seeds of doubt and suspicion, but Mike has brought in an anger that is creeping slowly through my body, strangling every other feeling and taking root.

Get out of here, my mind screams at a volume louder than anything else now.

I stumble out of the hotbox café, gulp the crisp air and begin pounding the pavement. If I continue at this manic rate, home is a twenty-minute walk away. But that's twenty minutes of stewing in my own thoughts: Nancy standing me up, Mike's blunt message, our argument last night and the way he just got up and left; he's never done that before.

Then I remember him disappearing into the alleyway and someone – Norman – already there, lurking. A shiver runs through me, and I realise I don't want to go home. I don't want to face all of that, and possibly more if Mike really isn't alone. As I slow my pace, wondering where to go instead, I look up ahead and spot him. Henry.

He's coming right towards me, casual as always with his hands tucked inside his coat pockets and his hair messy and ruffled. He sees me, and his face brightens with a smile that makes me feel... *noticed*. He waves, confident and unafraid of being seen, like a small child in a playground whose day is made when they find their favourite person at the end of the day. I'm slightly embarrassed by how... *wanted* it makes me feel. Then my stomach flips when I think of last night's texts. The way it had felt flirty, even if neither of us had *technically* crossed a line. I'm all hot inside, unsure if I feel awkward or excited to see him, but realising I've stopped and waited for him to come to me. Now I don't know how to react.

'Hey, stranger,' he says as he reaches me, making things easy as always. 'What are the odds?'

I laugh, a little breathless. 'Small world.'

He tilts his head, studying me. 'Are you okay?'

No, Henry, I'm not. But I can't begin to bore you with my crazy mind. 'I've just been stood up by a friend is all.'

'Some friend, but it's their loss. I'd never stand you up.'

And there it is again. That undercurrent of his that sweeps me away and warms me inside. I glance away, unable to take the heat of his without acknowledging what he said. How do I even reply to that?

'Listen,' he says casually, rescuing me once again, 'I was just about to grab lunch. Come with me.'

It's not a question, but it doesn't feel like an instruction either. It's soft – not begging – but inviting. 'Oh, I don–'

'Please, I insist,' he cuts in smoothly. 'You've been stood up, I'm *starving*, and I happen to know a great little Thai place just around the corner. You'll love it. Trust me?'

Now, that was a question. He's asking if I trust him, and I'm not sure if he's referring only to the restaurant recommendation. And right here, in this moment, I do trust him. I do want to go with him, more than I want to go home – and that's a first for me. I almost want to reach out and take Henry's hand. Almost. I don't, of course, but the decision is an easy one.

With excitement bubbling in my chest, I smile. 'Yeah, I trust you, Henry. Let's go.'

———

A steaming bowl of red curry is set down in front of me, giving off a zesty lime aroma that's rich and inviting. Across from me, Henry dives straight into the fish cakes that I wasn't brave enough to try. I hadn't admitted to him that this was the first time I'd stepped foot into a Thai restaurant. Or that I didn't know there was one so close to my house. Mike and I usually stick to the same, familiar culinary choices and rarely venture out into something new. Being here with Henry, trying a different cuisine... it feels a bit surreal.

'See!' He gestures to my plate with his fork. 'Told you this place was amazing.'

I nod my head. 'Yes, you're right, I must concede. This is good.'

'I love being right,' he replies with the biggest school-boy grin.

I'm rolling my eyes, but I can't help laughing at the same time. He's just so easy to be around. Even when I think of the texts back and forth last night, it was like messaging someone I'd known for years, yet with the excitement of still getting to know everything about them. None of this feels embarrassing, though I know in my gut it should feel horrid and awful and wrong. But it just feels... natural. I almost want to open up further, confide about Mike travelling for work and about Nancy ditching me, and what I think all of that means. But there's a part of me that doesn't want to scare him away with my suspicious and imaginative thoughts.

The way Henry leans in when I speak, his eyes locked on mine with undivided attention, and the way he shows an interest by asking questions, is refreshing. Even when we're both quiet, eating, I'm very... *aware* of him.

'So, tell me more...' he asks. 'I know you're a writer, but what do you actually *write?*'

I reply, more honestly than I usually do when I'm asked. 'I don't really like to label or restrict my writing. Broadly, it would be fantasy, but for me it's about creating new worlds and deep characters with big emotions and messy choices. Sometimes I might add a spice of magic.'

He lets out a low whistle. 'I had you pegged for more crime, police procedural stuff. I didn't envision you being such an escapist.'

'Real life can be boring.'

'Is there something in particular that you're escaping from?'

His gaze lingers, and I can't help but lower my own and focus on rolling a charm on my bracelet between my fingers. Why can't I look at him? More importantly, why can't I answer the question? Starting a family with Mike is all I've wanted for these past few years... I'm not trying to escape–

'You're doing it again.' Henry's voice cuts through.

I look up. 'What?'

'Fidgeting with your bracelet.' He nods to my wrist. 'You did it in my car, too, and I'm starting to think that you really do get nervous around me.'

'It's just a habit.'

'A nervous habit?'

I feel the tug of my lips, my own body wanting to betray me with a big, foolish grin, but I contain it... Despite Henry's cheeky comments and playful smile. He leans forward slightly, elbows resting on the table, waiting for my answer. I hesitate for a few moments, unsure about everything right now.

'You don't make me feel nervous, Henry,' I finally say, barely a whisper.

'Do I make you feel anything?' he copies my tone.

I breathe in, steady. 'Yes.'

'Ditto,' is all he says.

My chest beats rapidly from my own quick and truthful answer, so much so that I don't know what to say next. I don't know where to go from here. The restaurant is suddenly sweltering, and the light-headedness makes me feel as if I'm floating. I clear my throat and look away from the intensity in his eyes. I grab my drink, take a sip and then another, suddenly too aware of everything. Henry picks up his fork again, like he's letting it go. Like he's giving me space. But something just changed between us. And I know *he* feels it too.

CHAPTER TWENTY-FOUR

When Henry and I leave the restaurant, the late afternoon sky has lost its earlier brightness, the clouds dulling as we walk side by side. We've kept things light. Well, Henry has. My heart's been beating as loud as the Jumanji board game since we finished eating.

I'm glad of the fresh air, whipping around my cheeks and untethering me from the weightless balloon that had threatened to whisk me off to No Man's Land. I feel more grounded now, walking down the road with a friend, a neighbour, as he shares yet another hilarious story after a very innocent lunch together. That he insisted on paying for. But it definitely wasn't a date. Of course it wasn't, I have a... Mike.

Henry nudges me gently, a smile teasing. 'All right, don't judge me for this, but I once spent an entire morning pretending to be a drill sergeant to a bunch of fake cadets.'

I raise my eyebrows, intrigued. 'I hope I don't live to regret this... tell me more.'

'So me and a few mates decided to re-enact the iconic Jolly Boys Outing–' He stops dramatically and turns to me. 'Do you...'

'An episode from *Only Fool and Horses*. Yes, I know it.'

'You see, I knew I liked you.' We both feel it, but say nothing. Instead, Henry smiles an approval and we continue walking. 'Right, so anyway, we're in Margate and I went for a morning jog, to clear my head.'

'You were hungover.'

'I was hungover,' he agrees with a laugh. 'And I'm running along the seafront when I see this woman rounding up a group of kids. Four of them, all under the age of ten and they look depressed as hell. One's properly bawling her eyes out. I stopped to see if she was okay, the mother, I mean, because it was clear she was on her own. A single parent, I could tell. There's an amusement park in Margate called Dreamland, you probably know it, it's right on the seafront. Anyway, the mother had promised the kids an adventure before they left on a long car journey home, but it didn't open until 11am and they couldn't wait that late. The kids were gutted.'

'And this is where you had to get involved?'

He grins. 'Well, I couldn't just leave the family looking all sad and depressed, could I? Plus, I knew my mates wouldn't be out of bed before lunchtime.'

'So what did you do?' I ask, feeling invested now.

'I told them all to get inventive. Everyone had to get an object – from the mum's car or from anywhere around us – as long as it was free, not dangerous and within the area. We had buckets, a fold up chair, an umbrella, water bottles and coats. Then I just placed them around the beach, made an assault course that they all had to finish. It was great fun and the mum got to sit and chill with a coffee for a bit.'

I can't hide my smile. 'That's actually really sweet.'

Henry shrugs, playful, but a little sheepish. 'Well, it worked off my hangover.'

'That wasn't the only reason you helped out.'

'My mum was a single parent.' He pauses briefly, then shakes his head, as though shaking a memory away right in front of me, before launching right back in. 'My sister is a single mum, too, so I know it's not easy, and she's only got two kids. This woman had four. What a handful! I couldn't just leave them all sad. And she was chuffed, because they all looked knackered as they walked off to the car.'

'What did your mates say about it?'

I can't deny the unmistakable pull towards Henry. There's an electricity running through me that demands I know more about him. The way he speaks about his family, now and before, filled with love and laughter. I can imagine special occasions spent together, with the warmth of food and drinks and games and... noise. Not too dissimilar to Stef's house during Hunter's party, but worlds apart from my lonely birthday and the Christmases spent with Mike alone.

He's never wanted to invite his mum and brother over for the festive period, or visit them during it. I barely know them at all, really. Mike's always said that he and his mother have a difficult relationship, strained, and it's one of the reason he wanted to move out of his childhood home and in with me. I've always just accepted that, and not questioned him further on it, but now I can't help but wonder if it's me... Perhaps Mike doesn't think *I'm* good enough for his family.

'My mates?' Henry replies, dragging me from my reverie. 'They had no idea. Still, to this day, I've never told them. When I got back to the B&B, they were only just getting out of bed. Man, did I need a nap, but didn't want to explain why.'

I laugh out loud at the image of four little tearaways putting Henry through his paces more than he expected. 'You've got a big heart, GI Henry.'

He winks. 'You keep that to yourself, Ruby, otherwise you'll ruin my bachelor image.'

I'm still laughing as we stroll past the row of apartments and parked cars, until we reach the corner by Patty's house. It's a natural pause point, the place where our paths diverge.

I stop and glance around the cul-de-sac. My house is at the end of the road, and being within a hundred feet of my front door makes me feel nauseous. Where we're stood now, we're protected from view by my next-door neighbours' bushes and trees, but I half expect Mike to come walking down our path, into the street, demanding to know where I've been. Thoughts of Mike with Nancy come swimming back.

'Guess this is where we part ways,' Henry says, rocking back on his heels.

I nod, forcing a smile, my eyes keep flicking back down to my end of the street. Then Henry does something that makes my stomach jolt: he lifts a hand and waves. Not at me. Not at someone passing by. But at the dark house behind me. I spin quickly, my heart hammering, knowing it's *his* house. Norman's. There's a figure at the upstairs window, but they don't dart away like before, they just stand there. Motionless. Watching.

A shiver laces down my spine. 'You know him?'

Henry shrugs. 'No. Just thought I'd wave since he was staring at us.'

He gives a small chuckle, like it's nothing. But it's *not* nothing. Even from here, I can see the family resemblance – slight build, tall, pale features and dark hair – but it's not Norman.

'Billy,' I murmur.

But instantly, as if the sound of my whispering voice summoned something, the person moves away from the window. My eyes dart around the house, looking for signs of life elsewhere. A light, another window, the front door. But there's nothing. It's as if no one was ever there, at the window or in the rest of the house. There's only darkness.

'That was weird,' Henry says.

I swallow, my pulse loud in my ears, but I'm glad he's here. Glad he saw it with me, but his interest is already fading. He turns back to me, asking something else, saying something light-hearted again, but I barely hear him. All I can think about is that house, and the way someone is always at that window. The curtains always snapping shut, or now someone darting away from them, like whoever's behind the pane of glass doesn't want to be seen. But they clearly want to see everything that's going on outside, around them. What the hell is going on in there?

A chill settles deep within me. 'I should get going,' I say, forcing a steadiness into my voice. 'Thanks for lunch.'

Henry watches me for a second, like he's about to say something more, but I back away slightly. Moving further away from him and the dark house, forcing him to accept there won't be a long, drawn-out goodbye in the middle of the street.

He nods, and calls out, 'Anytime.'

I turn quickly then, speed walking to my front door as my skin prickles under the layer of clothes. Because someone *is* always watching from that window. And now, I'm not the only one who's noticed.

The house has been suffocating all evening. Mike's hangover, and our unresolved argument, has clung to him like a storm cloud. Again, I didn't have the audacity to mention Nancy. It's not something you can slip into conversation when there isn't one. The few words we *have* exchanged have been clipped, flat and nothing like the easy, laughter-filled afternoon I've had with Henry. Now, as I step into the bedroom, fresh from a shower, the difference feels even harsher. Mike is already in bed, propped up against the pillows, his attention fixed on some film.

The light from the TV screen flickers across his face, but he barely acknowledges me as I move around the room.

The air is stale, carrying the faint, lingering scent of beer. I can't be sure if it's last night's fumes or if he's indulged in a bit of hair of the dog. I think about cracking a window, but I *cannot* be bothered to start another fight.

I pull on my pyjamas, running the towel over my damp hair, then look over to my bedside table and I stop what I'm doing. My notebook isn't there. Nor is my special pen. I drop the towel and open the bedside table drawer. They're not there either. I crouch down, checking under the bed, pushing aside a stray sock and a hairband. Nothing. Mike still doesn't look away from the TV.

'Have you seen my notebook?' I ask, trying to sound normal, as if there isn't an uncomfortable grudge lodged between us.

He finally glances over, as if noticing me for the first time, but then looks back at the screen. 'What notebook?'

'The one that's *always* here.' I gesture to the empty space on the bedside table. 'Black with foiled butterflies, and my pen, my special personalised one from Mum.'

When he doesn't answer immediately, I set off to my office. I flick on the light, scan the desk – which is always tidy and home to my laptop and *office* notebook. I check the chair and the floor and behind my desk. It's not in here, as I knew it wouldn't be. I return to the bedroom, telling Mike as I scan in here again.

He exhales nosily through his nose, again not looking away from whatever it is he's watching. 'It's probably downstairs.'

'I don't take it downstairs.'

He finally meets my eyes, his expression heavy with impatience. 'Then maybe it's next door. You haven't looked properly.'

'I have looked properly.'

'Like you did when I found your phone in the fridge.'

It's my turn to huff, because this is not the same thing at all. I'd misplaced my phone when I was busy in the kitchen. My notebook and pen can't be misplaced because I remember, *without a doubt*, seeing them this morning when I woke up. Right here, as they always are. The pen definitely doesn't venture too far, my office at most, because it's one of the last gifts from Mum, and I'm so scared of losing it. It lives here, next to me, with my notebook for whenever I get a sparkling thought late at night that I don't want to forget.

'Did you go out today?'

'No.' He sounds bored.

'Was anyone else here?'

His eyes flick to mine. 'Who would be here?'

'I don't know, that's why I'm asking.' And even though this feels like an opportunity to say Nancy's name, something holds me back. I just can't. I feel stupid.

'Even if someone was here, Ruby, why would they be in our bedroom? And even more, *why* would they want to take your notebook?'

I notice he hasn't denied someone being here, but what hurts the most is his patronising chuckle at the end. I push down the threat of tears.

'It's my pen, too.' I hate the sound of my crumbling voice and clear my throat in an attempt to shake the sadness from it. 'Are you sure you didn't move it today?'

'Yes, I didn't even open the curtains in here today, so I was nowhere near your side of the bed.'

'Were you in the bedroom all day?'

'I pissed a few times, took a shit, went out to collect my Chinese–'

'So you did leave the house? You said you were in all day.'

He sighs. 'Oh, yeah, I popped out to get some lunch. I'm sure someone was lying in wait until I'd left the house to break in. They ignored all the TVs, the jewellery and the laptops to grab your little notebook and personalised pen. Thousands will be made on the black market with those.'

'Mike, that's unfair I–'

'Ruby,' he interrupts with a growl, 'it's a bloody notebook. Stop with the interrogation. It will turn up.'

'Will it?' The tightening feeling in my chest coils a little more.

Mike sighs again and rubs a hand down his face. 'Look, it's late. Things don't just disappear, do they? You'll find it tomorrow. I'll even help you look, okay?'

It's a question, but not one he really wants me to answer and so I hesitate. When he grabs the remote and turns the volume up a notch, it's clear that's the end to our conversation. Frustration scratches at my throat, I want to push back, to make him look at me, to apologise for how he just spoke, but the room already feels stale with old arguments. Instead, I say nothing and climb into bed. I keep a distance from Mike as I pull the duvet high over me, and stare at the ceiling, my thoughts racing. The notebook and pen aren't downstairs and they're not in my office. I *know* they were here this morning, and yet, somehow, now they're gone.

CHAPTER TWENTY-FIVE

You. You don't have a clue. No idea that I'm here, watching you, again.

The living room glows faintly, a golden halo spilling out from the small gap in the curtains. Small, maybe, but not so small that I can't see you. I wonder if you even notice little mistakes like that; how careless you are; how easily someone could be watching. Someone like me. It's a perfect view from here, really.

On the edge of the alleyway, protected by the night and the trees and the town houses either side, I see you sitting on the sofa. Legs tucked beneath you, cradling a mug in both hands like it's a lifeline, and covered with a blanket as always. You're quite the creature of habit, aren't you?

I can't see your face clearly, which saddens me. But I watch as you bring the mug closer to your mouth and can imagine your full, red lips pressing against the rim. I close my eyes briefly, visualising us together. Your lips are moving towards mine, instead, and you're pressing against me. I rub my hand over my trousers. *Calm down, you animal.*

It's fun, really, to watch you. Predictable Ruby. Always the same spot on the sofa, the same routine, the same tatty blanket. Even the same damn cup. It's like a flipping ritual. Predictable, ha! What I mean is boring. Don't you want to do something different and exciting and fun? I could be that to you, Ruby, if you let me. If you just dropped your guard...

I take a quick look around, but it's quiet in the cul-de-sac tonight. Too cold, too dark, for anyone to be out and about. Even on this nosey neighbourhood. So I have you all to myself. Though, I know I shouldn't stay long.

There's a restlessness about you tonight. Pulling at the blanket, moving around the sofa, phone up, phone down. You're all alone. Again. You hate it, don't you? Can't even get comfortable in your own home. I can see that. What would you do if you looked through the curtains at just the right spot and saw me? What would you do, Ruby?

I hope you wouldn't snap the curtains shut on me. I hope you wouldn't want to make me disappear. You're a beautiful, kind woman and I know I must stop this... But you're just so fragile, and I worry about you. I have to watch you.

If only you truly understood what you mean to me. It's weird to say that from my place in the shadows, I can admit that. We're so close to each other, really but... ah, I'm not ready to show my true self to you, Ruby. You have a hold over me, one that I never expected, and one that I can't explain. With your wild curly hair and the cute dusting of freckles on your cheeks... You're an enigma that I can't ignore. Trust me, I've tried to. But it's you, Ruby, it's your fault. I want to know more about you, everything I possibly can, because I just can't shake you from my mind. Even when I want to. *How* have you done this to me?

I shift my weight slightly, but keep to the darkness. The alleyway smells damp, earthy, from yesterday's rain and I've had enough. I've stood here for long enough. It's always the same. But then your eyes flick to the gap in the curtains, to my window into your world and I watch patiently, waiting and maybe even hoping that you see me. But you don't really look, you don't really pay attention. You stand up, walk towards the door and switch off the light.

The hallway lights up simultaneously and I wait a little longer. As one light turns off, another turns on, as if you're lighting your own flight path. Signalling your exact spot in the house at any given moment. Once you're in the bedroom, I briefly wonder if you'll forget to conceal yourself before you start undressing. But within seconds you're at the window, lingering slightly, probably scanning the area to make sure you're safe.

Good girl, you never know who's out here late at night. Though yet again you look, you don't really see. Because if you glanced at the shadows for long enough, you'd know you're not alone. I'm here, outside, watching you.

What I haven't decided, yet, is if I'll come inside tonight. Again.

CHAPTER TWENTY-SIX

Patty's house is warm, filled with the rich scent of herbal teas and coffee, biscuits and old books. I shrug off my coat in the hallway and take in the familiar cluttered-but-cosy space.

I shouldn't feel nervous – it's just the cul-de-sac's book club – but it's my first time joining them. Patty had finally sent a text to the Blackwood Close WhatsApp group with the promised date of the next book club meeting. She had explained about being off her feet for a while, but now she was fighting fit again and looked forward to welcoming everyone on the last Thursday of the month. It also left a bit of time for anyone who needed to catch up with the book.

Thoughtful like that, is Patty, and I couldn't help but wonder if it was done for Henry's benefit. I hadn't asked if he'd bothered to read it, but during our texting session last night, he had sworn he would be at the book club. It feels a little easier knowing I'm not the only newbie.

Patty beams when she catches me loitering in the doorway. 'Ah, Ruby, love! Right on time. Come in, come in, don't stand on ceremony.'

The room is already filled with chatter. I peer around to find sweet old Mrs Shah, perched carefully on a dining chair with her walking frame resting beside her. And there are two other neighbours I have never spoken to, but who I recognise from nods in the street. They live at number 26, right down the end of the cul-de-sac, and I've always assumed they're husband and wife, but I guess I should know better than to make assumptions. I've lived with Mike for years and he's not my husband.

My eyes then fall to *him* – Norman – and the shiver running down my spine forces me to stand taller, rigid. He's relaxed in the armchair nearest to the window, as if the seat belongs to him, watching everything with that unreadable gaze of his. He doesn't acknowledge me, doesn't even nod, and I briefly think back to the blunt way he spoke to me on the doorstep of this very house. Now, he just stares in that beady way, as if he's looking right through me.

It forces me to break away from him, but thankfully that means I find Henry. He's leaning against the bookshelf, looking more relaxed than I feel in a pose that just screams he's too cool for everyone here. But he chats effortlessly with Mr-number-26 anyway.

I desperately want Henry to look in my direction, but Patty interrupts my silent plea. 'Go and help yourself to a cuppa, love. Oh, and can you get one for Mrs Shah while you're in there, too. Milky as hell with three sugars. I don't know how she drinks that treacle.'

Slipping into the kitchen, I laugh at Patty's comment and am thankful, yet again, for the way she makes me feel like part of the furniture. When I finally return with our drinks, Mrs Shah accepts it with a smile and wraps her fingers around the mug.

'Oh, you are good, Ruby, thank you,' she says. Then her eyes drift across the room, to Henry. 'Lovely of him to take some time for Noah. He usually keeps to himself, and only really talks to Anna, his wife.'

I mentally thank Mrs Shah for offering up the other neighbours' names, so I don't have to refer to them as Mr and Mrs Number 26 for the entire evening.

'And he's very handsome, isn't he?' she continues, while nudging me slightly with her elbow.

'Who, Noah?' I wink.

She laughs and winks back. 'You naughty girl. We both know I mean our newest neighbour. If I were thirty... okay forty years younger, Henry would have to watch out.'

I join in with the quiet laughter, but the nervous edge to mine is like thunder in my ears.

'But I shouldn't really say that,' she says, and continues watching Henry for a second, tilting her head slightly. Then, almost to herself, she murmurs, 'Not when he looks so much like Patty's son.'

Her words hang in the air for a moment, so soft I almost wonder if I misheard her. I glance at Patty, who is busy fussing over a stack of books on the coffee table, completely oblivious. *Patty has a son?* I don't know why I'm surprised, but I am. My eyes flash to the framed photo on the bookcase, the one I saw the very first time I was here. The one she clearly didn't want to talk about. Of course it's her son, I can see that now, and probably knew it then, but respected her privacy and thought no more of it. But for over a month now, I've had more conversations with Patty than I ever have before. I've told her about Mike's business trips and she's talked about her late husband. She's sent me personal text messages, not just via the group, and we've discussed books or recent true crime documentaries. In all that time, she's never once mentioned a child. Never mentioned the young man in that photo is *her* son.

Mrs Shah takes a sip of her tea and says nothing more. She's left me with countless questions, but it's not the right time to interrogate the poor woman, so I take my place on the sofa. Just in time to be distracted again.

Patty claps her hands together, signalling the start of the meeting. 'Right, everyone, let's get to it! We're here to discuss *In Cold Blood*. Now, I want to know: how many of you *actually* finished it?'

'I didn't, I'm afraid,' Noah confesses a little too swiftly.

Now Henry looks right at me. A devilish, handsome and mischievous glint in his eyes, but Anna lets out a dramatic sigh and steals away our attention.

'I did,' she says. 'And I'm sorry, but I don't get why you chose this one, Patty. It's so violent and brutal... and *true*. That poor family. I found it difficult to sleep after I finished, worried someone was breaking into the house.'

Mrs Shah gasps. 'Yes, me too, I couldn't read it at night. I don't mind the police procedurals we've read before. But there was something about this one. I'm not sure, but I wasn't a fan of the style either.'

Anna jerks her hand out. 'Exactly, Mrs Shah. It read like a novel, but I know it was a true crime. So I was confused... was it all real?'

'That's the best part.' Patty steps in. 'Truman Capote created something new with this book.'

I nod, shifting in my seat. 'You're both right about the violence, but as you say it is based on a real crime. What Capote did, after an intensive period of research, was mix fact and fiction, creating one of the first non-fiction novels. I think it paved the way for true crime to become a popular genre.'

'But real-life crime shouldn't be entertainment.' Anna's

voice is more high-pitched than before, like she's outraged with my opinion.

'Yes, I get your meaning,' I reply. 'But crime captivates us all – the suspense, the tension, the need to know *why*. The true crime genre, books and television, allows us to look deeper into the darker human psyche.'

'But from a safe distance from the baddies,' Henry chips in.

'Good point,' Anna says, her tone a little lighter.

Henry smiles at her sweetly before continuing. 'And I was actually captivated with the book, because it took us through everything from the murder to the trial and, finally, the execution of the murderers themselves. As the reader, I was fully immersed in every aspect of the story.'

'You read it?' Obvious surprise in my tone.

He smirks. 'Of course. I take book club very seriously.'

'We'll see if that lasts,' Anna cuts in again, but laughter ripples through the group.

Henry reclines back in his chair again, and I notice how he and Norman strike up a conversation quickly. The Weird One hasn't contributed a single word to the discussion so far. What does he so suddenly have to say that is of interest to Henry? I don't want to focus on it, but it unsettles me. Why are they speaking in hushed tones, as if it's not a chat for everyone to hear? The dying daylight spills in through the window and casts shadows across Norman's face, making his expression even darker. But Henry's body language is relaxed, like he doesn't find the man strange at all.

'Oh, ignore those two.' Patty notices and follows my gaze. 'Norman's not big on group discussions, but he does love being here, so he usually manages to trap someone in a deep debate privately. And Henry's new, so Norman probably sees him as fresh meat.'

Her comment makes me smile. A fake smile, mind you.

Purely for her benefit, so she thinks I've accepted her version of events, of why Henry would be locked in a conversation with the man who gives me the heebie-jeebies. But it's really a ruse to hide all the thoughts spinning round and round my mind like a Catherine wheel that's just been ignited. That is until Anna, second-in-command to queen of interruptions, plonks herself on the sofa next to me. She demands to hear all about my books and writing career because, of course, she has a story she's dying to write.

Later that evening, after more chatter about my books – which I found completely cringe-worthy – and a brief debate over whether *In Cold Blood* is factually true, or if the author created scenes and characters to suit the story, Patty steers the conversation back to the logistics.

'Right, I'll add a poll to the WhatsApp group tomorrow with some ideas on our next read for you all to vote on.' Then she turns to my new bestie. 'Anna, you and Noah will be hosting, right, so once we've decided on a book, let us know what date is good for you next month.'

A book a month? Seems an excessive amount of time, but I guess these people have lives outside of the book world.

'Feel free to help yourselves to another drink, or take some biscuits home with you. I baked plenty,' Patty adds.

As everyone begins shifting, stretching or refilling their drinks, I get the strange sense that I've just sat through something significant. Like pieces of a puzzle have been placed in front of me – but I don't quite know how they fit together yet. Maybe it's Norman and Henry's quiet exchange. Maybe it's the fact that Mike is away, and I feel I'm doing something wrong, something behind his back. Or maybe it's Mrs Shah's whispered words... *He looks so much like Patty's son.* And yet Patty hasn't so much as mentioned him. I shake off the feeling and stand as Noah and Anna begin gathering their coats. Patty is already bustling around, collecting mugs and empty plates, insisting we don't help her tidy up.

'It'll give me something to do when you're all gone,' she says, straightening a chequered blanket on the back of the sofa.

One by one, we filter out of the living room and into the hallway to exchange goodbyes. Everyone except Norman. He's the first to the front door and hasn't muttered a word to anyone, but stops next to Patty to give her arm a slow rub, up and down. I internally gag for her, watching as she shakes her head at his touch. Right there, I see it, she's clearly as uncomfortable as I am with the creep. Then he simply pulls his coat tight around him and shuffles off into the night. I watch his retreating figure disappear into the darkness, across the street to his even darker house, my skin lacing with goosebumps.

Noah and Anna follow him, stepping out into the cool night with murmured promises about fixing a date for the next meeting, and searching for me on Amazon. I thank them, embarrassed, but also slightly perturbed by the fact no one else finds Norman's behaviour odd. Can it really just be me? Perhaps because I'm new to the circle, I just have to get used to his strange ways. Though, Henry seems to have managed to swing into their rhythm pretty quickly. He steps up beside me then, reaching for his own coat.

'You and Norman looked deep in conversation earlier,' I say, with a hint of a question about it.

Henry smiles widely, as though he's everyone's best friend already. 'Oh, old Smithy, yeah he was telling me all about his football playing and pre-retirement days. He's a funny guy.'

Funny? No, that's not the word I'd used to describe the old man. Intense springs to mind, weird and creepy, too, but before I can say anything further or ask about the nickname, Henry continues.

'You heading home?'

'That's the plan.'

'Fancy a nightcap?'

He's being suggestive with the way he looks at me, openly flirting, but I'm distracted by all the neighbours I've spoken to tonight and everything that's been said. Besides, Henry and I are inching towards *that* line, and once it's crossed, there's no coming back from it. Isn't it the whole reason why I haven't already confronted Mike? How can I accuse him of something when I'm freely messaging another man most evenings? But I'm rescued from responding to Henry when a hand touches my arm.

'Ruby, love, would you mind walking me home?' Mrs Shah asks gently. 'I know I'm only next door, but you're passing by mine to get to your house anyway.'

'Of course,' I reply without hesitation, but glance at Henry, who gives me a lopsided smile.

'Guess I'll have to drink alone, then.'

It's fate.

'You'll survive.'

Henry makes a show of sighing dramatically before turning serious. 'Are you both sure you don't want me to walk you?'

Mrs Shah shakes her head, adjusting her walking frame. 'No it's fine, dear. We like to have men in our lives, but we don't *need* them.'

I laugh at Henry's raised eyebrows and lack of comeback. 'Well, that's you told.'

'Hasn't it just.' He recovers, but I wonder if it's sarcasm or irritation. 'I'll leave you in Ruby's good hands then. Ladies, it's been a pleasure.'

With that, he steps outside, glancing back at us one final time with a mock tip of the hat. Just as I'm about to ask Mrs Shah if she's ready to go, Patty calls out our names and beckons us back inside the house. She complains that we've all left far too many biscuits and goodies, which we now have to split between the two of us, or else it'll be our fault when she doesn't fit into her jeans. I light-heartedly sigh and roll my eyes, which amuses Mrs Shah, and close the front door on our departed neighbours.

CHAPTER TWENTY-SEVEN

I unlock my front door nearly forty-five minutes later. After waiting while Patty divvied up the sweet treats, and then while Mrs Shah bent my ear on her front doorstep about her grandchildren, I wasn't sure what time I'd make it home. Not that I was in a hurry to return to the quiet.

I had actually wanted to question Mrs Shah about Patty's son, but I couldn't bring myself to gossip about the woman who had welcomed me so seamlessly into the group of neighbours. Especially after I'd shunned them for so many years. If I want answers, I'll have to grow up and ask Patty directly.

The house is as hot as a sauna, though I know I turned the heating off before heading out to the book club meeting. I strip off my coat and scarf, boots and handbag, and drop the Tupperware of biscuits on the counter nearest to the kitchen door. My whole being is trying to acknowledge the darkness, the quiet, but I'm ignoring it. Ignoring myself.

I refuse to feel scared every time I'm home alone. So I switch on lights as I move around the house, calm as a swan but secretly flapping on the inside as I climb the stairs and head straight for my bedroom. Whether it's knowing that's where my trusty golf club is, or because there's a security in having my bed up against the wall and my view on the door and window at any given time, I'm not sure. But it's the room I've felt the safest in when alone.

I refuse to check all of upstairs tonight, and head straight for my personal space, turning on the big light before I'm even fully inside the door. I tell Alexa to play some smooth tunes while I close the curtains and then pull a pair of pyjamas from the drawer. I changed the bedsheets this morning, and there's nothing better than new bedding, a warm shower and fresh nightwear.

But something feels off. There's an unfamiliar smell in here tonight. It's not my laundry and it wouldn't be one of Mike's aftershaves as he hasn't been here for days. I scan the room, my attention landing on the side of the bed, and my breath catches. My notebook. The *missing* notebook is there, on the bedside table, right where it belongs... just without my pen. *Why the hell isn't my pen with it?*

Heat rises from my stomach, snaking up my chest before crashing back down again. Over and over. My breathing becoming quick and noisy, heavily in and out of my nose like I've just run a marathon. My eyes keep scanning the room, looking for any movement, any other sign of something being wrong and out of place. It's then I notice the slight change in the duvet, on my side of the bed, right near the edge. The clear dent of someone's arse. Someone sat right there and returned my notebook to its rightful place. Someone's been in my house. Today. This evening, while I was out, because I know the notebook wasn't there before I left. Just like I know the bed sheets were freshly made.

I'm going to be sick.

I scan the room again, pulse hammering, still trapped on the spot because I don't know what to do. Because this doesn't make sense. Or have I been right all along? A terrifying thought bursts in my mind and I whisper for Alexa to stop. What if the person is still in my house? I hold my breath while I listen for unwanted sounds, and my heart pounds in my chest like a drum. The extractor fan in the bathroom is like a helicopter. I slowly reach into my back pocket for my phone.

Shit! It's in my handbag. Downstairs. Shit.

I gently step back into the hallway, practically on tiptoes, not wanting to disturb anything or anyone. My head swinging around like a meerkat to take in the hallway, the staircase, the closed doors. One step at a time, I make my way back down, each creak of the stairs loud enough to wake the dead. I stop at the bottom, gripping the handrail. I suddenly remember the golf club at the side of my bed. I need a weapon, but I can't go back for it. Not now.

Everything down here is still. Quiet. It feels empty, but how can I be sure? I glide along the hallway, my back to the wall, and reach out for my handbag. My eyes scan every corner while my hand struggles blindly to find my mobile. When my fingers finally grasp the weight of my phone, I feel a small pinch of relief. I could just leave, walk out of the front door, but where would I go?

I peer inside the living room. Empty. Gripping my phone, I walk into the kitchen and instantly look over to the knife block. No empty holes. All the knives are there. My heart beats faster as I make my way towards the back door, drawn by an instinct I want to ignore but can't. It's dark outside, the garden swallowed in shadow, but under the glow of the kitchen light, something doesn't look right. My brain scrambles as my fingers curl around the handle. I push it down and the door swings open.

Unlocked.

I didn't leave it unlocked. I *never* leave it unlocked.

A wave of nausea rolls through me, but I slam the door shut, twisting the lock so hard the force may well break it entirely. My entire body is shaking, but my mind is screaming at me, confirming what I've known for sure these past few months. Someone *has* been in my home. Someone came into my house, took my notebook and then returned to put it back in its place in my bedroom.

I run from the kitchen – away from the door that I know was not left unlocked – and into the living room. I'm not sure why, it doesn't bring more safety, but I feel slightly better being away from that door. I look down at my phone, tap my finger on it to bring it to life, look at the photo of Mike and I smiling in a stupid selfie. I should call him... No, he's not even in the country. He'll probably tell me I'm imagining everything anyway, and all this proves is that I did misplace the notebook. But I think of the imprint in the bedsheets, and I know I have to call someone. But Mike is a thousand miles away. I feel sick.

There hasn't been a peep from Nancy since she stood me up. And I can't bother Stef – not this late, not when she has Kelly and Hunter, not when she might be working. I stare at my phone, my fingers hovering over the screen. I *could* call the police, but what would I even say? That my notebook went missing and one of my doors was unlocked? That I *feel* like someone has been in the house? They'd ask if anything had been stolen, if I'd actually *seen* someone, if there were any signs of a break-in. And what do I have? An arse print on my bed. A missing notebook that isn't actually missing anymore. A gnawing, sickly dread in my stomach that I can't shake. That's not enough. They'd believe me even less than Mike.

My mind flits to Henry. It's only been an hour since I was last with him, and he had wanted to spend time with me. Right now, I really can't be alone. Before I can second-guess myself, I type out a message.

> Are you still awake?

Henry replies instantly.

> I am. Fancy that nightcap?

Relief crashes through me.

> No. But please can you come round to my house? Now!

He doesn't ask for details, doesn't question why I'm asking this for the first time since we started chatting, he just replies that he's coming.

I don't move from my spot in the living room, my back up against the wall. I can't move, my body won't let me. If I leave, it'll mean looking at the back door again, the one that was used to break in to my house, and I can't bring myself to do it. Or perhaps they broke in the front door and left via the back door. But how?

Seconds drag like hours, my heartbeat a heavy, erratic thud in my ears. I tell myself I should be checking the house, but the thought of walking round on my own, opening doors, peering into corners where someone *could* be, makes my throat tighten. No. I'll wait for Henry. My phone vibrates again, and I nearly drop it.

> I'm outside.

I don't even type a reply. I sprint to the front door, unlocking it so fast my fingers fumble on the latch. I rip it open and there he is – Henry – in the same jeans and hoodie as earlier, slightly out of breath like he's rushed to get here. As soon as he steps inside, I move without thinking and lean into him.

He embraces me immediately, not saying a word, just wraps his arms around me. His warmth and solidness make the tension snap in my shoulders. I realise how tightly I've been holding myself, like one wrong move might shatter me.

'What's wrong? What's happened?' His voice is gentle but urgent.

I step back from him and walk towards the kitchen. He follows. 'I was getting ready, after I got home and–' I shake my head, my words a tangled mess. 'Someone's returned my stolen notebook, I promise I searched the house for it and it wasn't here. Then the back door was open and I know I locked it, I always check.' I gulp in a sharp breath. 'Henry, someone has been in my house. I'm *sure* of it.'

His posture stiffens. 'And you didn't hear anything? See anyone?'

'No. Nothing.' My voice wavers. 'But I *know*... please believe me.'

Henry looks over his shoulder, back down the hallway. 'I'll check the house.'

'No,' I reply quickly, reaching for his arm. 'What if–'

'I'll be fine. Just stay here and keep your phone with you.'

I nod, swallowing hard, and let go of his sleeve. He disappears into the hallway, and I hear him walking around the living room, not quietly at all. I can imagine him checking behind the sofa, the curtains... They're daft images but it's all I can think of. Henry doesn't even look at me as he glides past the kitchen door and up the stairs swiftly and cautiously.

Only seconds pass, but the urge to call out to him is overwhelming, just to make sure he's still there, still okay. I glance at the phone instead, hoping the screen will light up with a message from him, reassure me he's fine, but that's a daft thought too. He's only upstairs. I can hear the doors opening, the lights switching on.

Finally, footsteps on the stairs. Steady and unhurried. Henry reappears, his brow furrowed. 'No sign of a break-in,' he says, but his tone doesn't feel dismissive. 'All the windows are closed, and it doesn't look like there's been any disturbances – none I can see anyway.'

I exhale shakily, but it doesn't bring relief. 'Then how did the notebook... and the door... and–'

The tears trickle down my face. I don't know what else to say. I know I'm right, but why do I feel so foolish?

Henry watches me for a moment before pulling me into his arms again. 'I believe you, Ruby, it's okay. Do you want to call the police?'

I shake my head along his torso. The energy zaps away from me, making me want to fall asleep right here where I'm standing, enveloped in Henry's warmth and safety and acceptance. He believes me. Without question. Without explanation. Even if I *am* wrong, he doesn't make me *feel* as though I am.

He lifts my head slightly, forcing us to lock eyes for a second before glancing at the back door. 'Ruby, do you want me to stay?'

CHAPTER TWENTY-EIGHT

You. You are a very naughty woman, Ruby.

You nearly caught me, right there in your kitchen. If only you had taken a few more steps inside the room, if only you'd turned on that light before making your way upstairs, you would have seen me.

I'll admit, it was quite thrilling. I've never been caught before. I've never wanted to be caught, of course, but I've never felt as alive as I do right now. What would we have done, face to face in what should have been your empty house. More importantly, what would I have done? My mission is always in and out. Discreet. Stealthy. Unseen. But you... you've changed things.

Panic did set in when you walked upstairs and I had to bolt out the back door. I was careless, in a rush, and didn't lock up behind me. I wanted to give your notebook back, but I wasn't ready for you to know it's me... Fuck! Now I'm furious with myself.

But I need to know what the mood in the house is like now. What you're going to do. So I stay hidden, nestled deep in the shadows of the alleyway. My spot. Watching you, and watching the lights go on and off to let me know where you are. I'm taking too many risks. I shouldn't be this close after nearly being spotted. It's *you*, Ruby, everything feels different with you and because of that I can't tear myself away. Not even now. Just imagine, if life hadn't changed, and you weren't on your own for days and days at a time, or if you had never embraced your neighbours, I might not have noticed you. *That* would have been a crime.

You're in the living room. Your spot. Though, something is wrong... you're not sitting down under the blanket as you usually do. You're jammed up against the wall, like you're scared. Why would you be... ah, you've found the notebook, haven't you? Now you know it was taken. Now you know it was returned. I feel a slight twinge of something. Guilt, perhaps. That's a first for me. I said that you were different, Ruby.

The smell of your bedroom will stay with me, even though I can't quite put my finger on what it is... There's a fruitiness – which could come from a flower – mixed with something comforting and warm, like you've been baking cookies. It's *so* sweet. So homely. So *you*. I wonder if it's your perfume or your fabric softener. Maybe it's a mixture of the two. In the quiet, I sat on the bed – on your side of the bed – where you sleep and dream and wish for more. I caught the scent from your pillow. I stroked your bedsheets. I wanted to lie down for a while, but I was worried you'd be home soon. I was right to worry, too, wasn't I, Ruby?

I ran my fingers over your notebook when I returned it, and I hope that now you'll be able to feel me on those pages the next time you use it. It was an honour to read your words – unpolished and raw and real. These characters that you write about. I have a secret, Ruby... in this very special notebook of yours, the words aren't for the worlds you create and the stories you tell. No, no, no, I don't believe that for one second. These are your dreams and your fantasies. I could feel the passion in those pages. You wish you had their lives. Not the boring, predictable one you're living. You want more.

The pink lipstick stashed away in the drawer of your bedside table. I've never seen it on your lips before, Ruby. It didn't look brand new, so I can only imagine that you try it on in secret, pose in front of the mirror with the hint of colour on your lips... But you don't wear it outside of the house. Are you too scared? Scared to try something new. Scared to be noticed. It's only a little blush pink, Ruby, why are you so shy?

I know you now. Maybe even better than you know yourself. It's amazing what you can find out about a person by looking through their things. The personal and private sides of themselves, that they don't show to others, not even those closest to them. The parts of them that are locked away in drawers, in wardrobes, in notebooks. I saw them. And now I see you, Ruby. More than just the way you fidget with your bracelet, or the way you bite your lip. More than that rainbow scarf you wear as your only pop of colour, or hiding behind your screen and characters. I've seen your hopes and your secrets, and I know you have something to hide.

I should leave. I should disappear into the night, the way I always do. But I stay, watching you study your phone. You feel exposed and violated, don't you, Ruby? You finally feel unsafe and alone. That's why you're up against the wall in your own home.

Ah, of course, you don't want to be alone. Who will you choose to contact in your time of need, Ruby? Who can you really trust right now? I exhale slowly, amused, and wait.

CHAPTER TWENTY-NINE

The living room feels big and endless in the dim light. The only glow comes from the floor lamp, casting long shadows along the walls. Or maybe it's because I feel smaller, lost, emotional squashed like the teeny-tiny version of Alice in Wonderland. Though I didn't drink anything to put me in this predicament. Maybe wine would help right now. No, Ruby, that's not the answer, not when everything is already so upside down.

Henry is settled on the sofa, one arm resting along the back, his legs stretched out as if he belongs here more than I do. But it doesn't feel uncomfortable. Quite the opposite, actually. I'm curled up at the other end, knees pulled and a blanket draped over me for warmth. The distance between us is on purpose. The fact I've asked another man to stay in my home, and actually want him here, is terrifying. Being closer to him right now would only confuse me further.

I should go to bed. But every time I think about walking up those stairs, stepping into my bedroom – where a stranger has been – it's just too nauseating. The thought of lying there, knowing someone touched my sheets, maybe my pillows and pyjamas, too, and could well have gone through my drawers and other things, makes my skin crawl. So I stay here, wrapped in the blanket, holding a cup of tea that's long since gone cold. Henry hasn't pushed me to speak or explain. We haven't even turned on the TV. He's just sat here with me, waiting.

'Thanks for not thinking I'm crazy,' I finally blurt out.

He shifts slightly, angles his body more towards mine. 'Why would I?'

'Notebooks and unlocked doors... you don't think it's my imagination?' I know how Mike would answer that question.

Henry turns his mouth down and shakes his head. 'You looked petrified when I got here, Ruby. That wasn't make-believe. I just wonder... No, never mind.'

'Please go on,' I beg, desperate to hear what he's thinking.

'Well, could Mike have accidentally moved the notebook and then just put it back where it belongs.'

Though I hate the question, second-guessing what I've told him, it's clear from Henry's tone that it's genuine. He's trying to find answers for me, so that I don't have to believe someone's been in my home.

I shake my head, definitely. 'No, I asked him about it. Plus, it *wasn't* there this morning when I changed the bedsheets, and Mike's been in Spain for three days. And that wouldn't explain the back door.' I search his face. Does he believe me? 'Henry, I double-check the doors, especially when I'm on my own.'

He raises his hands in surrender. 'I said I believe you, Ruby, and I mean it. I'm sure it's not nice to be on your own so much. When you're not used to it, I mean... Are you okay?'

I swallow hard. *No.* But the word doesn't come out.

Instead, I stare at the surface of my untouched tea, then exhale shakily before admitting, 'I *hate* being alone.'

Henry watches me, again waiting patiently, as though he senses that there's more to what I'm saying.

I let the silence stretch for a few moments, wondering if I

should open up to him. He's still a stranger, really, isn't he? But the contentment I feel around him is hard to ignore. 'My mum died during the pandemic. It wasn't Covid. It was... suicide.' The words come out like glass, sharp and painful, but there's no stopping them now. 'She was living alone. And I... I didn't notice she was gone until a whole day later. I should have noticed. I should have known something was wrong.'

Henry sits up a little straighter, fully turning his attention, and body, to me. 'Ruby... I'm so sorry...'

I shake my head, gripping the blanket tighter. 'I don't know if it was the isolation, or if she was already struggling, or if it was just... everything all at once. I just don't know, because she never told me. But she was in her house, alone, like that, for at least twenty-four hours before I went round and–'

My voice catches. I squeeze my eyes shut, willing myself not to fall apart.

Henry closes the gap between us on the sofa, his voice soft. 'It's not your fault.'

I let out a bitter laugh and open my eyes. 'That's what everyone says. But it doesn't stop the guilt, does it?'

His jaw tightens, and he exhales through his nose. 'No. It doesn't.' His expression shifts, and there's something in his eyes, something that tells me he understands.

I bite my lip, hesitating before I admit, 'I think about it a lot. What she must have felt in those final moments. Whether she thought about calling me. Whether if maybe she wanted to be saved. What was she thinking about that made her feel so alone in life? I know it's easy to let your mind wander to the bad places, but to think now that someone has been in my house... Perhaps I haven't been imagining anything, and the terrors of the real world are even more frightening than what's in my head. And then I think–' I break off, taking a slow breath. 'I think about what would happen if I ended up like my mum. Completely alone. No one noticing. No one around to pull me out of the depths of my emotions, or fears. Or darkness.'

These thoughts are ugly. Uncomfortable. I shouldn't be telling him this, but Henry doesn't flinch, he doesn't recoil at my words. Instead, he reaches out and gently rests his fingers on mine. My skin tingles at his touch.

'You won't,' he says firmly. The conviction in his voice makes my chest tighten. 'You can't compare yourself to your mum, Ruby. That was a hard time for a lot of people,' he continues. 'And you're not by yourself. Even when Mike isn't here... and when he is, too... you don't have to be alone.'

There's something else in his voice now. A desire. An urgency. I believe every word he's saying – as if he's promising me that I don't have to be alone, because *he* won't let me be. The stranger in my home, my mum, Mike, Henry. It's just all too much swimming through my mind, too many people to think of, too many emotions for one person to feel all at once.

I inch away, allowing our hands to part, and place the mug down. It's then I notice that Gran's vase is still on the side table, and I roll my eyes because it does in fact look better there than it does on the coffee table. I must have forgotten to move it back after the last time I was mad – no, disappointed – with Mike. And here I am, yet again, struggling with my emotions for my partner. I look to Henry, who is waiting for my response, and catch his sweet smile.

'You always this positive?' I ask.

He lets out a quiet chuckle, but there's no real humour in it. 'Far from it.'

But it's my turn to watch him. My turn to wait patiently, to see if he'll mirror me and open up. And after a short pause, he does.

'My dad left us when I was thirteen. Just... walked out one

day and never came back. No warning. No explanation. Just disappeared and left me, my mum and my sister.'

'And you've never seen him again?'

'Nope.' His jaw tightens again. 'I mean, don't worry, we know it was nothing sinister, but it was awful watching my mum call everyone they knew, she even called the police. It soon became clear he had left her – *us* – for someone else. Another family. My mum's never really got over it, and has never been with anyone else. She didn't fall apart completely, but she changed. I think, in some way, she was always waiting for him to walk back through the door and apologise for the lies. But he never did. Never has.'

'That must have been hard for you all.'

His eyes fall on me, apologetically. 'Gosh, Ruby, I'm not comparing my stupid father to your mum. He's out there somewhere; you've lost yours–'

'Hey, Henry, don't be silly.' It's my turn to reach out this time, but I only let my fingers briefly brush his knee. 'I know you weren't comparing. Everyone has their own grief, their own stories... their own baggage. Please don't even think you can't share something with me just because our experiences are different. Carry on, please.'

He smiles, a genuine one, and for the first time I understand what they say in books when they explain someone's smile reaching their eyes. I see it in Henry's.

'My sister is younger,' he continues. 'She was only seven when *he* left, and I didn't want her to feel like... like everything was breaking apart. So I took care of her, and my mum, too, as much as I could. I became the person who sorted things, did more around the house, who made sure everything was okay. I had to.'

I stare at him, my heart squeezing at the weight of his words, but I pull my hand back. 'That's a lot to carry at thirteen.'

Henry lets out a long breath. 'Yeah. It was.' He doesn't say anything for a moment, then glances at me. 'It's why I hate seeing people that I care about struggle. I want to help, however I can.'

Does that mean I'm someone he cares about? I daren't say those words out loud, because I fear his answer may well just push us along a path I'm worried we're already starting to stumble down. So we sit in the quiet, the weight of our pasts hanging between us. Two people shaped by loss, by absence and by the people we love who left too soon. A part of me wants to reach back out to him, to hold his hand, to hug him and allow him to hug me. But I don't.

Henry's next question drags me from those thoughts anyway. 'What about your father? Your mum and your gran, I know about, but–'

'He was a deadbeat like yours.' I stop quickly, to offer an apologetic grimace for insulting his dad, but the shake of his head tells me it's okay to continue. 'When my mum found out she was pregnant, he decided he didn't want to be a parent and left, in that easy way men can... Okay, I'm sorry, that's stereotypical and unfair.'

'Kinda, yeah... but I get it.'

'Anyway, she didn't waste any more time on him. Not that Gran would have let her... maybe it had a lasting effect she never spoke about. Because we never did speak about him. I heard Mum and Gran having quite a heated debate one day, when I was about fourteen. They had just found out he'd died. A car accident. There was pain in my mum's voice, I know that now, looking back, but my gran told her not to sit and dwell on things she couldn't change. My gran's like that,' I say with a laugh that has no humour.

'Doesn't that bother you? About your dad, I mean, dying and not knowing him?'

'No, why would it? Maybe I should have shown *some* interest in him when I was growing up; perhaps my mum wanted that, but I always saw it as he made his decision. So why should I care? He was just another stranger to me. That makes me sound cold, heartless, doesn't it?'

Henry exhales heavily. 'Maybe a little... but actually, I kinda understand where you're coming from.'

'I don't think I've ever told Mike any of that. Not properly.' I'm not sure if I meant to say that out loud, but it's another truth escaping into the ether tonight.

'Why not?'

'I'm not sure. It just... it doesn't feel like something *he* would understand. Like he wouldn't want to hear about it.'

Henry doesn't say anything to that. He doesn't have to. I shift on the sofa, adjusting the blanket around me. There's still a space between us, but it's not as large as before. Physically and emotionally. The fear I felt earlier, while I stood in the kitchen scared, isn't completely erased, but it's settled inside me differently. I think that's because of Henry, because I don't feel so utterly alone.

'What about you?' I ask. 'Have you told anyone about your dad?'

Henry tilts his head slightly, lips twitching into a small smile. 'No. Not properly either.'

'So we're just two messed-up people, using a current trauma to offload past traumas at stupid o'clock in the morning?'

He nods, comically, and stretches out into a relaxed, comfortable position again. 'Yes, it would seem we've successfully turned a terrifying night into a therapy session. Productive.'

I let out a breathy noise, but there's no real laugh in it. My body is exhausted, but my mind won't slow down. My thoughts continue to circle over everything. I run the hem of the blanket through my fingers. 'I can't go upstairs.'

'Then don't,' Henry replies without missing a beat. I glance at him, and he shrugs. 'Stay down here. Whatever makes you feel safe.'

It's such an easy offer, like it's the most natural thing in the world. 'What about you?'

'I'll stay right here, too. We have a blanket each and the sofa's big enough for us both.'

I shift, not entirely sure on what I was hoping his reply would be, but thankful that he's still prepared to stay with me.

He nudges me with a smirk. 'Put your feet up there and get comfy. I'll be on sentry duty.'

I roll my eyes, but his words settle something in me. I adjust my position on the sofa, so I'm curled up properly, with my body angled towards him. Henry leans back, shifting again until he's comfortable, stretching out his legs. There's still a tension knotted tight inside me, but I think I can finally pinpoint why.

'Mike wouldn't have believed me,' I whisper.

'About the notebook?'

I nod, tracing a seam in the fabric. 'And the door. He already told me that I had misplaced the notebook. If I phoned to tell him about the unlocked door, he would have said I was overreacting.'

'I noticed you don't have a Ring doorbell, or any other one that captures footage.'

'I looked at those once, but they weren't cheap and Mike said, as it's not our house, we can't just start drilling holes in the landlord's doorframe.'

Henry chuckles. 'There's loads of ways around drilling holes, and I'm sure your landlord wouldn't disapprove when it's something that makes their house safer. I can show you different options tomorrow.'

I smile and nod, as a way of thanking of him, but he continues to watch me, as if he's staring into my soul. His expression is steady, no doubt, no hesitation when he says softly, 'And *I* believe you.'

It takes an effort to swallow the lump in my throat. 'Thanks. Again.'

'Anytime. Anything you need.'

Henry closes his eyes, arms folded behind his head, like he's perfectly content just being here. And *I* believe *him*. He would do anything for me... but why, when we've only just met?

CHAPTER THIRTY

I blink awake, my body stiff from sleeping on the sofa, a dull ache running through my neck. For a second, I don't remember why I'm here, why I'm not upstairs in my bed. Then it all floods back – the unlocked door, the notebook, the sheer terror of last night. And Henry. I shift slightly under the blanket, my heart hammering as I turn my head, already knowing the answer because I can feel the body heat. He's still here. Of course he's still here.

Henry's not as stretched out as when we said goodnight. We're a bit tangled and touching, and the blankets are twisted around each other. He can't be comfortable, yet he looks so completely at peace. Unlike me. I turn away from him and lower my head into my hands. What the hell was I thinking? At the time, last night, it made perfect sense. I was scared, alone, and Henry was the only person I could think of who would come to me, and maybe the only person I really wanted here. Non-judgemental and wanting me in their company. But now, in the cold light of day, I feel... well, sort of flipping ridiculous.

Yes, my feelings are slightly muddled right now and yes, Henry is a brilliant bloke – looks and personality – but I don't really know him. I should have called a friend... okay, so Stef, I should have called Stef. What did I actually accomplish by having Henry here? Nothing changed, except that now I feel guilty as well as wretched about the whole damn thing. This house is mine and Mike's. If I'm having issues or fears, it's him I should be turning to, not Henry. Mike is my partner. And yet... it's Mike who isn't here.

This isn't even about what happened between Henry and me – which is nothing, because he was just being a good friend, a good neighbour – it's about what easily *could* have happened. There's a fine line, we all know the one, and I'm inching closer and closer to it every time I text Henry, every time I have a laugh with him, or have lunch with him, every time I feel more comfortable in his company. The thought makes my throat dry. There's a deep itch of shame covering my skin, like prickly heat that isn't satisfied until you practically claw your skin off.

I need to move.

I carefully peel the blanket off, shift my legs from under me and try not to wake Henry as I slide to my feet. I grab my phone from the coffee table and head to the kitchen, but I barely make it out of the room before I feel it vibrating in my hand.

Mike.

My stomach lurches. I swing my head around with that paranoia you feel, wondering if the person calling you can actually see you while you are debating whether to answer them, or to ignore their call completely. But Mike's in another country and has no idea Henry is asleep on our sofa.

I force myself to answer. 'Hey.'

There's a pause before Mike's voice comes through, groggy and thick with sleep. 'You're up early, I didn't actually think you'd answer.'

'Yeah, just–' I clear my throat. 'Didn't sleep well.'

I should tell him about the break-in... except there was no

'break-in' because nothing was broken or forced or even taken. Something was returned. So, I can't tell Mike, can I? It will be irresponsible Ruby who forgets to lock up properly and finds missing items days later where they always were.

'Everything okay?'

No. *Someone* was in our home. I panicked and I invited another man round. A neighbour you've never met, and he stayed the night. But I don't say any of that. Any of what I'm really thinking.

'It's fine, just couldn't really settle.'

There's a rustling sound from Mike's end, like he's shifting in bed. 'You should have called me. Well, I was out late, having dinner with the office lads, but I would have texted back.'

'It's fine. I don't like to bother you when you're away.' That's true... but why is it true? It's not as if Mike's working twenty-four seven. I press my fingers to my temples and change the subject. 'Are you still in bed?'

'Yeah. I'm getting up now because I have to go into the warehouse for a few hours before I heard off to the airport.'

'What time does your plane land?'

'Erm... About four-ish. UK time.' He hesitates. 'Maybe we could go out for dinner when I get in?'

I stare at the counter. Why am I so uncertain? Yesterday I would have grabbed on to the chance to make things normal between us again, to push aside the unsettled feeling we never fully addressed after our last fight. But now, I feel suffocated. This whole conversation feels strained. Henry, still sleeping on my sofa. Me, last night, letting him in without any hesitation, seeking him out instead of my partner. Instead of an old friend. What the hell am I doing?

'Ruby?'

I'm startled at Mike's loud tone. 'Yes, sorry. Sorry, that sounds good.'

'Okay.' He pauses again and I don't feel the urge to fill the silence. 'I'll text you when I land then.'

'Okay. I'll be ready.'

'Good. Right, I have to go or I'll be late for work.'

'Of course. Bye.'

'Bye, Ruby.'

What the hell was that?

I drop the phone onto the counter and puff the longest sigh. It's as if I was chatting with a cold caller. This is all wrong. I can't be this person. I can't be someone who lets these lines blur, who invites a man into her home while her partner is away, who lets herself feel this kind of doubt. I turn back towards the living room and watch Henry sleep from the doorway. Before he wakes up, before he leaves, I need to decide what I want.

The days blend together. It's been a week since the break-in, since my heart-to-heart with Henry, since Mike came home. We've welcomed in another new month and for the first time in a long time, I don't care. I got out of bed each day and moved through the house, but nothing feels right. I haven't written a word in my novel, I haven't answered any messages or even looked at the Blackwood Close WhatsApp group. I've barely eaten or held a conversation with Mike for longer than ten minutes. I haven't left the house. Not once.

At first, it made sense that if I stayed inside then no one could get in. There have been no doors left unlocked, and the windows only opened ajar to let in some fresh air for a brief time before I close them again. My notebook hasn't disappeared, but my engraved pen from Mum hasn't reappeared and that worries me. What if this uninvited stranger has plans to return the pen at another time. So, if I don't leave, they can't sneak in. Plus, Mike has been home all week, too, so there's been an extra layer of security to the house.

But Mike... Mike hasn't even noticed. He's worked the week as normal with loud calls and conference meetings. Some days I've sat in my office, as if I've been typing away thousands of words into my imaginary worlds. But I haven't. I've listened to him talk, not really knowing what he's saying, and waited to see if he notices that I've been quieter this week. Distant. If he asked me, then I'd tell him, I'd open up and confess what happened last week.

A few times I've peered out of my office window, at the apartment building over to the left, and have wondered which one Henry lives in. Can I see his bedroom window or living room window? Does he look out at my house? Last week, after I ended Mike's call, Henry woke up immediately, giving me no time to decide what – or who – it is I want.

He knew something wasn't right, and when he asked if I wanted him to leave, I said yes. Blamed the fact that Mike would be home soon and it was better that he wasn't still here. Henry didn't know it would be hours, the whole day practically, but I couldn't look at his perfect, friendly face any longer. I've tried not to think about him – Henry – and the way he made me feel safe. But by pushing him out, all I've thought about is someone being in my home and sitting on my bed. He has sent me a message, but I've left it unread. I can't face him or the questions he might ask.

Mike, on the other hand, doesn't ask any questions. I'm sure he thinks I visited Gran this week. And even the fact that I didn't is another guilty sucker punch to the gut.

The house is too loud during the day, when it's bright and safe, because no one would break in during the day. Then it's too quiet in the night, when everyone is sleeping, I can hear every creak of the floorboards, every rustle of the wind against the windows and every hum of the boiler.

I feel like someone is always outside. Of course, no one is when I look, but I can't bring myself to stare out into the darkness for too long because my eyes play tricks on me. They create figures out of the trees or the lampposts or the shadows. So I don't look for long. But what if someone is there, watching and waiting? I check the locks constantly. The back door, the front door, the windows. Again and again, my fingers pressing against the latches and the handles during the day and night. But my body still doesn't truly relax or sleep peacefully.

Once Mike has gone to bed, I do the final checks on the doors. I leave the kitchen door fully shut, because the handle rattles when it's opened and I know we'd hear that from upstairs. I leave the light on, too, and the one in the hallway, so I don't have to walk through the darkness. I make it as bright as I can, to dispel the night from the house, to avoid shadows on the walls. To avoid my own reflection in the windows. Just in case it isn't only mine reflecting back at me.

I'm not okay, and I don't know how to voice that to Mike without him making me feel crazy. Obsessed. Overreacting. Which is what I try telling myself I am doing: overreacting. Because nothing has happened since that night, so it *is* all in my head.

But sometimes, I wake up in the morning, and I feel... a shift. A change. Like something is just slightly wrong in the house and I spend the day trying to figure it out. A book angled differently on the shelf. A chair pulled back from the table. A mug not in the place I left it the previous day. I don't know if I moved them or if someone else did, but I do know one thing: if I don't leave the house, they can't get in.

The knock at the front door startles me. I freeze mid-step, heart hammering against my ribs. *Pull yourself together, Ruby, an intruder wouldn't signal their arrival.* But no one ever really knocks on our door apart from delivery drivers; I haven't ordered anything and it's too late for the daily post. Patty, possibly, though I'm pretty sure she would text first these days.

Henry...

I groan, and for the briefest of seconds consider not answering. But I know if he's made the effort, summoned the courage to come, then he won't leave until I face him, and if he keeps knocking it will only bring this to Mike's attention. So I scramble to the door and open it, just a fraction, just enough for my head to poke through – just enough to resemble Jack Nicholson from *The Shining*. The irony isn't lost on me as I search out Henry, standing on the other side, with his hands shoved into his coat pockets.

'You haven't answered any of my messages,' he says quickly.

I grip the doorframe, my pulse fluttering at the mere sight of him. I could end this now and just shut the door on him, send a clear message, but something in his face stops me. He doesn't just look frustrated, he looks worried and my heart swells for him. I glance over my shoulder. Mike. I shouldn't do this, but I step outside anyway, pulling the door with me as much as possible before leaving it slightly ajar so it doesn't lock me out.

The cool breeze whips around me and I rub my arms, keeping my voice low. 'I'm sorry I didn't reply.'

'Are you?' His tone isn't cruel, but it isn't soft either.

I look away because I am sorry, but there's nothing else for me to say. I shouldn't have to explain myself.

'I thought something might have happened to you, Ruby. You've been... AWOL. And I didn't know if it was because of what happened, with the break-in, I mean, or with me. So, I just had to come over and check you were okay.'

'That's kind, Henry, thank you.' I swallow the lump in my throat. 'I needed some time.'

'Time for what?'

To get over the way I feel when I'm with you. To pretend last week meant nothing. To convince myself that staying in this house keeps me safe, keeps the intruder from coming back.

Instead, I simply say I don't know, and Henry studies me for a few seconds, as if he's weighing up whether he believes me or not.

'I'm worried about you,' he says, his voice quieter. 'And I don't mean just the past week.'

I shift uncomfortably. 'I'm fine.'

Henry lets out a dry laugh. 'You're not leaving the house and I bet you haven't even told Mike that someone was here, returning things they'd stolen. You don't really feel safe at all, do you?'

My stomach clenches. His words hitting too close. I should lie, and brush it off – brush him off – but my lingering silence answers for me. It's all the confirmation Henry needs, I see it in the flare of his eyes.

'For crying out loud, Ruby,' he murmurs through gritted teeth. 'Why are you still here?'

I exhale sharply. 'Because I live here, Henry. It's my home. I have a life here with Mike.'

'Do you, though, really?'

This man is just my neighbour, someone I've known for a couple of months. Why am I so bothered about what he's saying? I never scream and shout at anyone, but right now that's exactly what I *want* to do. Only, it's not because he's wrong...

Henry steps closer. 'Ruby, I care about you. And I know you don't feel safe here, with or without Mike. You're shutting yourself off, but that's not going to solve anything. You don't have to stay here, you know that–' He cuts himself off, jaw clenching.

'I know what?'

Our eyes search each other's. And I do know. He's waiting for me to admit that I know he's right, that I don't feel safe here. That I don't feel happy. That I don't know what I want from life anymore. That I'm terrified someone is going to sneak back into my house and perhaps I will be here when they do.

But I can't. I can't admit any of it because if I say all those things out loud, they become truths that can't be taken back. And what happens then? So instead, I take a step back. Back into the house.

Henry watches me, a flicker of pain passing through his expression before it hardens again. 'You feel the same as me, Ruby. Don't you?'

My breath catches. And right there in that moment I know I should deny it. Deny everything he is saying, speak up and say something. Just lie. But I can't, because we both know the truth. Still, I shake my head – whether that's in answer to his question, or because I'm acting like I don't hear him, I don't know.

'It doesn't matter,' I simply say.

Henry looks away briefly, before locking his gaze back onto me. It's sharper now, laced with something almost like anger in the furrow of his forehead.

'It matters to me, Ruby. And it should matter to you.'

I grip my arms again, not due to the cold this time but rather forcing myself to stay steady. 'Henry, I can't do this.'

He doesn't respond right away. Just watches me, and then he nods. A single, small nod. Not because he agrees, but because he understands, and that's almost the worst part. He's just accepting it and letting me be. He steps back now, too, further away from the door.

'Fine. I won't push you anymore, Ruby.'

I wish relief was settling in my chest – relief that he's giving up – but it's not. It's heavy and painful and threatening tears.

'Lie to me, and say it's fine,' he continues. 'But at least stop lying to yourself.'

I don't respond. Because what the hell am I supposed to say to that? I am lying, aren't I? And not just right now to Henry's face.

He nods once more, then turns and walks away. I don't move until he's disappeared down the path and turned onto the street. Then I exhale the shudder of a long breath and pray it calms my body. The moment I turn back inside the house, I freeze. Mike is standing in the hallway, at the foot of the stairs, watching me.

How long has he been there?

'Just the neighbour,' I say, keeping my voice light, but realising he hadn't even asked me yet.

'Which one?'

I force a shrug. 'No one special.'

The words taste like a sour betrayal on my tongue. Mike doesn't question any further, but pads into the kitchen with his coffee cup dangling. Fear swirls in my stomach like a whirlpool, at what Mike could have overheard and at how long he was standing behind me. But the fear is tinged with something darker, something I'm refusing to admit aloud. *Regret.* For Henry, for Mike, for everything I don't know how to fix. And for the first time in the past week, I wish I had left the house. Because being trapped in here now feels worse than ever before.

CHAPTER THIRTY-ONE

The message notification flashes across my screen, and my anger boils instantly. It's a little over a month since Nancy left me sitting in the café alone. No response to the message I sent her that day, and since then there's still been no reply, no explanation, nothing. And now, just like that, she flings in a one-liner like nothing's happened. I stare at the message, reading it over and over again, spotting everything that's wrong with it.

> Hey, I know it's been a while. I'm sorry. How's everything?

It's too casual and too vague and too... emotionless. No kisses on the end or emojis or dramatics. If it wasn't Nancy's number, I'd put money on this text coming from a stranger. Perhaps she's testing the waters. She wants to see what my mood is before she goes any further. Though, Nancy's never been shy in telling people what she thinks, which makes this seem even more wrong.

If she's testing me, perhaps this is my chance to stop pussy-footing around everyone. Maybe it's *me* who shouldn't be shy in expressing my thoughts and feelings. I haven't done a good job of it with Mike or Henry, but friends are different. When you've been solid mates for almost two decades, things just work differently. You know each other on a different level than you do with a romantic partner. But just as I'm building myself to lay it on her, in only a way a best friend can, my mind cannonballs in those images once again. Mike in Spain. Nancy in Spain. Together. She's never once said she's now travelling for work, and that's what's so unsettling about all of this. Why hasn't she mentioned it?

Devil's advocate: I didn't tell her Mike was travelling for work, either.

But that's Mike's news. That's not the first thing you share with friends. Now, if I was taking business trips left and right, she and Stef would have been the first to know.

This ping-pong of arguments is draining my resolve, and I just need to send a goddamned reply now. This has gone on long enough. I'll be breezy and casual, like none of it matters, and let's see where Nancy goes from there. She'll be more likely to open up to me if she thinks I'm calm and receptive.

My knuckles ache from gripping the phone so tightly. But just as I loosen it and attempt writing my response, it starts ringing and jolts me from my thoughts. For a second, I half-expect to see Nancy's name flash up on the screen – she knows I'm online, have read her message, and she's panicking as much as I am. But it's an unknown number. I usually ignore anything withheld, but this time I click the answer button anyway, my nerves all over the place.

'Hello?'

There's a brief pause on the other end, then a voice – soft, careful, the way people sound when they're about to say something you don't want to hear.

'Is that Ruby Turner?'

'Yes, speaking.'

'Ruby, I'm so sorry for calling so late, I'm Angelo, the on-call doctor at your grandmother's care home. We thought you'd want to know… she isn't doing too great this evening. She's taken a turn, and we really think you should come in as soon as possible.'

My throat closes. I knew this would come, of course I did, Gran is almost ninety. But somehow, the shock still hits with a power that could knock me off my feet.

I grip the counter. 'I'll be there as quick as I can.'

Mike is already out of bed when I rush into the bedroom, pulling on a hoodie, his movements quick and purposeful, like he already knows what's happening. I open my mouth to tell him, explain, but before I can, he turns to me, his expression softer than it has been of late.

'I heard your phone ring. And then what you said, that you'd be as quick as you can. I thought it could only be your gran that would make you rush out at this hour.'

For the first time since his promotion, Mike looks at me properly. Not distracted by his phone. Not irritated at something I've said. Just here, with me, caring. Between shaky breaths, I tell him what the care home said, and grab items of clothes to throw on, instead of going in my pyjamas. Like that really matters; I just need to get out of here.

Mike grabs my arms, steadying me, and forces me to look at him. 'Calm down. You're no good to her in this state.'

'I know. I just need to get there.'

'Then come on. I'll drive you.'

'You don't have to–'

'Ruby.' Mike squeezes me gently. 'Of course I'm driving you.'

And just like that, the pressure that's been building between us for weeks, dissolves. He releases his grip and I follow him downstairs. My head is banging from it all, Nancy's message, the call about Gran, Mike's attentiveness and urgency.

'I'll grab your coat,' Mike calls out as he walks in and out of the living room and the kitchen. 'Shall I make a tea in one of your travel cups?'

I shake my head, my throat too tight for anything but air. It's only when he crouches to tie his trainers in front of me that the thought strikes. The conversation with Henry at the door earlier, and the things I was almost prepared to admit. The worry that perhaps Mike overheard. But Mike doesn't look like a man who is angry or suspicious right now; he just looks like Mike. And he's being the version I fell in love with. Dependable and caring, and here for me, knowing how important Gran is. Mike is steady. Reliable. Sensible. All the things I've always wanted.

He grabs the car keys from the console table and turns to me. 'Ready?'

No, I think.

The drive is mostly quiet. Mike keeps the radio low, just a soft murmur of voices filling the silence between us. The roads are empty and hardly anyone is out walking the streets. It should feel peaceful, but it doesn't. Nothing about this day or night feels peaceful. I stare out of the window, thinking how I didn't visit Gran this week and wondering if, because she was alone, she gave up a little bit. Allowed her body to give up. Because what's the point in being in this world if there's no one to share it with? If there's no one to visit you when you spend your days in a care home.

No, that's not Gran. I'm getting caught up in my own fears and worries, but she wouldn't. She's stronger than I am.

Mike reaches over and squeezes my thigh. Just for a second. Just long enough to remind me that he's here, with me, by my side. It should be a comforting touch, a welcoming one, but I feel numb to it.

The Maples Care Home looks exactly the same as always. Warm, clean, welcoming in a way that shouldn't feel clinical, but still does. Mike parks the car, right outside the front door, but neither of us moves right away.

I inhale sharply, forcing my shoulders back. 'I need to go in.'

'I'll come with you.'

I nod, but my mind is already moving ahead, already picturing what waits for me inside. The door is unlocked, and the man at reception recognises me immediately, though I know it's not the doctor who called me.

'Go straight through, Ms Turner,' he says, soft but formal. 'Your gran is awake and asking for you.'

The relief crashes against me. I'm not too late. Mike places a hand on my back as we walk down the corridor, another silent show of support, but it only highlights that I don't want to be touched right now. If I'm handled like glass then I'm at risk of breaking, and *I* have to be strong tonight.

There's a sadness to walking towards Gran's private room, and not the common room where we always meet. I'd once offered to get her a small television, so she didn't have to keep sharing the communal space, but she'd laughed and said that was a terrible idea. *If you voluntarily lock yourself away, you'll be stuck there forever,* she had said at the time. Those words never screamed at me so loud as they do now.

As we approach Gran's door, Mike slows and pulls his hand away. 'Ruby, I'll wait in the lounge. Give you two some time together.'

I glance up at him, surprised at yet another thoughtful gesture, and thankful he understands I need this moment with her alone. I give him the smallest of smiles, it's all I can muster, and he walks away, leaving me to steady myself before pushing open the door to Gran's room.

CHAPTER THIRTY-TWO

Gran's smaller than I remember. It's the first thing I notice, but then when's the last time I saw her lying in bed? Gran is always dressed, hair up and sat in her wheelchair by the window. Now, she looks tiny and frail beneath those stark white hospital-type sheets.

But her eyes are bright when she sees me. 'There's my girl.'

I laugh, though it comes out like a breath, too shaky, too thin. 'Hey, Gran.'

She points to the chair beside her bed, and I move quickly, sitting down, gripping her hand like I can hold on to her forever. We don't say anything for a while, and I wonder if it's because she can't, because it hurts to speak. I know that's why I haven't.

Gran, as always, breaks the silence. 'You look tired.'

'So do you.'

'Ha!' She squeezes my hand weakly. 'I was waiting for you.'

My chest tightens. Is this it? Does she mean she's been waiting to die, tonight, but needed to see me first. They say that happens, don't they? Your loved ones, when they know it's time, hang on and wait until they've seen every last person that means something to them. But to witness it first-hand, to actually be in that moment right now, makes me choke on my own words. I need to say something meaningful to Gran. It needs to count, but I'm lost.

'I'm here,' is all I can muster.

We sit like this, quietly – which is very unlike us – for some time. I don't know how long, but long enough to scare me. I shift my hand in hers when I notice her eyes have been closed for a while. Fear gripping me. But she replies by wiggling her fingers, letting me know she's still here, and the warmth of her skin is a fragile comfort.

'You've got that look on your face,' Gran says suddenly, and I fix my eyes on her.

'What look's that?'

'The one that says you're about to cry.'

The night is full of weak laughs. 'I'm not.'

'Don't lie to an old woman on her deathbed.'

Her words hit like a heavy-weight's punch. If I wasn't already sitting, they'd have knocked me down. I shake my head, gripping her hand tighter. 'Don't say that.'

She smiles softly, her thumb brushing the back of my hand. 'I'm not afraid, you know.'

'I am.'

'Oh, my girl.'

I exhale sharply. 'Gran, if you go... that's it. I have no one, no family. I'm alone.' The words spill out before I can stop them.

'You've got yourself.'

'That's not enough.'

She sighs again, a long, tired sound. 'Ruby, life isn't about collecting people or hanging on to people just so you don't feel alone.'

'But you had Grandad, and then Mum, and then me. You had a family.'

'And I lost your mum and grandad. Because that's life.'

The silence stretches between us until she squeezes my hand again. A little weaker this time, I notice, but I know it's because she hasn't finished with what she wants me to understand.

'Ruby, I know what it's like to think you can't exist without the people you love. But you do. You keep going, every single day, and you honour their memory by speaking their names. They were here and they mattered in your life. The world doesn't stop spinning because someone leaves it. That's the sad truth. I know it, you know it. Everybody bloody knows it, but doesn't want to talk about it. Ruby, my dear, no parent should have to bury their child.' She pauses to catch her breath. 'But life isn't a permanent thing, and the ones we love will leave us – by choice or by death. Some of us aren't here to cure cancer or fly to the moon, or make an impact on the world that can be measured. Some of us are here, quietly, just to guide our loved ones through life.'

She stops again for a moment, though I know she has more to say. I'm just not sure if my heart can hear much more.

'Ruby, saying goodbye to someone forever is the saddest act we all share in this world. But a lot of that sadness is because we're the ones left here to *feel* the pain. I won't be here anymore, because I'll be up there, dancing in the sky and feeling no pain.'

'Gran!'

She coughs a chuckle. 'I'm serious, Ruby. Grieve us and miss us, but don't let it control you. If you do, you'll miss out on so much living. You'll miss out on finding new people who make everything worthwhile again.'

Her voice is softer now, but her words remain heavy. Because what if I don't? What if I never find someone that makes it okay to live in a world without Mum and Gran?

She shifts slightly in the bed. 'You remind me of her, you know.'

I stiffen. 'Mum?'

She nods. 'Same stubborn streak. Same way of overthinking yourself into misery.'

'Great.'

'You remind me of her... but you're *not* her, Ruby. You're you and you're more fierce and capable than you give yourself credit. You have a wicked imagination, and a cracking sense of humour. Don't deprive people of that because you're scared. I've never been worried about you.. Your mum, my daughter, she was lost. You know that, don't you?'

A chill seeps into my chest. 'Yes, I know. But what I don't know is *why*. Why was she lost? Why didn't she turn to us?'

'From the moment your father left her, she felt alone. Unwanted. It didn't matter how many times I told her otherwise, told her what a creep and loser he was,' Gran continues. 'Being left like that, pregnant, did something to her. It made her feel like she was always on the outside, looking in and not belonging. Waiting for someone to tell her she belonged to *something*. Though I'm always thankful it brought me you, Ruby, I'll hate that man long after I've taken my last breath, for what he did to my daughter.'

'I didn't realise he... I don't know. I didn't know that's how she felt about him. That it could make her feel so alone and abandoned.'

'Don't ever let another person dictate your place in this world, my girl,' Gran says, quiet but firm. 'Your mother didn't know how to ask for help, and so she became... lost. If only one of us had *known* how lost she really was.'

Gran's words linger in the air like fireflies.

In my own way, isn't that what I've been doing? Pushing people away, not standing up for myself or questioning things, pretending everything is fine with Mike and allowing Henry to walk away. Being lost and quietly floating along, instead of making my waves and *feeling* something real.

I rub my chest, swallowing an ache that's forming there. 'No, I won't let that happen.'

Gran closes her eyes. 'I hope not.'

I watch her chest rise and fall softly and slowly, thankful she doesn't sound as though she's in pain. I haven't even asked her if she is. The quietness surrounding us feels wrong and strange and... off. The last time we were this sombre together was just after Mum died. Now here we are again, in the clutch of death.

It's selfish of me, I know, but I clear my throat. Hoping the small noise will rouse Gran, bring her back to me for a little while longer tonight. It works, and I lightly draw her hand deeper into mine while she blinks her eyes open.

'Tell me something, Ruby,' she begins as if she hadn't been asleep at all. 'If you could be a flower, which would you be?'

I frown, though she gazes into the distance rather than at me. 'Gran?'

'Humour me.'

'A rose.' I barely think of an answer, unsure where this is leading.

She coughs a laugh. 'A rose is too common. Why would you not even pick your favourite flower?'

'I don't have a favourite flower, Gran.'

Now she looks at me and frowns.

'I haven't loved lilies since Mum's funeral.'

'Okay, I'll let you have that one. But I still want a thoughtful answer to my question.'

I close my eyes and take a minute this time. Gran used to love sitting in her garden, before moving here to the care home. I know they've encouraged her to get outside, into the fresh air, but her body's been too weak for anything green-fingers related. And if she can't dig and sow herself, Gran ain't interested. I shouldn't be so surprised that she wants to have a conversation like this.

'Hyacinth,' I finally reply, sure she'll be pleased with my not-so-easy choice this time. So I'm surprised when her frowns deepens further at me. 'What's wrong with that? I do like them. The way the petals look so fragile, but there's so many of them that they stand tall.'

'It's an interesting choice, actually, Ruby. I'm impressed.' She inhales deeply. 'I guess it's fitting that you're drawn to another flower that surrounds itself with so many meanings. Depending on the colour, of course, hyacinths are linked with a deep desire for forgiveness...'

She trails off for a moment, and I want to tell her it doesn't really mean anything. I just thought of a flower, like she asked. But then why didn't I choose daisy or sunflower or peony.

'They are beautiful flowers, Ruby, but another quite sorrowful one to pick if you were going to be one. Don't spend your life looking for absolution.'

'Gran, it's just a flower.'

'Hmmm. So you're not feeling guilty about anything?'

I hesitate for a moment. Why would she ask me that, right now, when I'm in the thick of guilt and remorse? Feeling lost and confused.

'Well, maybe, but how did you know?'

She hoots. 'I didn't, dear. But now I'm intrigued.'

I sigh, resigned to the fact she'll have to be told something. I can't lie to her, I never have been able to and I know I can't start now, so close to the end. But I also don't want to worry her, so decide not to mention Mum's pen and the notebook, and suspected break-in, which is what I really should start calling it. Instead, with the thought of flowers and forgiveness, I tell her all about Henry, surprised at how I wax lyrical about a man I hardly know. She watches me carefully, the whole time I'm talking about the two men in my life, as though I've been retelling an old favourite bedtime story.

Then, her voice low, she asks, 'It's real, isn't it? How you feel about this Henry.'

I open my mouth, but close it again before saying anything. There are no words because... my mind's gone blank.

Gran shifts her hand against mine, her grip gentle but firm. 'You know, when I married your grandad, I was so sure about the kind of man he was.'

'You two were perfect together. Marriage goals.'

She hums. 'Well, we weren't *perfect*, dear. No marriage is. But you put each other first and you make compromises and sacrifices. You're a team.'

I study her tired face. 'Did you ever... wonder what if there was someone else out there for you, that maybe you hadn't even met yet?'

'Not for a second.'

'But how can you ever be one hundred per cent sure?'

She loosens her hold on me. 'You can't, but if you think it for one moment, then you're not with the right person.'

I inhale deeply, understanding exactly what she means but wishing I'd never voiced any of this. Wishing I hadn't asked her that stupid question. It showed the doubt I have in my relationship with Mike. Not only to Gran, but to me.

'You can't live your life with the wrong man out of guilt, Ruby. You can't help who you love.'

'I love Mike,' I say quickly. Too quickly. 'He's good to me, and we've been together a long time–'

'Six years ain't a long time, my girl, trust me.' Gran moves against her pillow. 'You don't almost make it ninety years in this world without learning a thing or two.'

No, six years wouldn't feel like a significant period to an eighty-nine-year-old-woman. But it's significant to me, and you can't turn your back on that because a handsome new neighbour walks by. But even if I explain that, I know Gran would argue it further. I can see it in her eyes, despite the tiredness, there's a scowl to them that tells me to listen up.

'Ruby, my dear, I wish you many, many years in this game of life. It's a privilege, remember that because not everyone has this time on their side.' We hold each other's gaze. 'So you better bloody well spend it with the right person.'

She finishes with a slight smile and a weak wink, but I can't say anything in return. Her words, her warning, sit heavy, swirling around like a moody cloud that refuses to leave. Gran's eyelids flutter, the weight of sleep tugs at her again after the sermon she's just delivered. Maybe she hasn't taken such a bad turn as everyone seems to think.

'You head off home now, Ruby, love,' she whispers. 'I need to get some beauty sleep.'

There's something in her voice, a returned strength and force, that tells me it's okay to go. 'I'll come back tomorrow, okay, Gran?'

'Yes, love, that would be nice. Bring some flowers with you.'

I can't help but smile at that, and wish I'd asked which flower she would choose to be. That'll be my first question to her tomorrow. I lightly kiss her on the forehead, and squeeze her hand gently one more time before letting go.

CHAPTER THIRTY-THREE

You. You don't see me. I keep my distance because I have to.

This is the way it has to be for now, because I'm still figuring you out, Ruby. You're not an easy person to read. You walk along the high street, hands stuffed into your coat pockets, your head down against the wind. You don't look around or scan your surroundings or take any notice when you're outside your house. You should.

I watch you stop outside a bookshop, staring at the display in the window, it's one of your pleasures. I'd like to know more about what pleases you, what you love, other than your books. It's so easy to get lost in another world, isn't it, Ruby. That's exactly what's happening here, to me, I'm getting lost in your world. You run your fingers over the strap of your bag, a subconscious nervous motion, before moving on. Do you sense something? Something in the air that pulls at you, making you not go in today, making you not sniff at the old pages of the second-hand books. The way I know you like to.

Everything happens for a reason.

I follow on, keeping up with you, but making sure the space

between us is just right. I'm close enough to watch, but far enough to be nothing more than a shadow.

You pause at the florist, gazing at the bouquets wrapped in cellophane. Bright colours against the grey street. Your grey life. It makes me sad for you, because I really think you could be as bright as your name. There's a hesitation in your fingertips as yet again you brush the petals of the lilies. You do that a lot, too, but again you don't buy them. You never do. And it makes me think of the vase in your living room... the flowers in it are fake. You never buy these fresh ones, even though it's clear you love them. Is it because you don't want to replace them each week when they wilt and die? I guess there is something comforting in knowing you'll always be greeted by pretty, colourful flowers when you enter the room. Never dead and rotting petals.

You move further, your steps a little slower now, like something is tapping at the edges of your mind. I wonder if the unease is creeping in yet. As if that faint, inexplicable feeling of being watched is settling under your skin. A group of teenagers pass between us, and I let them buffer the space, let them become the noise between us. I move with them, step for step, weaving in the ebb and flow of the street. You reach for your phone, glance at the screen, then slip it back into your pocket without unlocking it. Restless and unaware.

The crowd thins as you turn onto a quieter road, where the foot traffic is less and the hum of the high street fades just a little. I have to be careful here. I can't let you see me. Not now.

There's a café up ahead, and you slow down, roll your shoulders like you're trying to shake something off. What is it, Ruby? I peer over the top of a car, tapping my phone as if I'm replying to a text, to a friend, though how funny is that because I have fewer friends in this world than you do.

You glance over the tables outside the café, watch a couple talking, a man drumming on his laptop, a barista wiping down a spilled mess. It's as if you're waiting for something, or someone. And just when I wonder if you do have a girlfriend to meet up with, you turn and carry on moving.

A car engine rumbles behind me and I shift, allowing it to mask my next few steps. The café's window catches your reflection as you pass and for a fleeting second, I wonder if you'll see me. But you don't. You never do, Ruby. For someone living in such a nervous state, why do you never really see what's happening right in front of you?

Don't think I haven't noticed you're walking the long way home. Avoiding the alleyway that would bring you right to your house. Another quick glance over your shoulder. Are you starting to feel it now? That flicker of something unseen, the whisper of my breath curling in the air. I feel a tingle, Ruby, deep inside me. Our skin prickles because of each other. I know you *feel* me, you just don't see me. Not yet. But you will.

CHAPTER THIRTY-FOUR

Gran let go.

Mike and I weren't long in the house, kicking off our shoes and debating a cup of tea before bed, when the second dreaded call came from the care home. Gran passed away in her sleep. A final heart attack, but one she wouldn't have even been aware of. I thank God for that, at least, and I'm not even a religious person. But we have a way of doing that, don't we, atheists. Pleading and praying when the time suits us. It's a comfort. Though, I clearly wasn't being heard on the drive home, when I prayed that Gran would make it another day. Make it to another visit, with flowers this time. Make it to give me another stern telling of what's what.

She let go. That's what they say when someone slips away from life. When their body decides it's time. Like it was a choice. Like she simply loosened her grip and drifted into something easier, something softer, leaving me here to hold on to a world that feels too empty, too quiet, too wrong.

She let go, and now I have to keep holding on without her. Instead of bringing fresh flowers and finding out which she'd choose, today will be filled with nothing. Nothing except regret and exhaustion. A new anniversary marked on the calendar that will haunt me forever.

My hand shakes as I slide my mug away. Tea never really cures the pain and hurt, but it's a routine to go through to keep busy. Keep things normal. Gran would scold me for saying that about today's date. Wasn't she just pleading with me to embrace life. But this isn't just about Gran, is it? It's about Mum too, and about being alone in this world in a completely different way, like never before. I have no parents, no grandparents, no siblings, no children, no husband.

Grief is a cruel thing. It forces you to examine every single thing, yet is the very reason you have the strength to do nothing all. It steals moments and replaces them with only memories that will fade over time. It rewires your brain, replacing warmth with ache, happiness with regret. When Mum died, I thought I'd drown in it, the grief, and let it swallow me whole. I stopped eating, and sleeping, and truly believed life would never feel normal again...

The power of my writing, of my books, in creating my characters and the worlds they live in is what saved me then. Now it'll be Gran's words that keep me from going under. Wasn't that the entire significance of my last conversation with her? She held on for as long as she could to knock me into place, to ensure I don't fall into a heap again. Mum's death had been so sudden, so unnatural, so unfair. It happened in the middle of a crisis that swallowed the world whole, and I wasn't the only one adrift from life. Like many, I'd been helpless, watching from a distance, forced to grieve alone. I was unprepared. But Gran's passing is different, painful yes, of course, but natural, and we had the chance to say goodbye in a loving way that I'll never forget. It doesn't feel the same as with losing Mum.

Gran's voice, teasing but firm as always, saying things like,

Don't go moping around like a lost lamb, Ruby, and *Life is for living, girl. You can grieve, but you bloody well keep moving.*

It's been two weeks since she passed, but I can still hear her, in my mind, crystal-clear. I've done all the things I need to do. Registered her death, collected the certificate, met with the funeral directors. I've chosen the flowers and the hymns and let the few people left in her life know the funeral details. It's felt easier to handle this time, smoother and maybe even a bit more methodical and transactional – I guess that's what comes with a natural death at a ripe old age. So that's everything, really. I've buried my head in it all, because it's actually easier than dealing with my life. Which is, it's helped me put off the next big thing I have to do. Gran wouldn't hold that against me, but she also wouldn't want me waiting too much longer either.

Mike has been helpful. Supportive, in that steady, dependable way he always is, because he's the logistics side of our partnership. I'm grateful for him, I am, but in the spirit of being honest with myself, as Gran would want, the spark is fading. I feel it deep within me, as much as I don't want to because he's been my constant for so many years. Mike has been the kindest version of himself. He's rubbed my back when I've gone quiet and zoned out from watching TV; he's made me tea and toast in the morning when yet again I haven't been in the office writing; and he's held my hand at the funeral directors. But it's all been so distant.

There have been no cuddles and no whispered reassurances in the dark. There's definitely been no intimacy. Until last night, when he reached across to me in bed. But it wasn't comforting. It wasn't making love. It was a routine for him – well, for me too – just a quick fumble in the dark that left him satisfied before he rolled over and drifted off to sleep. And as I lay there, staring at the ceiling and feeling nothing, a horrible thought crept into my mind before I could stop it. I feel ashamed to even think it again today, but I can't shift it from my mind.

I hope that wasn't the time that it worked. I hope that wasn't the time we created a life. The realisation clawed at my throat last night, like I was swallowing razor blades, and the wound is still fresh now.

I've spent the last hour pacing the house, pretending to look at hymns for Gran's funeral, when they've already been chosen, and the jobs on my list have all been ticked off. Mike has gone out with his brother again for another pint, and it didn't annoy me when he said he was going.

I fully hated being alone here before, but now I walk the quiet hallway, trailing my fingers along the walls, feeling detached from this house in a way I never have before. I don't know if this feels like home anymore. Mike and I have lived here for five years, with the belief we were starting a family. But if that were true, why does he never talk about it? Why does he never share his hopes and dreams and worries that we're *still* trying. Have these bricks and mortar ever really felt like home, or have I imagined it all? Ruby with the overactive imagination strikes again, perhaps, because isn't that what my nearest and dearest think of me?

I press my palms to my eyes, needing to stop this doubt and second-guessing, wondering what other people think. This is my life, and I can't let grief swallow me. I make a promise to myself, and to Gran. Yes, I will cry and ache and miss her forever. But I will bloody well keep moving, too, because if Gran taught me anything, it's that life doesn't wait. So neither will I.

And right here in this moment, I know exactly what it is that I want.

CHAPTER THIRTY-FIVE

My phone vibrates on the kitchen counter, and I grab it, expecting it to be Mike, but it's not. It's Henry. As if he knows my thoughts have more recently been consumed by him.

> Ruby, I know you want me to stay away, but I couldn't not get in touch. I just found out... I'm so sorry about your gran. Patty told me. I'm here if you need me! 🤍

It's a simple message, but it's thoughtful and genuine. Henry's thinking of me and he's reached out because he cares and wants to know how I'm doing. Still, guilt tinges my heart. Just because Mike is in the pub right now doesn't mean he doesn't care. I'm sure he needs a break from me and my grief. It can be intense when your partner isn't wading through it with you. My hands tremble as I re-read Henry's text, and it sparks an urge within me that I can no longer ignore. I don't *want* to ignore. Who cares that we barely know each other? You can't help how you feel, and sometimes you have to trust it. So, I stay true to my promise and walk out of my front door towards Henry's.

I don't let myself overthink this, and I don't slow down for a moment to see if anyone is watching or standing at their windows. For once, I don't care. My feet carry me forward and I don't even realise how fast I'm walking until I find myself outside his apartment building, my breath coming in gasps. But I'm caught short, because I don't even know which apartment Henry lives in. Or if he's even home alone at the moment. I let out a small, breathless laugh, shaking my head at myself.

Yesterday, last week, the other month, this would have stopped me in my tracks. I'd have taken it as a sign to turn around and go home. But not today. I pull out my phone from my back pocket, mirroring exactly what he did for me when I needed him the most.

I'm outside.

I stare at the message the second it sends, and wait for Henry to come online. When he does, instantly, my stomach plummets. I wait for a reply, but nothing comes. Instead, the main door to the apartment building opens and Henry's there with a quizzical frown and a hopeful smile. Neither of us speak, but as his eyes sweep over me, something animalistic is unleashed within me. A desire I've never felt before. Henry doesn't ask why I'm here, he just pulls back the door and I follow him through to apartment one.

So that's how he got to the entrance so fast.

The moment the door shuts behind us, I'm certain this is what I want. All I see is Henry, not his apartment or furniture or what colour the carpet is, just him. But he hesitates, like he's holding back, unsure of me. So I move first, closing the space between us, and grab his T-shirt, pulling him to me. This is so far from who I am, that I briefly wonder if I'm having a very heated dream. But the second his mouth crashes against mine, I stop thinking altogether.

It's *hot*. Like we've both been waiting too long for this exact moment, despite only knowing each other for a few months. He groans against my lips and his hands slide to my waist, gripping me tightly. What we're doing is so wrong, but the fierce, hot heat spreads down my body like wildfire. Henry pulls back just enough to look at me. His eyes are darker, heavier than I've ever seen them.

'Ruby,' he murmurs.

'Yeah?'

'You sure?'

I know exactly what he's asking, and I know this is the moment where I could stop it all. Where I *should* stop it all. Because this is the line. The line no person should cross when they've already set up a home and a life with someone else.

'Yes,' I reply softly, allowing Henry to lead me to his bedroom.

It's amazing the release that comes in the aftermath of passion. Or lust in this case. Yes, I am attracted to Henry, and we click in a way that feels natural and different. But now we're finished, the absolute horror of what I've done to Mike has cosied-up and sits heavy on my chest. The weight of this, this dark betrayal, is crushing, and if I didn't recognise myself in the moments leading up to it... well, I'm a complete stranger to myself now.

I look over at Henry. We're a tangled mess of limbs and bedsheets and sweat. He looks happy and content, of course he does. Why would he feel any guilt about his behaviour when he's free and single?

He looks at me now, with the most genuine and happy

smile, as he rearranges himself and then props up on one elbow facing me. 'I've wanted that to happen since the moment I first saw you,' he says. 'You okay?'

The guilt catches in my throat for a moment and I nod first, pushing it down. 'Yes, I'm fine, it's just...'

His faces changes, as if I've wounded a small child.

'You're not staying?'

'I can't, Henry.' And I want to explain further, but he wouldn't understand the full weight of my remorse right now.

'You're going back to him? To *Mike*? After that, after us being together?' He spits Mike's name out and my stomach drops.

'It's not as simple as that.'

'Yes it is, Ruby,' he replies, louder than I think he intended, and fully sits up so he's resting against the headboard.

I mirror his movement. 'I know I've just changed everything–'

'Well, that's something.'

I glance a side-eye look at him, one of those that means he needs to calm down. Though his frustrations are reasonable, of course they are, I need him to understand my uncertainty. Yes, I made a promise to myself to *live* my life, but all I've really done here is complicate everything.

'I do have feelings for you, Henry, but they're all tied up in a bunch, and I'm with Mike, and the thought of what I've just done to our relationship... I'm disgusted with myself.' Henry tries to interrupt but I hold my hand up and continue. 'It's not fair on him and things have escalated. Yes, I came here to you, and this is what I wanted. What I still want, but... this is crazy.'

Henry's twists his body to me now. 'What's crazy?'

A manic laugh escapes my lips. 'At the beginning of the year, I didn't know a soul on my street. Now I've been in their homes, know the books they're reading and the way they take their tea. Mike and I had plans to start a family and he was the only person I saw – other than my gran – for weeks on end. Now my gran is gone and I'm in another man's bed.'

The reality of it all is exhausting, and this whimsical promise I've made to myself has already landed me in some real shit.

'I don't want to lose you now, Ruby,' Henry finally says, forcing me to look at him.

There is such an attraction, such a pull, towards him, it knocks me a little more every time I look at him. I wasn't lying when I said I knew what I wanted now. I do want Henry – with such a force that it's a little bit terrifying, actually. But I also know that lying and cheating behind Mike's back is not the person I am.

'Henry, I just need some time.'

'Okay,' he quickly replies. 'I get that. You've gone through a lot, and I admire you for not wanting to be a cheater. So I can wait. I'll wait for as long as you need me to.'

He says it so genuinely that a smile pushes through all of my confusion. He leans forward, and my skin prickles with nervous anticipation, but a single kiss on the cheek is all he gives me. Our heads rest there for a moment, until I whisper that I have to leave. Henry nods gently and moves away to let me get up. The confidence I had while stripping off my clothes has long since left the room, and now I'm stranded with embarrassment instead, half-naked, looking for my jumper.

'Here you go.' Henry grabs it from the floor by his side of the bed and hands it to me. 'I'll walk you out.'

'You don't have to–'

'You're not a booty call, Ruby.'

I laugh quietly, and it helps lift some of the uneasiness in the room. Although, that feeling seems confined only to me, as

Henry busies himself around the room collecting his clothes and dressing, humming all the while.

Back at the main entrance of the apartment building, we take up the same positions we had earlier – Henry stood in the doorway, me on the outside facing him – but everything is completely different now.

'Don't take too much time, will you, Ruby? Henry says with a wink as he leans on the doorframe.

I roll my eyes, wanting to say *don't rush me,* but I know he's trying to keep things light. Making sure I don't forget the things I've promised.

'I'll see you soon?'

He pauses, then gives a small nod. 'Yes. You will.'

His voice is lower, rougher, and I can't be sure if the tone is a promise or a warning, but he doesn't give me a chance to dwell on it further as he steps outside of the building and lands another kiss on my cheek. It's warm and lingering, and it takes everything inside of me not to lean into it. I turn, breaking from his touch, and walk away. I don't look back because I know with a worryingly certainty, he will be watching me.

CHAPTER THIRTY-SIX

As I turn the corner onto the cul-de-sac, my mind in overdrive with all the questions I cannot answer, I spot Patty at the end of her pathway, looking unsure of herself. I speed up, wanting to make sure everything is okay, and it's then I spot that although she's wearing a coat, she's also still got her slippers on. I call out her name, once, twice, before she finally turns around and answers.

'Oh, hello, love,' she says, with a bright smile that should dispel my worries.

'Are you all right, Patty?' I peer down to her footwear, so I don't have to say anything out loud.

She follows my gaze and then looks up and laughs. 'I just quickly popped to Mrs Shah's house and quite frankly couldn't be bothered to swap out of these. They're comfy.'

I look to Mrs Shah's house, but the front door is closed. There's no reason it would still be open, I guess. I quickly glance behind me and as is so often the case, those curtains at the top of the dark house are shut. But it's just as I'm turning back to Patty that I notice the flash of bright blonde hair in the wind as a figure walks down the alleyway and out of sight.

'Is that the lady who let me into your house the other week?' I ask, quite rudely, without even thinking. Patty just nods. 'Who is she?'

'Just a friend,' she replies, but then glances in the direction I've just come from. 'Where are you coming from?'

'Just a friend's.'

'Touché.'

We both let out a small laugh and I shake my head. My own guilt is so heightened that everything around me feels suspicious. I try to think whether Patty was stood in her favourite spot at the window when I passed by to Henry's – but I didn't even look. I took nothing in during my hell-bent, savage journey to his apartment, and I curse myself for that now.

'I'm so sorry, again, about your grandmother, Ruby.' Patty's words pull me from my thoughts. 'When you texted me, to explain why you wouldn't be at Anna's and Noah's for book club, my heart just went out to you.'

'Thanks, Patty, that means a lot to me.'

She gestures to her front door then. 'Would you like to come in for a cuppa? You can tell me all about her.'

I dither for a moment. Any other time I would jump at the chance to speak about Gran, but my head is all over the place between Mike and Henry. And with that, a new layer of guilt seeps into my soul that the men in my life are consuming everything.

'Do you mind if I take a rain check please, Patty?'

She smiles. 'Are you sure, love? We don't have to talk about her if you're not ready, but it helps to not sit in your grief alone.'

Patty lost her husband some years ago, before we moved into the neighbourhood, that much I know. So she understands living with grief, and I appreciate her reaching out to me with support. The thought of her son, who she hasn't told me about, slips into my mind. But this isn't the time. There's enough already vying for my attention.

'Thanks for the offer, Patty, I really do appreciate it, but I have a lot on at the moment. Another time?'

She waves a hand between us. 'Of course, I completely understand. You know me, I just love company, especially yours. If there's anything I can help with, when it comes to the arrangements, you just give me a shout.'

I murmur another thank you, and promise to pop in to her soon. Then I wait until she's safely inside with the door closed.

Later that evening, home alone and for once thankful that Mike is pulling an all-dayer at the pub, I hear a faint noise at the front door. It's so quiet that the sound barely registers at first. I pull the blanket from my legs and stand up from my spot on the sofa. Padding towards the front door, I half-expect to open it and find Mike in a drunken heap having dropped to the ground while attempting to put the key in the lock.

But I don't need to open the door, because once I'm in the hallway my eyes land on something sitting on the welcome mat. A folded piece of paper. No envelope, no takeaway menu, no junk-mail leaflet – just a single sheet of white paper. I quickly squint out of the door's glass panel, holding my breath so I can hear the faintest sound, but there's nothing. No noise and no one standing there. I reach down and unfold the piece of paper.

Tut, tut, tut. Ruby. You are a naughty, naughty girl.

For a moment, my brain stalls, like a worn-out engine refusing to turn on. Then, as I re-read the handwritten note, dread rushes through me, a surge of panic so strong I might vomit right here on the wooden floor. I stare at the words, my vision blurring, and my entire body trembles.

Someone knows. Someone knows about me and Henry? Is it the same person who's been in my house? I whip my head up, scanning the hallway, as if I'll find a shadow lurking behind me. I run to the back door and yank the handle down, but this time it is locked.

First my notebook and pen are taken and later returned – well, not the pen. Now, on the day I cheat on Mike, a note is hand-delivered through my letter box. Someone is watching me. And it's as if they want me to know that, rather than physically harming me, they want to mess with me, freak me out. But who? Who could it be? I spin around the kitchen, walking to the staircase and dropping down onto the first step, my thoughts dizzy.

Norman? It has to be him – or his nephew – one or both of them are always lurking in that dark house, on the street, as if they're watching anything and everything. Didn't Norman himself tell me, warn me even, that he sees everything.

What if it's Patty? She was outside when I left Henry's and asked me where I had been. I took it in jest because it was *me* being nosey and questioning, but what if she was letting me know then that she had seen. She's been so welcoming lately, so friendly, but that could be fake. Isn't she always watching, too?

Then, another sickening thought. What if it's Mike? What if he already knows and he wrote this just to watch me unravel? I want to be honest with him, but haven't I believed that he could be with one of my best friends? Wasn't he standing at the bottom of the stairs when I was outside speaking with Henry? It wouldn't have been difficult to understand how charged and emotional our conversation had been, if he'd overheard. And if he had, I'd then lied to him further.

No, what am I thinking? Mike would never do this. And

ultimately, don't I want Mike to know? I want to be honest about what happened with Henry, and my feelings towards him, so whoever wrote this note has no clout. Unless they get to Mike first. Unless they had hoped Mike would pick up this note, get mad, get angry at me. Are they nearby, wanting to watch it all play out? But if someone really is watching me, then they know I'm home alone, again.

This downward spiral all started when Mike got promoted and started travelling. So that's their point with this note, they *want* me to know they know; they want me to know they're in control.

The retching feeling returns and the walls begin to close in. The house, the cul-de-sac, the neighbours, everything suddenly feels like a trap I have to get out of. I *need* to get out of... right now, before my imagination drives me crazy. I might not know who's watching me, or watching the house, but there is someone who owes me answers. And right now, that is something I *can* control.

CHAPTER THIRTY-SEVEN

I stand outside Nancy's flat, my heart hammering against my chest. I shouldn't feel nervous. This is Nancy, one of my best friends, a person I've known since university... though, do I really know her at all? The unanswered texts, the missed meet-up and, most of all, the nagging suspicion I can't shake: Nancy was *secretly* in Spain at the same time as Mike. With everything that's happening in my life at the moment, being so unsure of everything and everyone, this needs to be answered before I can move forward.

I take a breath and knock on the door. Seconds pass. Then a minute, and I raise my hand to knock again when I hear movement on the other side. The door swings open, and there she is, my friend who I haven't seen in months, wearing an oversized hoodie I recognise from our uni days and her blonde hair piled into a messy bun. Always effortless beauty.

Nancy visibly flinches. 'Ruby?'

I don't miss the flicker of a shadow cross her face – shock, maybe, or guilt. I'm in bed with those feelings and am starting to know them well.

'You stood me up. Weeks ago.' My voice is even, but my grip tightens around the strap of my handbag.

She sighs. 'I know. I was going to message, I just–'

'No, Nancy. No more texts or excuses. You said you'd explain everything. So explain.'

She hesitates, and then I see it again in her eyes. It *is* guilt. If she hasn't done anything wrong, then she wouldn't wear this wretched look on her face. I'm right, my suspicions of her and Mike are bang on, and we've all been unfaithful now.

Nancy steps back then, pulling the door open wider. 'Come in.'

I step inside, my stomach knotting tighter, and walk down the hallway which leads into the open-plan kitchen and living room. It's a home I know so well – warm, an organised mess, with the scent of candles always burning – but today it feels strange. I turn my focus to Nancy, who moves towards the kitchen, flicking on the kettle like this is any other visit.

'I don't need tea, Nancy. I need answers.'

'I know.' She doesn't look at me. 'I swear, I was going to tell you.'

I've had enough of this prelude. 'Tell me what? That you were in Spain with Mike? Is that why you didn't tell me you were travelling for work, too? Because you two were together.'

Nancy's head snaps up, her eyes wide. 'Mike was in Spain?'

It's too fast, too genuine, and I instantly believe she didn't know, yet I ask her again anyway. For my own sanity. 'You really didn't know?'

She shakes her head. 'I had no idea. I mean – Jesus, Ruby, you think I was there with him?'

I don't answer and the silence is enough.

She lets out a sharp, humourless laugh. 'You really think I'd do that to you?'

But that's the problem, I don't know what I think anymore. I don't know what I believe or what I want. I had worked myself up so much that the two of them being together had to be true, that it even helped push me to another man. But now that I'm here and can see my friend's face, I don't know anything at all.

'Then why?' I begin. 'Why did you say you'd explain everything? What the hell were you talking about?'

Nancy exhales loudly, and she wears that same look again, the one I've been calling guilt – so sure that's what it was…

'Mike messaged me.' Her voice is quieter now.

'What? When? Why?' I rush out the confusing questions.

'Just before your birthday,' she continues, and I don't interrupt now, needing to hear everything. 'He said he'd been following my Instagram and wanted to let me know I looked "smoking hot" and I felt so sick because… because, Ruby, then I *knew*… He hasn't changed, all these years and he's just that same old Mike.'

A cold, creeping nausea spreads through me. 'What do you mean, *same old Mike*?'

Nancy's fingers curl around the edge of the counter. 'I never told you, Rubes, and I'm sorry. I know I should have, but I was scared and then I was just… a coward.'

'Scared of what?'

She looks at me now, straight on, and I can already see the truth in her pained expression. 'Scared you wouldn't believe me.'

The room spins slowly, threatening to knock me down. 'I wouldn't believe what, Nance?'

'That Mike–' She exhales loudly again, sharply. 'That Mike tried to force himself on me.'

The words don't make sense at first. Like they belong to a different conversation, a different reality, and I just stare at my friend.

'It was years ago,' she rushes on. 'Not long after you two

started dating, and you were head over heels for him, Ruby. Smitten. I didn't know how to tell you.'

A thick pressure builds in my chest and I feel behind me for the sofa, sitting down with the weight of a brick. *Just after we started dating.* When I had been completely besotted with him, when I'd thought Mike was everything and I couldn't quite believe he had chosen plain little me.

'We were all out drinking,' Nancy continues, and joins me on the sofa. 'You had left the pub early because you had work the next morning, and Mike offered to walk me home.' She stops, clearly not wanting to share anymore and as much as I want to console her, tell her it's okay to speak the truth, my own words are choked-up, unable to escape. Instead, I reach out my hand to hers and look her in the eyes, knowing that although my world is about to fall apart, hers already has.

'He was drunk,' she finally says. 'I was drunk, too, and I thought he was just being nice. My best friend's new boyfriend trying to make a good impression. But when we got to my front door, he... he kissed me.'

A lone tear runs down my cheek and I squeeze her hand tighter.

'Ruby, I pushed him off instantly, I swear to God I did. I told him he was wasted and that he needed to go home. But he–' Her voice falters. 'He tried again. Then he had his hands all over me, making their way up my top and pushing me back against the door–'

'Oh, Nancy,' I cry out and pull my friend into a hug. She isn't crying, she isn't wailing, she is calm and controlled, and it hits me then that she's probably had this conversation with me in her head over and over and over. She's already cried.

I pull back from her. 'I'm so sorry.'

'Don't you apologise. It's not your fault.'

I shake my head. 'I'm sorry you felt as though you couldn't tell me.'

She closes her eyes, inhaling shakily. 'Somehow, I freed myself from his grip, got inside and locked the door. He knocked for a while, telling me not to be mad, saying he was just messing around, but I couldn't tell you. Because when I saw you the next day, you were so happy and telling me how much you had already fallen for him and how great he was. I didn't want to ruin that for you, and just had to hope and pray it really was the drink. That it was a one-time stupid drunken mistake. Over the years, we've never mentioned it and he's never given me a reason to think of him like that again.'

My breath is short and shallow. Mike: the man I built my life with, and the man I thought I knew. Steady, reasonable, logical Mike, who never makes waves and is so controlled in everything he does. Then I picture this Mike that Nancy's talking about, the Mike I wasn't there to see. Drunk. Forceful. Ignoring Nancy's no. I want to cry out, shout at Nancy for not telling me and for allowing me to be with someone like that for so many years, but I can't. Because if she had told me back then, would I have believed her? I don't know, and I feel sick with that realisation. But this isn't about me, or Mike for that matter; this is about Nancy and actually, right now, all I have to do is be here for my friend.

The house is dark when I step inside. I close the door gently, as if the walls themselves might crack under the pressure bubbling inside of me. I'm still reeling from Nancy's words, from the image of Mike trying to force himself on her. Deep down, I believe her, of course I do, but it still doesn't seem real. Can I really have lived with someone for five years and not seen that side to them? Or *have* I seen it, but just didn't... what? Didn't want to see it, so never acknowledged it?

My feet guide me towards the living room, on autopilot, and I spot Mike's coat thrown over a chair, dropped without a thought, and his shoes by the door, toppled over like he kicked them off carelessly. Of course he did. The faint smell of beer lingers in the air. He's home. I hesitate in the doorway because I've been prepared to confront him.

On the journey home from Nancy's, I had my words thought out, my anger coiled tightly but contained, ready to be released. I'd planned to come home to an empty house, to sit with my thoughts, to let the weight of what I'd learned settle before I faced him. But he's already here, and suddenly, I don't know what to do. The coward in me, used to the quiet life and going along with everything, has returned so quickly.

Mike's sprawled on the sofa, TV remote in hand, legs stretched out. The dim blue light from the screen casts shadows across his face. He doesn't notice me at first, not until I walk further into the room. The gnawing uncertainty follows like my own shadow. Then his gaze lifts to mine, slow and unfocused.

'Hey.' His voice is thick, lazy, the way it always is when he's been drinking.

I stare at him. Something in me had expected – hoped – that he would look different. But he's just Mike, same as always. Only now... he's not.

'I didn't expect you to be home yet.' I try to keep my voice neutral, part of me wishing I was the type of person who could shout and scream and openly confront him for what I know he's done to my friend.

He shrugs. 'Had enough of people. I'm knackered.' He lifts his beer, tipping the bottle toward me. 'You want one?'

I shake my head, slowly lowering myself into the chair opposite him instead of beside him. His brows furrow slightly at that, like he notices the distance between us. But then he yawns, rubbing a hand over his face, and the moment passes. He reaches for the remote, flicking through channels, his attention gone from me again. Bored of me – not for the first time – like I'm just... just part of the furniture. I study him. The beer and the looseness in his body, and a thought grips me so hard I'm winded by it.

Is this what Nancy saw that night? The Mike who had been drinking and didn't care. The Mike who thought a kiss wasn't a big deal and that he could have what he wanted, when he wanted. The Mike who ignored the word no. Sour bile settles in my mouth.

How many times have I sat with him like this, watching him knock back another beer and listening to one of his stories about work or a night out? Not asking about me or what I've been up to, because before his promotion, what did I do without him?

How many times have I excused things because he was tired, because he'd had a long week, or because we'd had an argument and I needed to make it up to him? I think back to all the times I brushed off his moods, the sharp words, the way he made me feel small without meaning to – telling me I'd imagined things and roughly taking me on the stairs.

Has Mike always been the man that Nancy saw all those years ago?

I think of our more recent disagreements. The way he hated when I pushed back, when I questioned things. The way he dismissed my paranoia about someone chasing me down the road and into the alleyway, about someone taking my notebook and pen. Isn't that the reason I didn't tell him that the book had been returned? Has he ever really listened to me?

'You're quiet,' he murmurs, setting his bottle down.

'Just tired.' It's not a lie, I am tired. Tired of trying to work out who it is I'm living with, and what the hell I'm supposed to do with Nancy's revelation.

Mike just nods, like my answer satisfies him. But I'm far from satisfied, because the truth is, I'm questioning everything I know and everything I see. And I don't know if I recognise the man in front of me at all. The man I've loved for six years, my perfect partner, now looks like a complete stranger.

CHAPTER THIRTY-EIGHT

The sun hangs low in the sky, stretching out and making the afternoons feel brighter and longer again, and with it, the street feels more alive than it has done in months. The neighbours have started flocking outside again, gathering in little chatty bubbles of animated conversation at the end of driveways, leaning against fences, their voices carrying around the cul-de-sac.

I used to watch them from my window, always wondering what they were talking about, never feeling like I belonged in those casual little groups. But today, something feels different. Maybe it's everything that's happened, and the realisation that I don't want to keep isolating myself. Maybe it's the fact that Mike has escaped, yet again travelling for work, and I've been left with the weight of indecision.

We had two days together. Two days between Nancy painting an ugly picture of Mike and him leaving for Spain. I said nothing. I walked around this house like a ghost, and didn't confront him at all.

Or maybe it's because I spy Henry with the group today. He hasn't contacted me since I left his apartment, and I know that's what I asked for, but today I could do with some friendliness. Some voices and chatter that isn't filled with dread and decisions. Could I really just walk out and join my neighbours? I never have before, not when they've been out in their numbers.

To hell with it, why not? It's not like I have anything else to lose at this point.

There's no need for a jacket: April brings with it a warm and welcome sunshine, so I slide my keys into my jeans pocket and make my way towards Patty and Henry down the street outside Anna's house. She's there, too, of course, as is a mixed-race lady with a small yippy dog at her heel, and that's when I notice *him*, Norman, and I instantly want to turn around and go home.

But Anna notices me approaching and calls out. 'Oh, Ruby! We were just talking about you.'

What the hell? Why would they be discussing me? Henry and Patty are gossiping about me with some neighbour I barely recognise and *him*.

Patty picks up the conversational baton. 'Yes, we were just telling Sadie here all about you and your books, the famous author of Blackwood Close.'

'I'm hardly famous, Patty.' My chest tightens and heat pinches at my cheeks. I can't even look in Henry's direction. Why in God's name did I come out to join them?

'Oh, please, your books are amazing. I just wish I could think up stories like you,' Anna says, giving me a knowing smile – she had promised to look me up before leaving Patty's book club. 'This is Sadie. I don't think you two have met.'

I give a weak smile, but Sadie honestly doesn't seem too interested in me or my books. I get the distinct impression she's here more for the neighbourhood gossip than to make new friends. The poised look on her face tells me if she could telepathically instruct her dog to piss on me, his tiny leg would be cocked against my ankle right now.

Still doing my utmost to not look at either of the men in the group – though for two very different reasons – and wishing I hadn't come and interrupted them all, I nervously attempt to engage.

'That's really kind of you to say, Anna, I'm glad you enjoyed them.'

'Well...' Anna draws out the word, ensuring she now has everyone's attention. 'I actually had an idea. Maybe we could have the next book club at your place, Ruby?'

The suggestion blindsides me. 'Oh, I–'

'What a great idea,' Patty chimes in, nodding enthusiastically. 'Book club at an actual author's house.'

Before I can think of a way to politely decline, a low deep voice breaks in. 'We could read one of yours.' I know who that voice belongs to without looking. *Weird* Norman.

My throat is raw at the thought of inviting him into my home. 'I mean, well, maybe, but it would depend on the date.'

'Ooh, that's an interesting idea,' Anna agrees with *him*, and then turns to me. 'We could pencil in a June date. Plenty of time, and gives everyone a chance to catch up with me on your books and lets you get organised.'

I force a smile, but my stomach twists. *Book club at my house.* With everything that's been happening, that's the *last* thing I need. But before I can protest further, or look to Henry with a plea for help, a figure emerging from the bleakness of the alleyway catches my eye. I realise then that I haven't walked through it since I was followed home. I watch intently now as a young lad, hoodie pulled up and hands shoved into his pockets, heads straight towards us. He stands on the edge, not saying hello or interacting, and no one really pays much attention to him. Except Norman, who I can't help but notice looks between me and the strange newcomer a couple of times before clearing his throat.

'Right, I best be off,' he mutters, nodding to the lad. 'Keep the WhatsApp group updated with dates.'

'Will do, Norman, catch you later,' Anna calls out.

The others all say goodbye to the man, too, even Sadie. Though her attention is then quickly turned to Henry and I wonder if he's the real reason she's out here chatting to her neighbours. I watch the weird pair fall into step together, walking away without so much as a word to one another.

'That's Billy,' Patty leans in and whispers. 'Norman's nephew. I was telling you about him.'

Though she didn't need to clarify it for me. I knew it was him by the way they looked at each other, by the way they look slightly alike and by his physique – the same one that's been looking out at me from the top window of the dark house.

'Strange young man,' Sadie offers, 'but he keeps himself to himself.'

I glance back towards Norman's house, but they're both gone now, like ghosts slipping back into their deathly shadows. My body shivers, and that old turn of phrase, someone just walked over my grave, couldn't feel more apt.

Patty pats my arm. 'You okay, love?'

'Yeah. Just a lot going on.' I nod, but still can't look in Henry's direction. If I do, everyone will know what we've done and how I feel. But then, someone already does, don't they?

'That's why hosting the book club will be good for you,' she continues.

Will it? All my neighbours in my space when it doesn't really feel like mine at all anymore, when I don't know who I can trust, when someone – possibly one of them – has already forced themselves into my house. But it's too late to back out now because they've all made the plans and, once again, I feel like something is happening around me that's beyond my control.

I regret joining them so much that I quickly make my excuses and turn to leave. I had thought that their comfort and friendship, that Henry's warm smile, would make me feel better, but it's had the complete opposite effect. Seeing Billy close-up like that, watching him and Norman walking down the street, has left me cold. I've never been able to put my finger on *why* I feel that way, but my gran's voice screams in my head once again, telling me to trust my instinct.

Just as I place the key in my front door, a hand touches my shoulder and I yelp out, swinging around with my fists clenched. To my surprise, it's Henry.

'Hey, you didn't say a word to me out there, Ruby.' He holds his hands up, knowing he's given me a fright.

I puff loudly. 'Right back at you.'

'I know, sorry, I felt a bit awkward when you joined us.'

'Charming.' But I fully understand.

'Weird, wasn't it, when all I wanted to do was put my arms around you.'

'Henry–'

'I know, I know, don't worry. I wouldn't do that in front of witnesses. You've told me you need time to figure things out and that's exactly what I'm giving you.'

Something about what he says causes a sharp inhale of breath. Because we already have witnesses, don't we? Henry needs to know about the note and so I tell him everything. Quickly and briefly, though, because I'm mindful of how busy the cul-de-sac is today, and who knows which of them we can trust.

'That's a bit freaky, Ruby, especially after your notebook and the back door.'

'No need to remind me. It's all I'm thinking of... as well as a lot of other shit.'

Henry reaches up to my face and his thumb caresses my cheek. 'Do you want to go to the police? I'll come with you, of course.'

I close my eyes and lean into his touch, and his entire hand cups my cheek warmly. I shake my head, knowing the police will blame my overactive imagination when I don't have any real proof.

'Well, I'm here if you change your mind,' he says, gently removing his hand and bending down to lightly kiss my cheek.

When I open my eyes again, my gaze is drawn to something just over Henry's shoulder. A hooded figure standing at the mouth of the alleyway, motionless, watching us.

'It's Billy,' I whisper.

Henry pulls back and frowns at me. 'What?'

I nod in the young man's direction, but as Henry turns around Billy bolts down the alleyway. My voice is full of panic as I repeat through gritted teeth that he was watching us, confident Henry will shrug it off and tell me I'm imagining things. But to my surprise, Henry tells me to stay put and legs it after the lad. He's gone just as fast and I'm left standing on my doorstep alone, glancing around the street to make sure no one else is watching, that they've all returned to their homes, to their own business.

It feels forever before Henry returns, only slightly panting from the chase. He's shaking his head as he walks up the path back to me and all I can do is stare at him, wide-eyed and waiting.

'No one's there,' he says when he reaches me.

'What do you mean? You saw him, Billy, you saw—'

'I saw the figure of someone, but by the time I got to the alleyway, whoever it was, was gone.'

'It was Billy,' I reiterate with an edge to the man's name, 'and I don't understand. When you got through the alleyway you should have at least seen him running up the street.'

Henry shakes his head. 'The street was empty. No one was there. Billy or otherwise.'

I frown, pausing to recall the last five minutes, trying to decipher the memory that's already becoming hazy... No, no it's not, someone *was* stood there watching us, watching Henry stroke and kiss my cheek. It was a hooded man, the same hoodie I saw Billy wearing only moments before when he walked away with his uncle.

'Norman,' I squeal. 'We should knock on Norman's door and confront him.'

'About what?' Henry's releases a loud puff of air.

'About us being watched.'

'You saw someone pause at the alleyway, being nosey and looking over at a couple on their doorstep, that's all, Ruby–'

'We're not a couple.'

He rolls his eyes. 'You know what I mean. That alleyway is used by loads of people, not just us lot who live on this street. It's a shortcut to the high street.'

And there it is, another person in my life subtly alluding to my overactive imagination. But I did see Billy... well *someone*. I did see *someone* watching us and I don't believe it was just a nosey passer-by. Sure, they would glance over, but they wouldn't stop and face us full on. No, I am not imagining this.

Something changes about Henry's face, his expression softens, as if he knows how he's just made me feel – like Mike would.

'Let's knock at Norman's.' He backtracks unexpectedly.

'But you don't believe me.'

'I said *I* didn't see his nephew, but you believe you did and that's all that matters. I'm sorry, I should have said that straight away.' He strokes my arm. 'Look, Norman's a nice guy, let's go knock together and see what's what, yeah?'

Now I feel like a total idiot. Knocking on my weird neighbour's door to accuse his nephew of watching me in public. But is it really just that? Wouldn't it also mean that his nephew's leaving me icky notes, stealing my things and entering my house? How can I even prove that to Norman? While Henry peers at me, waiting, and the unanswered questions spin around my frazzled brain, my phone vibrates in my back pocket. It jolts me out of my tangled mess of thoughts like a lifeline, saving me.

'Sorry, Henry, hold that thought.' I reach for my phone.

Stef. A flicker of relief stirs inside me. A small, fleeting moment of lightness and familiarity and friendship, pulling me away from... what is this? Preparing to rampage round to my neighbour's house, making wild accusations with the man I cheated on my partner with. I'm getting out of hand. I open her message.

Hey, can you come over? It's important.

The lightness vanishes, and I read it again, a headache brewing.

'Everything okay?' Henry asks when I say nothing.

I shrug, reading the message a final time before slipping the phone back into my pocket.

I look up at Henry. 'It's Stef. I have to go.'

'Is she okay? Do you need me to come with you?'

'No, but thank you. Girl stuff.'

I'm not sure why I phrase it like that. Perhaps I think it will make him drop it, leave me be so I can get to Stef, because she isn't the dramatic type. She doesn't throw words like *important* around, all cryptic, if it doesn't mean something. If she says it's important, then it is.

'Do you need me to drive you?' he asks.

I shake the keys I've been holding since trying to get inside my home. If only I hadn't joined the gossiping crowd for a bit of neighbourly chit-chat.

'Maybe I can pop over to Norman's on my own then.'

I chew the inside of my lip, unsure of what to say. I mean, a few minutes ago Henry made it seem as if I had him running after a complete stranger who then disappeared into a puff of magic once they'd got through the alleyway.

'Look, Henry, let's just leave it–'

'Are you sure? I don't mind. Norman is all right, I've spoken to him a few times.'

But I've already taken off, walking towards my car parked at the side of the house, because in comparison to my friend needing me, this isn't important anymore.

'It's fine, really, I was probably imagining things. Thanks. Speak later,' I call over my shoulder and jump in the car.

I start the engine and watch Henry walking away, down my path and right onto the street towards his own home. I hope that's where he does go, and not to Norman's house. I can only imagine how my accusations would sound to my weird neighbour, and the thought of him and the man I... the man I'm attracted to, laughing at me and dismissing what I believe I saw, makes my stomach flip.

Before I drive off, I reach for my phone again and reply to Stef, telling her I'm on my way. I then throw Billy and Henry and Norman to the back of my mind as I pull out of the cul-de-sac, not even glancing around to see if I can spot anyone. I don't want them dominating my thoughts, not when my friend clearly needs me.

The drive to Stef's passed in a blur, and I'm already outside her house and turning off the engine. A niggling worry kept creeping in throughout the journey, though, ignoring all my efforts to push it away. I hope everyone is okay, Hunter and Kelly, and I pray Stef's just had a row with her wife and needs a shoulder to cry on. Well, a shoulder to rant on is more Stef's style.

As I walk up the pathway, the door opens almost immediately. Stef looks awful. Baggy joggers, an oversized jumper and her braids messily pulled up on the top of her head. This may well be how she likes to lounge at home these days, but it's so far from the well-kept friend I've come to know over the years.

'Hey,' she says, her voice as exhausted as she looks. 'Come in.'

She steps aside, and I walk in, my heart beating slightly faster now. I can feel it. The *wrongness* of this moment because Stef isn't herself. She doesn't make a joke about her chilled-out attire, or tell me to make myself at home. The house isn't alive with the playful noise of Hunter, or Kelly in the kitchen making a cuppa. Stef's too quiet – the house is too quiet.

In the kitchen, I turn to Stef. 'Where's Hunter? And Kelly?'

'At her mum's house.'

That's all she gives. Then she walks past me and busies herself with the kettle, mugs, teabags. I want to tell her to stop, to take over, but I can see she needs something to do, something to keep her body busy. That's who she is, the energiser bunny, always on the go. But none of this is energetic today; it's routine. Motions.

I sit down at the dining table. The silence is thick, pressing itself against my skin, and I bite at the skin around my nails until Stef finally lowers herself into the chair across from me.

'I don't know how to say this,' she murmurs.

I feel for my friend, knowing this is the moment she has to tell me why Kelly's left her. Why their marriage has fallen apart. I reach for my tea, just to have something else to do with my hands. Stef looks up at me, and for the first time since I walked in, I see it – the grief, sitting heavy in her eyes, pushing her shoulders down.

'Kelly lost the baby.'

Her words knock the air right out of me. It's not what I had expected at all, and for a second, I don't react. I don't speak. My brain won't process any words properly, and the irony of that smacks me across the face. Stef didn't ask me to come just to sit here like a dummy.

'I'm so, so sorry,' I quickly rush out the words, then reach across the table, grab her hand and tightly squeeze it. What else do I say?

Stef lets out a shaky breath before she starts speaking. 'It happened two nights ago. Kelly just started bleeding. Why is it always during the night, when everything is calm and quiet and you're happily lying in bed together, then you get shocked right out of your existence?' she asks, but doesn't wait – or really want – an answer. 'We went to A&E, but there was nothing they could do. There was nothing I could do. And I call myself a paramedic.'

'Oh, Stef, no, don't do that. You can't blame yourself.'

She shakes her head. 'I didn't even cry at first. I just... I kept thinking I'd wake up and it wouldn't be real. That it was some horrible mistake.' Her voice cracks and she lets out a small, broken laugh to cover it. 'But it is real. It's so fucking real and I don't know how to deal with this pain.'

Tears sting my eyes. 'Why didn't you call me? Or tell me to come round sooner?'

'Because you have enough going on with losing your gran. You don't need my grief, too.' She squeezes my hand back. 'And I don't know, Rubes, I just didn't want to hear one more person tell me that everything's gonna be okay. Because it's not okay.'

'I would never–'

'I know. I know.' She lets go of my hand and wipes the silent tears, so I take a minute to do the same. 'That's why I texted you today. Kelly took Hunter to her mum's because he doesn't understand what's going on and she can help look after him. She's distraught and I'm not sure how I'm supposed to comfort her right now. Then the house was so bloody silent, and I knew that if I asked you to come, you would, and that you wouldn't try to say all the right things – you'd just be here.'

And she's right, I have no idea what to say or even what the right thing to say would be. I can't begin to imagine what she's going through. Stef has spent her whole career dealing with emergencies – has probably gone to many houses at the very moment women are losing their babies – held people's hands as they've taken their last breaths. She's built for chaos and devastation.

But nothing – nothing – prepared her for this. For her own chaos and devastation. So I say nothing. I just sit with her, in the silence of her kitchen, which doesn't feel so lonely when it's shared with someone you love, and I join Stef in her grief.

CHAPTER THIRTY-NINE

You. You were meant to be different, Ruby.

I see the way you check the doors now, and the windows, you double-check everything. Pressing your fingers against the locks, as if you would know whether they've been tampered with. You think you're being careful, doing everything right, but the truth is, it's too late for any of that. I'm ahead of you now.

You noticed when your notebook was gone, filled with all your stories and hopes and secrets, but it was my *choice* to return it. To return it alone, without your specially engraved pen because that's mine now. Your treasures have become mine. But you still don't *understand.* Did you think it was a trick, or a game? Did you even check it properly? The words I left for you.

No, Ruby, you didn't and it's pissed me off. *You've* pissed me off. I kept the pen, not to be mean to you, please understand that, but because I know it matters to you. And you matter to me. But that was before, before you–

No, I can't even say it. I get so angry.

I've stood in your room while you sleep, listening to your breath, watching over you when no one else would, to make sure you haven't felt lonely. I've touched your things, held them close and breathed you in. I've stood where you've stood and lain where you've lain.

You sleep so still, Ruby, so quiet, so different from the frantic and irrational person you've become when you're awake. I could have whispered your name, just to see what you'd do, but I didn't. I let you rest, just watching over you. I've noticed your vulnerable grip around the golf club and I've worried about you. What must go through that mind of yours to think you'd need it? I've followed you in the dark, making sure nothing happened to you because I've *protected* you. I'll always protect you.

At least, that's what I *used* to do.

Because how do you repay me, Ruby? Just look at what you've done. You've thrown it all back in my face by continually making bad choices, straying from the correct path, trusting the wrong people. You were supposed to be different, but you've allowed yourself to be distracted so much that now your mind is clouded and your judgement is weak. You look in the mirror but don't see what I see – someone lost, someone who needs guidance. And you *do* need guidance, don't you, Ruby? You don't know what's best for you. But I do. Why can't you see that?

I needed it to go right for me this time, not like it did with *her*. Because, Ruby, you're not my first. There was one I loved before you. And so I've tried to be patient with you, I really have, I've tried to give you the space and distance you need. I wanted to let you come to the truth on your own. But you're too far gone, and I can see that's been my mistake because I've grown tired of it. Tired of waiting and being patient. Tired of you just not understanding, not making good decisions. It's disappointing and frustrating, and for the first time, I'm really not sure what to do next with you.

I can't just keep watching, Ruby.

Maybe it's time for me to step out of the shadows.

CHAPTER FORTY

Ashes to ashes, dust to dust. Ashes to ashes, dust to dust.

That part of the ceremony replays in my mind. Over and over again. The priest's words, the thundering soil hitting Gran's coffin, are like a private sermon on repeat. The others have all left. I told Mike to go ahead without me, to attend the wake at the care home on my behalf, that I'd follow on shortly.

I'm not sure if I will, and I'm not sure if he believed me, because he hesitated, brows furrowing, but didn't argue. He just gave me a small nod, squeezed my arm and walked away, leaving me here. Alone. I didn't want him to stay with me, or even touch me, and I haven't looked him fully in the eyes since Nancy. But I also haven't confronted him, still, and although I hate myself for it, I knew I had to get through today first. Say goodbye to Gran.

I didn't speak to Henry either. He hovered in the distance of the cemetery, just watching, and gave a small smile when he saw me notice him. It was kind of him to come, for me, to pay his respects to a woman he never even met. But I don't have the energy to confront him either right now.

So it's just me and the fresh mound of earth, the raw wound

of a burial. I watched as the men covered the opening with soil once everyone had gone. They were waiting for me to leave, too, but I said they could go ahead with me here. Part of me needed to see it, the disturbed, uneven ground where Gran is buried underneath.

But that's not the thing that's kept me here, rooted to the spot. No. It's the sunshine on my face as I stand here waiting for a sign. From her, or from my mum, or from myself? I don't know, but I need a sign because I need answers. The weight of the day is pressing down on me, but it's not just the grief, it's everything.

It's waking up this morning, avoiding Mike and quietly getting ready for my final goodbye to Gran. It's reaching for my rainbow-coloured scarf that she gifted me many birthdays ago, knowing I didn't need it on this glorious sunny May afternoon, but wanting it as a piece of her with me. It's the feeling of dread that knocked me down when it wasn't hanging on the coat stand. Not misplaced. Not forgotten or hung up in the wrong place. Gone. Taken.

Someone has been inside my home. Again.

Since the first time, when my notebook vanished only to be later returned, part of me has been trying to rationalise it all. Not going to the police, or confiding in Mike – back when I wanted to confide in him, that is – because I knew what they'd say. I knew it would be put down to my imagination, so I accepted it and tried to believe it was just that. My own creativity biting me on the arse. But this, Gran's gift to me, a scarf that only sits in one place by the front door, this confirms it. I am *not* imagining things. This is not my paranoia.

I exhale slowly, focusing on the grave again. My mind racing. I've never felt so numb, and it's not due to the sadness – this is not a new feeling. I have lain on the floor and cried with my grief. But there's more – this is all too much on top of losing

Gran, on top of the world demanding everyone pick themselves up while they're mourning, and carry on.

This is Nancy confessing she's always known Mike has had a darker side to him. This is me now looking at him in a different way. This is Stef losing her unborn baby and feeling lost. This is me cheating with another man. This is the note and my possessions going missing; this is knowing someone is watching me.

It's too much for anyone to handle. Then to also add—

I close my eyes, physically turn my head away from my own thoughts. If only it were that easy to escape them. I wrap my arms tighter around myself, shivering, not from any cold wind – there's actually a soft warmth in the air today – but from the sheer weight of everything that's happened lately. From a solitary writer with a boring life to a tangled mess of a person who hasn't switched on her laptop in weeks, and who can't be sure if she can trust the man she's sharing a bed with.

I stare at Gran's grave, wishing she were here to tell me what to do, and wishing I wasn't so goddamn alone. Then, as if they knew there hasn't been a moment I needed them more, I hear them softly approach from behind me. Their footsteps slow, but I don't turn around, I don't move until I feel the warmth of their arms slipping through mine. One on each side of me. Nancy and Stef.

For a long while, none of us speak. We just stand there, with the sun on our faces at the foot of Gran's resting place, our arms linking as we hold each other up from the weight of everything trying to drag us down.

Stef is the first to break the silence. 'Your gran was a wickedly amazing woman, and we'll all miss her.'

'Yeah.' I nod, swallowing hard.

Nancy squeezes in tighter. 'And we're here for you. No matter what.'

I let out a slow, shaky sigh, staring down at the ground. Neither of my friends know what's been going on, and I wonder if perhaps I should have reached out to them ages ago. If they knew how much I've kept from them, would they still be standing here?

Yes, Ruby, for crying out loud, and I remember the promise I made to myself, and to Gran. Perhaps this is exactly the sign I was hoping for, and this is not the time to be like Mum; this is the time to reach out and ask for help.

'I think I'm pregnant.' The words spill out before I can stop them. Before I can second-guess if I should say them.

Both Nancy's and Stef's arms stiffen, pulling us all tighter together, but neither one of them says anything. The tears roll down my face then, as I turn to Stef with a new wave of guilt crashing against me.

'Stef, I'm sorry,' I whisper. 'I shouldn't have just blurted it out like that. Not after–'

'Hey,' Stef interrupts softly, turning to face me fully. 'Don't. It's okay.' She pulls me into a hug, holding me tight, and I drag Nancy in to join us. I sink into their warmth, their steadiness, and then pull back to wipe the tears away.

'And I'm sorry to you, too,' I say to Nancy.

'For what?'

'For making you think that I wouldn't have believed you.'

It hits me then, the anger that's been simmering under the surface of my grief and the fear of being alone. All this time, Nancy has been just as scared as I have been about not being believed.

My breathing speeds up a notch as I glower between my two friends. 'How could he have done this? Mike... how dare he? I could just... I could just *kill* him. Nancy, I am so sorry.'

'You've got nothing to be sorry about. I'm the one who's sorry for letting you stay with a man like that,' Nancy says, with a glimmer of rage of her own. 'But why are you still there? Just get away from him and don't ever think about him again.'

Why am I still in the house with him? It's a bloody good question. Again, I've let this idea of being alone, of not being safe by myself, rule how I live. I've assumed Mike wants exactly what I want – a family – but is that really what I want *with him*? Have I let this fear of mine keep me locked away, living a lie?

When I think of the Mike that Nancy has shown me, though it was six years ago, it makes me wonder if that's who he's been all along. When he goes out with his brother, or his mates, or even while he's working in Spain. Has he always been lying to me? Perhaps I've just seen the man I've *wanted* to see, and not the one he really is.

'Neither of you two are to blame.' Stef's voice is solid and resolute. 'Nancy told me everything just before your gran's funeral, and I never want to hear you two saying sorry about this again. That responsibility lies with *Mike*.'

She says his name with such spite, like he's a poison to be watchful of. I guess he is, I was just too blind to see it.

'I haven't taken a test yet.' The words leave my mouth in a near-whisper, almost embarrassed to admit it. 'I just *feel* it. I'm never late.'

'Then we'll go get one.' Stef says it so simply, so matter-of-fact, like it's nothing more than a grocery item to tick off the list.

Nancy nods. 'And a bottle of wine.'

'Wine?'

'For after,' she says, giving me a pointed look. 'Because a baby with Mike... we may all want to drown our sorrows.'

Henry's face flashes in front of me but, of course, my friends know nothing about him. There's no time to protest, or argue or hesitate, as Stef and Nancy lead me from the cemetery and out to the street before I can stop them. I hear them making plans, such as where the nearest shop is and the fact that Nancy's house is the closest to where we are. My feet move on autopilot. I'm hearing them speak but not really listening, dazed – but for once, not in the weak and mild manner I normally feel.

We don't linger in the shop, and I don't remember much of anything. One second we're outside, and the next we're in Nancy's house, the door shut behind us, the test clutched tightly in my hand like a secret I don't want to let go of. The three of us sit huddled in Nancy's living room, the wine glasses already half full on the coffee table. The bottle sits between them like an offering, but I haven't taken a sip. My hands curl around the stem of my glass, but I don't bring it to my lips, it's just to give my fingers something to do.

Nancy watches me expectantly. 'We know there's something else. There's more going on, so spill.'

I take a deep breath, because there's no point in hiding anything anymore. The slow creep of resentment has pulled up a chair and refuses to leave. I tell them everything. About Henry, about the note, about someone watching me and being in my house, the scarf, the notebook and pen and the back door being left unlocked. Nancy's eyes widen with every new revelation and Stef rubs her forehead, like she's trying to process it all. When I finally finish, there's a long silence.

'You need to go to the police,' Nancy suddenly blurts out.

I shake my head. 'What's the point?'

'This isn't just *one* thing going missing now, it's multiple things. Someone is coming into your house, Ruby. There could be fingerprints on your notebook– Wait, you didn't mention the pen being returned... Was it just the book?'

'Yes.'

'That's strange–'

'The police will just give me a crime reference number thingy and tell me there's nothing they can do,' I continue. 'Or worse, they'll tell me I'm overreacting.'

Nancy's jaw tightens. 'Mike's been making you think that for years. That doesn't mean it's true.'

Stef is quiet, staring down at her hands, before she finally speaks. 'Rubes...' She hesitates. 'We talked about this a few months ago, in the café, remember? About how your worst fear was someone breaking in, violating your space.' She meets my gaze. 'Could you... could you be misplacing things? Could this be–'

'Stef!' Nancy warns.

'No, I'm not saying she's making it up,' Stef rushes to explain. 'I'm saying... could it be her mind playing tricks? Stress, grief, everything happening at once?' She looks at me again, almost pleading now. 'It just... it feels like a lot, doesn't it?'

The sting of her words makes me sink further back into the sofa. I almost want to neck that glass of wine now. Although, at the same time, I understand why she's asking. I *have* been in my own head too much lately, carrying too much alone. But I won't deny it any longer, and I won't be made to feel like I'm making everything up. I may well be a storyteller, but this is no fantasy world with fake characters, this is my life.

'Yes, Stef, it is a lot,' I agree and reach for the pregnancy test box. 'So maybe I should find out for sure if I'm about to add to this personal whirlwind.'

My friends exchange glances, then both nod as I stand and turn towards the bathroom. Behind me, I hear the clink of wine glasses as they fill them both back up, their voices dropping into a hushed murmur, and I know they're whispering about me. Worrying about me, maybe, hopefully. But I close them off, shutting the door behind me and stare at my reflection in the bathroom mirror. I look pale, stretched thin, a woman who barely recognises herself anymore.

This isn't how it was supposed to happen. All those times of hoping, of wanting, of taking tests in secret, peeking at the results and always bracing for disappointment. Now I already know because I can feel it, deep down, in my gut. Maybe it's this, this difference happening to my body is what's forcing the change to my mind and attitude, too. Finally allowing the anger to knock through the floodgates of the weak character I *have* been playing in my own life story. Seeing past Mike and the quiet, secluded women he's made me become. Refusing to crumble because a coward is sending me cryptic notes and trying to scare me. Not anymore, I won't allow it.

Still, I go through the motions of taking the test. While I wait, I give all my overwhelming emotions a seat at this table, and accept the crushing weight of reality. Because for so long, I've wanted this. A family. A baby. A future. I just never in my wildest dreams pictured it the way it's playing out. Mike and Henry, and the fact I lay with them both within a twenty-four-hour time frame. I squeeze my eyes shut. *Who the hell have I become?*

There's a knock at the door, pulling me back to life, and Nancy's voice travels through. 'You okay in there?'

I inhale deeply and glance down at the test, the result clear in its little window.

No.

No, I'm not okay.

CHAPTER FORTY-ONE

The walk home from Nancy's house is longer than I remember. But I needed it. I don't take the shortcut from the high street that would lead me through the alleyway, of course. Rather, I stick to the roads, weaving through the terraced streets and letting the last of the day's sunshine hit my face. The sky is a hazy hue of peach and lilac, the kind of softness that belongs to the summer, not to grief. It doesn't match the day. It doesn't match me.

I should have gone to the wake, really, because that's the done thing after funerals. People gather, they share stories, they eat bland sandwiches and sip bad coffee or flat beer, trying to take comfort in each other's presence. But I couldn't do it, and Gran wouldn't hold it against me. I think she'd quite like this new side of me, the side who couldn't give a rat's arse what other people think and what the *done* thing is. I haven't even spoken to Mike. I don't know if he's home yet, or if he's still waiting for me at the wake, wondering where the hell I am.

And now, inching closer to my claustrophobic home, I realise it's time to make some tough decisions. It's time to tell Mike I know what he did to Nancy, and it's even time to call the police. They would never accuse me of having an overactive imagination with everything that's actually happened.

But I'm distracted as I slow to a stop outside Henry's apartment building when I spot him sitting on the front step. With his long legs stretched out in front of him, arms resting lazily over his knees, he looks up and I watch his expression change the moment he sees me. It's warm, expectant, and I wonder, briefly, if he's been sat here waiting for me. Just a few weeks ago that would have made my heart race, and maybe it still does a little, because he is perfect. But things aren't the same.

Henry pushes himself up, brushing his hands over his trousers. 'Hey, you.'

'Hey.'

I want to say more, so much more, but I can't just blurt it out here on the street. So instead there's a moment of quiet. It's heavy and complicated. Does he feel it, too?

'Thanks for coming to the funeral.' I quickly fill the silence before he can.

Henry shrugs. 'Of course. I wanted to be there. For you.'

I should tell him, shouldn't I? Yes, right here on that street, because didn't I just say to myself I don't care what other people think.

Henry, I'm pregnant. But I slept with my long-term partner the day before my one-night stand with you, so the baby could well be yours, or it could belong to Mike. The man I've recently discovered pushed himself on my best friend, who doesn't like to hear the word no from me, and who could have treated countless other women in the same way.

A heavy cloud hangs over me and Henry, and we both scramble to speak. Words fall from our mouths at the same time and we interrupt each other so nothing is clear. He laughs and I tell him to go first.

'I, uh, was just going to say I lost my keys.' He scratches the back of his head. 'That's why I'm sat here looking quite the loser. I'm locked out.'

'Oh no.' *So he wasn't waiting for me. Of course not, Ruby.* 'Can't one of your neighbours buzz you in?'

'Well, yeah, but that would only get me into the building. I don't have a spare key for my apartment on me.'

He laughs again, in that warm way he does, not taking the piss out of me but just being... *nice.* I on the other hand feel foolish.

'Anyway,' Henry continues. 'Norman's on his way over to help me.'

Norman. The mere mention of that man's name makes my skin crawl, and I don't want to be here when he arrives. Although I haven't made a list of all the people who could be preying on me, my weird neighbour would probably be at the top of it.

I tuck the wind-swept hair behind my ear and step back. 'I'm sorry, Henry, I can't stick around.'

His brow furrows slightly. 'I did notice a car parked outside your place. It looked like one of the women from the funeral. Is that who's stealing you away from me in my hour of need?'

I rack my brain. Who on earth could he mean? I have no idea, but I seize the excuse and apologise again for leaving him stranded on his doorstep.

'Yeah sure, no problem, Ruby. Of course, you have to go.'

Henry trips over his words, and I feel sorry for him, I do, but I can't stay and be faced with that creepy man. Why does no one else seem to feel that way in his company? I race round the corner, trying to recall the other women who were at Gran's funeral earlier, but remembering no one in particular.

Inhaling deeply, I drop the speed of my steps as my house comes into view. I force myself to shake off the paranoia, because if this was anything sinister, the unexpected guest wouldn't park up outside my house. And that's when I see her – Lesley – sitting in the driver's seat of a red Ford Focus. She smiles as soon as our eyes meet, but doesn't get out of the car. Instead, she discreetly nods her head to the left, instructing me to get in the passenger's side.

I hesitate, because what the actual fuck? Have I misjudged everything recently, and actually it's Lesley who's been following me, watching me, sending me unnerving messages? No, of course not: this is my gran's nurse, not some stranger lurking in the shadows. I can trust her. Although this seems very cloak and dagger, and I'm not sure I have the capacity to deal with anything else. But this obviously has to do with Gran and I can't ignore that. So I jump in the car as per Lesley's non-verbal command.

'Hi, Ruby,' she greets me as soon as the door shuts behind me. 'Sorry for the lack of professionalism. I took your address from your gran's next-of-kin forms.'

'It's fine, but is everything okay?'

She nods, but I catch her looking out the windows, around the street. She's more on edge than me. 'I left the wake while Mike was still there, hoping to find you here, Ruby. But I'm not sure how much time we have until he comes back. So I better make this quick.'

'Mike?' I repeat, stunned. Why would Gran's nurse be worrying about Mike?

She doesn't answer, but she swivels in her seat and grabs a white envelope from the backseat, my name written on the front just visible. A gasp shudders from my mouth as I remember the white piece of paper dropped through my letter box not so long ago. Is this all connected?

'Lesley, please explain what's going on,' I stutter.

'Sorry, Ruby,' she says as she hands me the envelope. 'But

this is from your gran. I wanted to give it to you at the funeral, but couldn't get you alone and then you didn't come back to the care home with everyone else.'

I take it from her, and see now that it is in fact Gran's handwriting scrawled across it. *Ruby,* that's all it says. But that doesn't explain Mike–

'I found this in one of her drawers, after she passed on,' Lesley continues and my head spins. 'There was a piece of paper attached to it with a paperclip.'

She pulls that from her coat pocket now and I see my own handwriting staring back at me. My number. My note to Lesley. The one I had scribbled down weeks and weeks ago during a visit with Gran. I forgot I had asked her to pass it along to the nurse, asking for her help so perhaps I could communicate with Gran more. Why hadn't Gran given it to Lesley? She put it on this envelope deliberately so the nurse would hand-deliver it to me after her death? My gran wasn't one to beat about the bush, or hide away from what she felt, so what could she have written in here that she couldn't tell me when she was alive?

'Have you read it?' I ask.

She shakes her head firmly, assuring me she wouldn't and that it's still sealed. But there's a sadness in her eyes that unsettles me.

'Why are you giving me this in your car, Lesley? Why are you worried about Mike coming home and catching us talking?'

Her eyes dart from left to right again, and she's clearly uncomfortable. 'When Elsie deteriorated and you came to sit with her, I wanted to talk to you before you left. You know, go through some things and discuss any plans. What you'd want us to do with her belongings, stuff like that.'

Though the questions and the rage soar through my body, I don't interrupt her. I need to hear every single word she has to say.

'But I bumped into Mike, in the common room, and he was very insistent that you two were leaving and that you weren't to be bothered with trivial things right now. And then about Elsie's belongings... he told me to get rid of anything that wasn't *valuable*–'

'He said what?' I can't help myself.

Lesley nods. 'I had hoped that he didn't say it to be cruel, but more that he was trying to spare you any more pain, trying to help. But then when he came by the care home last week, to see if we did have anything "valuable" of Elsie's... Well, something just didn't sit right with me. So I wanted to come give you this in person. Directly.'

'That wasn't his place to decide. They are *my* gran's possessions.'

'I know, Ruby, I know,' she says quietly. 'And all of Elsie's things have been boxed up and waiting for you to collect or discard or whatever you choose as her next of kin. It's just, the more I thought of it, of what he said, and his emphasis on the word valuable, I didn't like it.'

'Thank you,' is all I say, because my mouth has gone dry.

How could Mike tell them to throw away my gran's things, without consulting me first. And then something else Lesley said hits me.

'Mike couldn't have come by last week, he was in Spain, working. Unless he came before or–'

'It was last Wednesday.'

I shake my head. 'Oh, no, it couldn't have been, I'm afraid you have that wrong, he was in Spain from Tuesday and didn't get home until last Friday afternoon.'

Lesley grimaces, then pulls her lips in a taut line. If she's wrong about that, perhaps she's wrong about what Mike said to her. About Gran's things. He asked her to put them aside is all, until I could come and deal with it all.

'I'm not wrong, Ruby. My shift last week was Wednesday to Saturday, and Mike came just after I'd started for the day.'

She doesn't grasp the importance of what she's saying to me. If Mike wasn't in Spain last week, like he'd told me, then where the hell was he?

Lesley continues anyway, as if she isn't dropping grenades into my life. 'It's when I was packing up Elsie's belongings that I found that envelope. The note on it, addressed to me, from you, felt like a sign. It felt important, and I couldn't just leave it packed away in boxes that you may well never come for.'

My stomach drops and I just sit there, blinking at her as my mind scrambles to make sense of it. But no matter how I spin it, it's just not right. Mike told Lesley to get rid of everything that wasn't valuable. What exactly wasn't valuable in his eyes? Does he care that little for me that he wouldn't see a problem with this? Was he trying to erase Gran and her memories from my life because he didn't want to deal with my grief again?

Lesley reaches out and touches my hand gently. 'I'm sorry, Ruby, I really do have to get back to the care home.'

I thank her again, nodding as she says goodbye and sorry and gives her condolences a final time. Once I'm out of the car and on the pavement in front of my house, I don't move. Motionless, I watch as Lesley switches on the engine and drives out of the cul-de-sac. I wait for the sadness and fear to wash over me, as it always does. Except this time it doesn't, because my head is spinning with such anger, such fury, I feel as if I could explode.

Whatever it is that Gran wants to say, this letter signifies so much more than just her last words to me. It's my missing things, the note, the break-in, the truths I'm discovering about Mike. It's one burning question demanding an answer.

Who the hell am I living with?

272

CHAPTER FORTY-TWO

I'm still in the same spot, debating if I should go in the house and hunt down Mike's passport. Won't it have been stamped each time he entered Spain? It could disprove Lesley's accusation... but I don't even know if that's a thing now, because it's been so long since I travelled abroad. There has to be some kind of paper trail for his work trips. Boarding passes? No, those don't *have* to be printed anymore. Receipts for hotels and restaurants? He'll have a work credit card for those expenses, and I don't know what their system is, but it's probably all calculated online now too. Perhaps I could...

No, snooping through his phone has always been something I've vowed never to do to Mike. To any partner, in fact, because it smears all trust in a relationship. But what trust do we have at all right now? I should just pack my bag and leave. After everything Nancy has told me, I have no reason to stay here with him. Instinctively, my hand rests on my stomach, but before I have a moment to make the right decision, footsteps echo across the pavement. I look up to my right and see him. Mike. His pace is brisk, purposeful, and when he sees me, his expression hardens.

'There you are.' His voice is sharp, laced with irritation. 'Jesus, Ruby. You just left me there? At the wake? With a bunch of old people talking about your gran?'

My fists clench at his tone, the way he says it, as if it was a burden to be there at all. As if he did *me* some great favour by attending. The fury that has been simmering beneath the surface all day rises, ready to boil over.

'I told you to go ahead. I needed time alone.' My voice is tight, controlled, but there's a bitterness underneath it. This is Mike, but I have no idea who he really is.

'Oh, come off it. *Go ahead.* You never bloody showed at all and now you're here outside the house as if you're waiting for someone. What about me?'

I turn, face him full on, my teeth gritted. 'It's always about you, isn't it, Mike?'

He throws his hands up in the air. 'What is wrong with you, woman? I'm being so patient but you've been acting weird for weeks. And now, it's like you're just avoiding me. Disappearing. Keeping secrets–'

'Keeping secrets? Oh, that's bloody rich coming from you.'

Mike's face flickers with something – annoyance, defensiveness, I can't be sure – but he readjusts his mask quickly.

'What the hell is that supposed to mean?'

I don't answer. I can't do this out here, not where the entire street can witness it. They'll be typing out WhatsApp messages to each other in seconds. Without another word, I walk up the path to our house. After unlocking the front door, I throw a look over my shoulder to Mike.

'Come inside.'

For a brief moment, I think he won't follow. That he'll turn on his heel and walk away. But then I hear him huff, hear his boots on the gravel, and I step inside. The hallway feels like it's shrunk, thick and suffocating, so I move into the living room, drop my handbag to the floor and spin to face Mike.

'Where do I start?' My voice trembles, but not from fear. From sheer rage. 'Maybe with Spain? Or Nancy? Or the fact that you tried to get rid of Gran's things before I even had a chance to sort through them myself?'

Mike exhales sharply, shaking his head. 'Oh, for fuck's sake, Ruby. You're spiralling.'

'*Spiralling?*' I let out a sharp laugh. 'You lied, Mike. You told me you were in Spain last week for work, except you weren't, were you? So, where were you?'

His jaw clenches, but he doesn't answer me. He doesn't deny it or admit it, he just stares at me with a look of pure annoyance. He doesn't like what I'm saying or that I'm confronting him. But I really don't care; his silence only pushes me on.

'And Nancy... Did you *really* think that she'd never tell me what you did to her?'

A slight twitch to his lips. But it feels more like smugness now than irritation. Is he pleased that I've found out?

'I didn't do anything to your friend,' he growls. 'She wanted me. She'd been flirting with me all night then changed her mind when the time came. Like so many of you.'

It's Mike's voice, I hear it so clearly now, the venom in the way he speaks. Yet, it's nothing new to my ears. I've heard him like this – towards me, towards other people – but I never recognised it before.

'And Spain?' I ask again.

He puffs loudly, moves further into the living room, but I stand my ground. 'There's never been any Spain, Ruby.'

It's a punch straight to the gut. 'What do you mean?'

Mike rolls his eyes, perches on the sofa with his legs spread open, and folds his arms across his chest. 'My company never asked me to work in their Spanish office, Ruby.'

'You were fired?'

At least he has the courtesy to look at me now.

'Nope, I wasn't fired. I've been working from home as normal... just not *this* home.'

He must see the confusion written all over my face because he stands up again, so we're eye to eye, and takes a deep breath.

'I wasn't going to be with you forever,' he says with a cruel, casual shrug. 'I met someone else, and I guess I wanted to test the waters with her before leaving you and this place. So, I made up the Spain trips to give me some time with her, and you lapped it up. Really, I was surprised how easy it was to live a double life.'

I think back to everything that's happened over the last four months. Everything that's changed in my life is because Mike got promoted and started travelling, leaving me alone. Except he was never in another country.

'All those delayed flights, tired from travelling, and having no reception in the warehouse to call me... it was all lies?' The lump in my throat chokes me.

Mike looks away, not out of shame but as if he's bored. Bored of this conversation. Bored of me. But I continue anyway.

'And this other woman... you love her?'

He rolls his head side to side, the way you do when you have a pain in your neck, and sighs heavily at me again. 'It's not about love, Ruby. But this... us, it hasn't been working for me. Not for a while now—'

'But we were trying for a baby, Mike. Why would you do that if you knew... if you knew deep down that you never planned on staying with me?'

He barks a laugh so harsh, so unexpected, I flinch. '*You* wanted a family, Ruby, I never said I did. Then when you started banging on about us getting tested, that was it for me, we were dead in the water.'

'No, Mike. What are you talking about? You're lying again. We moved into this house and said we were ready to–'

'When did I say that? Did you ever hear those words come out of my mouth?'

He stops then and glares at me with dark, thundery eyes – darker than I've ever seen before – like he's possessed. I'm speechless for a moment, memories whirling around my mind, because he did say he wanted those things. He told me he loved me, hundreds of times since we've been together, and he did say he wanted a baby with me. He did say he wanted this to be our family home...

Didn't he?

I step closer, fists trembling at my sides and scream, 'You absolute bastard.'

Mike barely flinches. He looks at me the way someone might look at a pathetic stray dog.

'You see, Ruby, I didn't. I never fucking said those actual words to you. I've never wanted a fucking baby.'

'I'm pregnant.' The words fall from my mouth like shattered glass.

Silence crashes into the room and Mike just continues to stare at me. His head tilts, eyes narrowing as if he's trying to process what I just said. And then he starts laughing. It's not joyous or happy, it's a cruel, biting laugh that turns my blood to ice.

'You think it's mine?' His voice now as loud as mine. 'Fucking hell, you really are delusional.'

'What... what do you mean? Why wouldn't I?'

Mike steps forward, an amused expression dancing on his face. 'I had a vasectomy, Ruby, years and years ago, even before we were together. I know what you women are like, trying to trap successful men like me. Guess that little *miracle* of yours isn't mine after all.'

'You're fucking lying,' I screech, my voice sounding nothing like me, as though the rush of adrenaline from all these secrets has taken over my body.

A knock at the door startles me, but Mike lets out a low, dark chuckle.

'Well, *that* is convenient. Think it's lover boy come to claim his kid?'

'What? Who?' My thoughts swirls.

'You know exactly who.' He lets out another sharp, humourless laugh. 'You think I don't know, Ruby? You think I'm as stupid and naïve as you? I've seen you with the pretty boy neighbour.'

How could he–

The conversation with Henry at the door, Mike must have been eavesdropping. And if he hasn't ever been out of the country, who knows what else he might have seen, or if he's been looking through my phone... and then a realisation crashes into me as heavy and as forceful as a tidal wave. If Mike's never been in Spain, could it be him? Could he have been sneaking around the house, taking things and posting notes? Watching me, making me believe I had a stalker, when I thought he was a thousand miles away?

CHAPTER FORTY-THREE

The knock at the door comes again. Sharp, insistent, and cuts through this suffocating silence like a blade. My heart is hammering and my fists are still clenched, Mike's words ringing in my head, but the knocking is relentless. Urgent.

Mike perches again, just on the arm of the sofa this time, and watches me like he's just won a boxing tournament.

'Well, go on then,' he drawls, tilting his head toward the door. 'Let's see if it is lover boy. We wouldn't want to keep him waiting, would we?'

I feel sick, but I force myself to do as Mike instructs. Not because he tells me to, but because I don't want to be in this house alone with *him* any longer than I have to be. I pull open the door and, of course, Henry stands there, brows furrowed. His gaze sweeps over me with a flash of concern.

'What's going on?' He rushes out the words, looking past me, looking at Mike. 'I felt like you wanted to say more to me before, outside my house, and I know I shouldn't be here, but I heard you shouting and screaming from outside and I–'

Mike lets out a low, cruel laugh from behind me. 'Are you here to play hero?'

'I'm here to check on Ruby.' Henry's voice is low and controlled, but he steps forward with such a force that I instinctively put my hand to his chest. His heart is pounding as fast as mine.

'I'm fine,' I whisper. 'Everything's fine.'

But I move my hand away and step back into the house, back into the living room to face Mike. When I hear Henry closing the door and following me in, I'm grateful, confident I could rely on him not to leave me with this... stranger. He places a hand on the small of my back, and Mike straightens, pulling himself from the sofa, and walks a few steps towards us. His smirk makes my skin crawl.

'Well, lover boy,' he sneers. 'You've joined us at just the right time. We've been discussing some exciting news. Ruby's pregnant.'

Henry's fingers flex along my body, and I lower my head because this isn't the way he should have found out. He looks at me, searching my face, and I can see his mind working, putting the pieces together.

'Oh and don't worry, it's *definitely* not mine by the way,' Mike adds, before folding his arms again.

'Ruby?' Henry asks, his voice quieter now.

I shake my head, unsure of how to explain, but before I can say anything, Mike claps his hands together, like he's enjoying a show.

'Go on then, tell him,' he taunts. 'Tell him how you fucked the two of us, and how it must have been within a short space of time because you thought it could be mine.'

'Shut up,' I snap, my voice finally coming back to me, loud and vicious. 'Just shut up, Mike.'

But Mike laughs *again*. 'Why, Ruby? You don't like the truth?' He shifts his gaze back to Henry, lips curling in

280

amusement. 'Did you think she was different, mate? Sorry to tell you she's not, she's nothing but a lying little sl–'

Henry moves before I even register it. He steps past me, straight into Mike's space, his jaw clenched so tight it looks painful.

'Don't finish that sentence, *mate*,' Henry warns, his voice dangerously low.

Mike's eyes grow wide, with a flicker of something... a flash of uncertainty, maybe. He clearly wasn't expecting Henry to have the courage to stand up to him. He's not used to that in this house.

'Everyone's a little touchy about the truth,' Mike finally says.

But Henry doesn't back down, and continues to defend me. 'You have no idea what you've thrown away.'

'Oh, please, she's hardly girlfriend of the year. Neither of you had a problem shagging in secret, behind my back, did you?'

My breath catches. 'Mike, stop–'

'Or what?' he scoffs, stepping up to Henry, chest to chest. 'Lover boy here gonna protect your honour? Show me what a real man he is?'

For the longest minute, Henry doesn't move. His fists are clenched at his sides, his entire body is stiff, and I know he doesn't want to do this. He doesn't want to sink to Mike's level because he's not like that, he's not a bully.

Mike smirks. 'That's what I thought–' And he throws the first punch.

It happens so fast and I flinch at the sound, at the impact of Mike's knuckles against Henry's face, snapping me out of my frozen state. Henry staggers back, his lip split open, blood beads in the corner of his mouth. But he doesn't seem to feel it, or care, as he slowly lifts his head to Mike. Both their chests rise and fall heavily.

Henry doesn't hold back. He swings this time, his fist

connecting with Mike's jaw in a brutal, forceful blow. Mike stumbles, crashes into the coffee table and sends it skidding across the floor. He scrambles to his feet, but Henry's on him again, grabbing the front of his shirt to pull him up and shove him hard against the wall.

'Henry, stop!' I scream, stepping forward, but neither of them hear me.

Mike sneers, shoving Henry back and swings wildly again. Henry ducks out of the way and throws another punch to Mike's ribs, making him grunt in pain. But Mike shoves Henry hard enough to send him stumbling back a few steps, giving Mike just enough time to grab the crystal vase from the side table, the artificial flowers scattering like moths, and he swings it with full force—

I scream as it crashes into Henry's head. He goes down with a hard thud. Mike stands there, chest heaving, still gripping the vase, blood dripping from the corner of it. His eyes dart to me.

'Look what you made me do, Ruby!'

I shriek out, dropping to my knees beside Henry and press my shaking hands to his chest.

'Henry,' I call out. 'Henry, wake up.'

Mike jerks, stepping back calmly and lowering the vase to the floor. I scream at him, yell at him to call an ambulance, to get help, but he just continues to walk backwards out of the room. And then, he bolts for the front door. It crashes against the interior wall as he runs out into the early evening, leaving me with Henry.

I scramble around, grabbing my handbag from the floor and rummage inside for my phone. *Come on, I know it's in here!* But my entire body shakes with shock. I keep calling out Henry's name as I feel for my mobile.

The face ID won't work: my ugly crying has stopped the phone from recognising me. My fingers tremble as I tap the emergency button rather than entering my passcode. As I press 999, the sound of the front door swinging shut grabs my attention. I'm flooded with relief that Mike has returned to help. Just as my thumb is about to crash down on the green call button, I hear a voice. A voice I don't recognise.

'Put the phone down please, Ruby.'

I spin around, but it's not Mike standing in the doorway. It's Billy.

CHAPTER FORTY-FOUR

Billy reminds me of my nightmare, the dark figure standing in the doorway of my bedroom. Motionless, heavy breathing, posture eerily casual. My attention quickly darts to his face and I watch him take in the chaos of my living room. The furniture in disarray, frames and ornaments knocked over and smashed, and Henry unconscious on the floor and losing blood. Oh, the blood. It's so thick and so dark, and it just keeps glugging out like boiling lava, soaking into the floorboards.

'I said, put the phone down, Ruby,' Billy repeats.

He doesn't scream or shout, but it's the unnerving softness of his voice that forces me to do as I'm instructed, again, and I lower my mobile. Gently pressing my thumb where it had hovered seconds before, placing the screen facing down so he doesn't see its light, and praying that the call connects. There's no time to check as Billy steps further inside. He quickly scans the room again before he reaches down and picks up the massive roll of black duct tape that's fallen out of Mike's tool case – another thing knocked over during the fight. I gasp in a mouthful of air that shudders in my chest as I half sob and half laugh at what's unfolding in front of me.

Why didn't I put everything back in its place?

Billy slowly moves the tape between his hands, passing it from one to the other, and though his actions feel measured and menacing, his deep frown and eyes frantically looking around show he's confused. Unsure. As if this isn't planned, and he has no idea what he's about to do next. And that's what's terrifying me.

I hang my head and take a deep breath praying that the call connected.

'Help!' I scream. 'He's going to kill me. Blackwood–'

A fist wallops the side of my head and I topple to the floor. I briefly squint through my eyes, and find myself within kissing distance of Henry's bloodied face and glassy eyes. I cry out, from the pain and from the realisation that Henry's already dead, and I'm here alone with the person I've feared the most.

I must have passed out, because when I come to, I'm leaning up against the sofa. The duct tape covering my mouth and haphazardly wrapped around my wrists, binding them together, and around my ankles, keeping them together too. I squint through the pain and watch Billy pace the room. He's murmuring as he walks up and down, as though he's having a conversation with himself. I quickly search for my phone, before he notices that I'm awake again, but I can't see it. Did Billy find it? Did the call even go through?

Then I spot it, screen still facing down, close to Henry's feet. I think that's where I put it... I'm not sure. I need to get help, but what can I do? I'm helpless.

There's only one thing for it: I need to get Billy's attention. He looks so deep in thought, it confuses me. Why is he staying here when Henry is lifeless on the floor? The puddle of Henry's blood just inches from staining Billy's bright white trainers. Why wouldn't he leave when this has nothing to do with him? Or else... is he going to kill *me*? I can't just sit here bound and gagged. I grunt and mutter, forcing Billy to look at me.

I'm surprised when he pulls the duct tape from my mouth, as if he really wants to hear what I have to say, and I trip over my words. Even more so when he grabs my face so roughly, so tightly, the pain sears through my head again. Why is he so mad? I start mumbling apologies, though I don't know why I'm sorry; I don't know what I've done. But he's not listening, he doesn't care and I'm clearly not saying the right thing. My eyes fall to Henry then, I don't want to see him, I know he's already dead and the tears stream down my face.

I think of my baby. The one I've wanted and pined for, for so long, who will come into this world with no father. *If* they come into this world. If I make it out of Billy's hold alive. But it's my unborn child that forces me to stop crying, who urges me to communicate with this crazed young man who seems to be as confused as I am.

'Billy,' I call his name softly, but he flinches as though I've slapped him.

'I didn't do that.' He points at Henry.

I nod, ignoring the pain. 'I know, I know, you don't have to worry. It was my partner, Mike, I'm a witness to that.'

He begins pacing again, his fingers moving in the air like he's calculating something. He seems happy with my answer, that I know he's not to blame. But that still doesn't explain why he hasn't left.

'If you could just call an ambulance–'

'It's too late, he's dead.'

I whimper. 'For me then. Could you help me?'

Billy spins, crouching in front of me again, and the spittle flies from his mouth.

'I tried to help you, Ruby. But you chose him.' He flings his head in Henry's direction. 'You let him touch you. When it should have been me. I'm the one who's been looking after you when your boyfriend pissed off. I'm the one who's been watching you sleep at night, leaving you little messages. You didn't even read them all and that hurts me.'

He's off again in one easy swoop, but he doesn't pace any further. He just stands over me, glaring and ugly as if he's deciding what to do with me. I watch him for a moment, and finally take in his face now he's not cloaked by a window or a hoodie, or the shadows. I would have guessed he was a teenager, rather than in his twenties as Patty had said, purely because of his acne-scarred skin. His greasy, unkempt hair. The type of young lad who makes me feel as though I'm already in my forties, I look and feel so much more mature in his presence. There's an innocence about that. He can't look me in the eyes, not for long anyway, and the weight of not knowing what to do around me weighs down his hunched shoulders.

All this time, it's been Billy. I knew he had been watching me from the window of the dark house; I knew he had been at the alleyway. I had been right all along. But to hear he's been watching me sleep, that he's walked around my house, while I've been here, makes me shake. If he's brazen enough to do that, what else is he capable of?

But there has to be a reason why he's never hurt me before, why he's never touched me before, and I use that knowledge.

'I'm sorry I hurt you, Billy, by choosing Henry. I was confused. I didn't know it was you all this time.'

His head turns, eerie and slowly, like he's assessing if I'm telling the truth. Wondering if he can trust my words.

'I'm sorry if I missed your clues,' I continue. 'I've been going through a lot lately, and I haven't been myself.'

He nods his head. 'I read the condolences cards. I'm sorry about your gran, Ruby.'

I feel sick at how genuine he sounds. But he says no more than that. I remember Patty calling him non-verbal, when she first spoke about him, and I had assumed she meant he was autistic. Now I get the feeling his lack of verbal communication was a choice. It's not that he can't talk to people, it's that he doesn't want to. He doesn't have the social skills to hold a conversation.

I so desperately want him to speak more right now, tell me everything like they do in the films and at the end of books. Isn't this the moment when they confess everything? But then, again, this isn't a story, this is my life. So despite the fear clawing at my chest, I push on, keep him talking, praying someone heard my screams, pleading that Mike will have a change of heart.

'Thanks, Billy.' I take a breath. 'How have you... I mean, how have you been getting in to protect me?'

He smiles now, like a child about to show off. He reaches into his pocket and pulls out a keychain with two keys.

'My uncle has some uses.'

So he's had both keys, one for the front door and one for the back. *I* didn't leave my kitchen door unlocked; *Billy* just forgot to lock it when he left that night. That's why the doors haven't been tampered with. I *knew* Norman was involved too, but how–

'He's a retired locksmith,' Billy adds, as though reading my mind.

The discarded memories return. Of Henry referring to Norman as Smithy after their conversation at the book club. It wasn't a football nickname; it was his profession. And it was why Henry waited on his doorstep for Norman when he was locked out. Norman was going to help him get in. My weird neighbour had the tools and skills to open any lock he wanted.

Then, before either of us can speak any further, the distant wail of police sirens cuts through the silence. The blue light flooding through the window, spinning and twirling in unison with the welcome noise.

Billy becomes erratic at the interruption, running around the confined space of the living room and I think for a moment, *this is it.* He's going to grab the vase and finish me off so I can't tell a soul about him and what he's been doing to me for months.

My breath comes in sharp, ragged gasps, waiting for him to strike. But nothing comes. Instead, Billy sprints out of the room and in the direction of the kitchen.

As footsteps crash up the pathway and through my front door, I hear the rattle from the wooden fence in the garden as Billy scales it, running off into the night. I scream to the officers, warning them that Billy's done a runner out the back, and then lower my head and allow my tears to fall freely.

CHAPTER FORTY-FIVE

It's a week since I've been back here, to my house on Blackwood Close, and I feel so detached from it, so far removed, as if I haven't lived here for five years. It doesn't look the same or feel the same, and it certainly doesn't feel like home. I was taken to the hospital for a check-up, just as a routine; I guess they have to do that with a bound and bruised woman. I told the nurses about the baby, too, and although it's early days, they didn't seem worried. I've stayed at Nancy's house since that night.

Now, I sit at the dining table, staring at the faint marks on the wood where Mike used to put his beer bottles down without a coaster. Nancy potters in the background, collecting some of my things, and across from me sit two police officers. I can't remember their names, because I've spoken to so many of them over the past seven days. Today we have officer one and officer two. They wanted to run over some final details with me. I had some questions of my own, and it was also an excuse to get some of my own clean underwear.

I've since learnt that Billy was arrested. The stupid lad had only gone as far as his uncle's house. They found him, in bed, pretending to watch TV, and he protested to all the accusations until they took him to the police station. The officers informed me that Billy didn't communicate with them much, but they learnt a lot from Norman.

'Billy's history isn't pretty, Ruby,' officer one explains. 'He had a restraining order against him. It would seem he moved in with his uncle because his mother was afraid she couldn't cope with his declining mental health and obsessive behaviour.'

'Obsessive?' I repeat.

'Another woman he fixated on,' she continues. 'She had made complaints, things going missing, a break-in – no tampered doors or strange notes – but there was no real evidence against Billy. He was never physical with her–'

'Well I'm glad you let him roam off to a new home and find a new obsession in me. Maybe if you had listened to that woman's complaints, he wouldn't have tied me up and... God knows what else he could have done if he hadn't been disturbed.'

I'll never know what Billy had intended to do. He was mad at me for being with Henry and not noticing him. I was saved because my call *had* gone through. The operator had stayed on the call and heard everything, but they'd also received another call from my next-door neighbour about 'some kind of disturbance' – and for that kind of nosiness, I'll always be thankful.

'Billy moved in with his uncle in an attempt at a fresh start. His mother spoke very highly of Norman. Very thankful for his support and generosity, but is adamant that they were both unaware Billy was learning his uncle's trade or using his tools.'

The mention of Norman, and how she refers to him, riles something in me. 'And you honestly believe that Norman wasn't aware of what his nephew was doing? He knew. I *know* he did.'

'There's no evidence that Norman was involved,' officer two says. 'We searched the house thoroughly and found nothing.

Norman's record is clean, with no employers or customers having ever logged an issue with him or his work.'

'Billy knew how to get in and out of my house, how to copy my keys to have a set for himself, how to move around my house without making a sound. That isn't normal–'

'He learned a technique used by locksmiths called lock bumping. It wouldn't cause any visibly damage that you would have noticed. Once he gained entrance that first time, he copied your keys to keep a set for himself. All the equipment was found in his uncle's workshop.'

'But Norman is retired. Why does he still have all the equipment that allows him – or anyone else, in fact – to discreetly *bump* into peoples' doors and then copy their keys?'

'He was a self-employed man, and has every right to still have his trade workshop.' Officer one again. 'But Norman insists he had no idea Billy was using those tools to get into your house. We can only use the evidence we have.'

The police did find my rainbow scarf. It was under Billy's bed, and even that feels weird to me. He had returned my notebook, so why would he keep my other things. Why hasn't my pen been found? Surely he would have kept it with my scarf? I'll never believe that Norman wasn't involved, in some way, but I can see there's no use pushing it with these two.

Mike's also been arrested. They found him at his mother's house in shock, so I'm told, at how the whole thing played out. He's claiming self-defence, and while I do understand that he and Henry were fighting, it was a fist fight. Mike introduced a weapon, and I saw a demon in his eyes when he swung the vase to the side of Henry's head. I shudder now as it replays in my mind. I know I'll be needed at some point in the future to give evidence, but for now, the further I can stay away from Mike – the lying, cheating waste of space – the happier I'll be.

Henry died in the living room, before the paramedics could

even get in and help him. The sheer force of that crystal on his skull, on his brain, had been too much. I'll see his dark blood puddled on the floor in my nightmares forever.

The police said they'll ask Henry's family if I can have the funeral details, when that's all been arranged, and I nod silently, encouraging them to do so. But the truth is, I'm not sure if I'd even go. What would I say to his poor mother, and sister, and his niece and nephew? Just the thought of them could reduce me to a crying mess... And would I then feel compelled to tell them that I'm carrying his baby, too? Be a part of their lives? No, I'm not ready for any of that.

I show the officers out, but don't dare look in the living room – I never want to see it, or Gran's crystal vase, again. After they say goodbye, I watch as Patty walks up my pathway in a floral summer dress, and a smile on her face. She's trying to be friendly, I know, but it just feels all too soon for merriment and hugs. I don't invite her in, not to be rude or mean, but because I don't need another drawn-out conversation. Nancy calls out about grabbing my laptop and toiletries from upstairs, and it gives me a moment to talk to my neighbour.

'I'm sorry you're leaving the Close, Ruby,' she says, and leans on the doorframe.

'I can't stay here.'

'No, no, I understand.' She pauses, and it's clear that she hasn't come here just to say goodbye. 'I wanted to apologise, really.'

'For what?'

Patty looks to the floor for a moment, as though she needs a final push of encouragement. 'For lying to you, Ruby,' she finally says, and locks eyes with me. 'When you asked about Norman being in my house, and I told you that you must be mistaken...'

'He had been in your house, hadn't he?'

She nods slowly. 'Yes, but it wasn't anything sinister. Not

like his horrid nephew did to you. I knew Norman was there because... well, because we've been having a bit of a *thing* on and off for a while.'

I recoil at Patty's confession. The unexpectedness of it floors me, and if I knew it wouldn't completely hurt her feelings, I'd openly cringe at the image of them together. Norman... the man I've always thought so weird and so creepy... Patty was having a fling with him, and Henry thought he was funny. Perhaps I judged Norman when I shouldn't have.

'Anyway,' she says. 'I didn't want you going without knowing the truth, and knowing that I was sorry.'

'Why didn't you tell me before?'

'I... I didn't want everyone knowing my business.' She rolls her eyes, and I know she feels the irony of her words. Blackwood Close's neighbourhood watch. 'People round here are used to seeing me with my Harold, and I don't want to be the talk of the street. Especially when not everyone knows how to take Norman.'

'Well, thanks for telling me now, Patty, I appreciate it.' She turns to leave, but I call out to her. 'Just one more thing.'

'Yes, Columbo?'

She smiles and I laugh despite myself. 'Mrs Shah said you had a son, and I pointed out that photo in your house that time, remember? But you never mentioned him to me, not during any of the chats we had.'

Her face turns sombre. 'Because not every story is a happy one to share, Ruby.'

'Don't I know it.' I raise my eyebrows high.

'My son, Christopher, stopped talking to me many, many years ago. His father and I – well, his father – didn't agree with his life choices. We all said hurtful things and never spoke again. When Harold passed away just before the pandemic, I begged Christopher to come to the funeral, but he refused. He said he'd come, but only to nail down the coffin on that homophobic son of a bitch. Those were his words.'

'Oh, Patty, I'm sorry.' I reach out and rub her arm. 'But those aren't your views, surely?'

She shakes her head. 'They weren't then, when Christopher found his now-husband, but I didn't go against Harold. I didn't stand up for my son. And I know that's why Christopher is holding a grudge over me. But I know he's happy, and that's all that matters.'

'How do you know?'

'Christopher was married before, to a woman, for almost a decade, until he admitted to her that he never loved her in a romantic way, and was doing it to fit in to what was expected of him. She's a lovely woman and we stay in contact. She's still friends with Christopher, and every now and then she gives me little updates about his life.'

The pieces form together in my mind. 'The blonde woman who let me into your house that first day.'

'Yes, that's Beth.' She taps me on the hand and smiles. 'We'll miss you at the next book club. Our very own published author.'

If only she realised it was that very message she'd sent to the Blackwood Close's WhatsApp group which had set off Billy's obsession with me. There's no point in telling her, because I'm sure it will only fuel the gossip, and I'd rather be yesterday's news sooner than later.

'Where are you going?' she asks then.

'I'm not sure yet.'

Which is the honest answer, but would I tell her now even if I knew? Patty's a lovely lady, and I've enjoyed chatting with her about our shared love of books. But hasn't she highlighted how little anyone can know their neighbours. Even those you consider to be a pal. Nancy, too, really. She's proved that you could go years without knowing what's happened in your best friend's past. And Mike... Well, Mike has been the mightiest blow to the face when it comes to living with an utter stranger.

'Don't forget to set up that Royal Mail redirect thingy.' Patty interrupts my thoughts. 'It's very handy.'

I smile at her. At her way of always being in the know about everything.

'Good tip, Patty, thanks.'

She rubs my arm one final time before saying goodbye, and while she has been a lovely neighbour over these past few strange months, I can't say for sure if we'll ever speak again.

CHAPTER FORTY-SIX

You. You, my dearest Ruby have messed with my head and got me into more trouble than anyone ever has before.

I came to live with my uncle Norman because I needed help. Help my mum couldn't give me. Help getting out of my own head. And he did just that... he taught me a trade that he had spent his whole life perfecting. He told me it was an important job. A *responsible* job. Now he knows that I took what he was teaching me and turned it into something... wrong. Something criminal. I hope he won't get into trouble.

He began explaining the basics of his craft, in an attempt to keep me busy, and maybe even to restart his own little company, and I was intrigued. Then that nosey neighbour Patty introduced you to the WhatsApp Group and I became... *excited*.

You have to understand that I never wanted to even be in that stupid group, but my uncle thought it would be good for me. Meet new and different people, mature people. Then you popped in, a famous writer among us, and I tingled with something that I had felt only once before. A thrill that drove me mad in finding out everything I could about you. It wasn't too hard, because of your websites and many, many books on Amazon. I've always found a place of peace while reading – the words and characters much friendlier and kinder than people are in real life. I was utterly and truly lost in your worlds and in the words you wrote.

This world isn't kind, Ruby, you must know that. Especially now, when I'm not there to watch over you. People will become super fans of your books and want to know you. We've all seen *Misery*. All I wanted to do was to protect you from all of that... But then you chose *him*. Is it because he's older, and taller, and has his own apartment? Looks like bloody Clarke Kent without the specs and cape. Well, he *did* look like him. My uncle's been to see me and explained everything that happened with him and your fellow. I'm sorry about it. I'm sorry you didn't choose me. It's your fault that Henry is dead, so perhaps I was lucky to escape you.

Escape... some escape when I've been detained. Under some mental health act, my mum said. It was nice to see her, though she didn't stay long. She didn't want to look at me, I could tell, like I've embarrassed her, shamed her. Anyway, *detained*, can you believe that? I didn't even hurt you. Or Henry. Yes, I had to hit you that once, but you kept shouting and screaming and I was scared. Yes, I copied your keys and watched you sleep, but it was just to be close to you. My *intention* was never to hurt you. Just watch you. Just help you make better choices.

But I don't bother telling them, any of those people in charge who ask, and I don't bother explaining. Why should I? Even when you speak to them, they don't listen. Friends, family, strangers... they hear the words, but they never really *understand*.

So I'll be good, do whatever it takes to get out of here – shame I can't copy the keys for these doors! Until then, I'll stay locked in the world of books. *Write your own story*, Ruby, I'll keep reading your words forever.

EPILOGUE
ONE YEAR LATER

I never thought I'd live any further from London than its suburbs. But when I stumbled on a listing of a beautiful, thatched cottage in Yorkshire, my heart knew it had to be mine. That I had to make the move. Surrounded by rolling fields, winding country lanes, the occasional speck of a farmhouse in the distance. That's it. No houses or apartment buildings within spitting distance, no WhatsApp groups and gossiping neighbours leaning on each other's fences. It's peaceful and quiet, with a solitude that isn't lonely or scary.

We've been here a few months, but there's still boxes to unpack – having a newborn who doesn't sleep without being held doesn't leave much time for home decor. I think of Henry, and how he had said something similar about boxes being everywhere when he moved into his apartment.

My eyes sting when I picture his face, which is a daily occurrence, really, because already our son looks the image of him. I decided not to attend Henry's funeral, and even after all this time, I'm not sure if it's a decision I'll regret or not. But somewhere along the way, the newspapers picked up on a *story* about a man who was murdered in the home of a local author and tried to run with it.

By the grace of God, Mike owned up to what he did and pleaded guilty to manslaughter, which meant there was never a trial. The journalists and reporters still hounded me for a while after his sentencing. It cemented things in my mind then: I didn't want the world knowing I was pregnant. I didn't want to be known to everyone. And with the help of my two true friends Nancy and Stef, I hid for months to get myself sorted, and I no longer write under the name Ruby Turner.

I peer over at Conor, my son, asleep in the Moses basket next to me on the sofa, and know one day he'll have so many questions about his dad and where he came from. Perhaps the same ones I should have asked about my own father. But I know now that Mum was protecting me from things I didn't need to know about, and from people who didn't need to be in my life.

A shadow of guilt chills my skin for not telling Henry's family about the existence of his son, but for now it feels like the right thing to do for Conor. The living room is bathed in an early summer sunshine and I'm taking the brief moment on my own to pack away some things.

That's when I come across a shoebox in one of the moving crates. I lift the lid and peer inside. It contains items I no longer want or need, because they remind me of the lowest point in my life. But they're also things I can't let go of. My rainbow-coloured scarf and my notebook. I thumb through the pages, as I did many times last year, and stop at one in particular. Even if I had looked inside before Billy hinted at his note, I'm not sure I would have noticed that he'd left a mark. In between my notes and ramblings and crossings-out, he had penned the initial B followed by a heart and then a R initial. It clearly meant a lot to him, enough to make him mad at me for not spotting it.

I wrap the book back in the scarf, and return them to the shoebox. Gran's letter is in here, too. Not because it's as triggering as the other two items, but because it reminds me of the courage I need – and the belief I should have in myself. I take it out now, just to hear Gran's voice through the words again.

> *My dearest Ruby,*
> *Life is too short to live in the shadows of someone else. Don't be afraid of things you can't control. Live in beautiful colour and grab every opportunity with both hands. When you get to my age, you will realise there are no rules in life, other than the ones we make for ourselves. Don't keep apologising, don't let anyone make you feel small and most importantly, don't forget to trust your gut.*
> *Gran x*

I return her letter to the shoebox, too, and place it on the top shelf of the bookcase. Far out of sight, but there if I ever need to remind myself of her words.

The screen on my phone lights up, showing an image of the postman standing at my gate at the end of the pathway. I may not have many neighbours now, but I'd be stupid not to have fitted an electric gate and a camera doorbell. Just as Henry had once advised.

I take the baby monitor with me, leaving Conor where he's restful, and go outside, down the short pathway to meet the postman. I need to sign for a small package, a redirected one, and I'm surprised there's still post coming from Blackwood Close. I step back inside the house, nudging the door shut with my hip and stop just inside to set down the baby monitor. I could hear Conor from here, but I like the security of being able to see him at all times, too.

I tear open the padded envelope and reach inside. My

breath hitching as my fingers wrap around something smooth and I pull out my engraved pen. The one gifted to me by Mum, the one Billy took from my home, the one the police could never find. In that moment, I know this has been sent by Norman because he's the only person who could. It's been a whole year since I discovered who Mike really was, since he murdered Henry, and since Billy was arrested, why would Norman wait so long to return it to me?

Perhaps my neighbours had been right about the *weird one* actually being a nice guy, and I have to believe this means Norman wasn't involved in everything Billy did to me. I have to believe it means Norman is just replacing something that doesn't belong to him. I have to believe he's using the anniversary as a signal, as a way of making sure I know it's been sent by him.

I have to believe and hope it's all those things, because I can't live in fear for the rest of my life.

Still, I press firmly on the front door, twist both locks – top and bottom – and fix the chain in place. Just in case. Because if the past year has taught me anything, it's that you never know who you're living with or who you're living next to. And no one, absolutely no one, is perfect.

THE END

ALSO BY TARA LYONS

STANDALONE SUSPENSE THRILLER

The Paramedic's Daughter

THE DI HAMILTON SERIES

In the Shadows

No Safe Home

Deadly Friendship

The Stranger Within

A FESTIVE SHORT MURDER MYSTERY

A Christmas Crime

ACKNOWLEDGEMENTS

My first thanks goes to *you*, dear reader, for buying and reading *The Perfect Stranger*. It's been a while since I last put pen to paper (or fingers to keyboard, really), but this story played out over and over in my mind for some time. It has been such a pleasure to let the words flow again, and I can only hope you enjoyed Ruby's story.

A massive thanks to my mum, Val, and my partner, Daniel, for giving me the gift of time. This book was written in the quiet hours while everyone slept, in the early mornings before the day really got started, during the weekends and school holidays, but wouldn't have been possible at all without you both giving me the space to do so.

The amazing duo of editor Clare Law and proofreader Shirley Khan, you both went above and beyond to help me craft my words, reassure me from start to finish and catch any inconsistencies. The words *thank you* just don't seem enough, but I hope you feel the weight behind them.

To my two trusty early readers Trish Dixon and Maria Lee, thank you for always being so honest with me. This book is better because of you both.

Then to a dear group of friends who made time to read an advanced copy, thank you so much for your ongoing support. From my first book to this one, your encouragement and friendship has always been unwavering — and it means the world to me.

And finally to the dynamite team at Bloodhound Books, thank you for believing I had another book inside me! For the fantastic cover, the marketing, the support and everything else in between that goes on behind the scenes, thank you.

A NOTE FROM THE PUBLISHER

Thank you for reading this book. If you enjoyed it please do consider leaving a review on Amazon to help others find it too.

We hate typos. All of our books have been rigorously edited and proofread, but sometimes mistakes do slip through. If you have spotted a typo, please do let us know and we can get it amended within hours.

info@bloodhoundbooks.com